A CIRCUS MAXIMUS

A CIRCUS MAXIMUS

JOHN ANTHONY McKENNA

Epigraph Books
Rhinebeck, New York

Hardcover ISBN 978-1-954744-90-5
Paperback ISBN 978-1-954744-91-2
eBook ISBN 978-1-954744-92-9

Library of Congress Control Number 2022914022

Book and cover design by Colin Rolfe

Epigraph Books
22 East Market Street, Suite 304
Rhinebeck, NY 12572
(845) 876-4861
epigraphps.com

AUTHOR'S NOTE

Deep appreciation is extended to family, friends, colleagues and acquaintances who supported and shaped the arc of this experience. Your collective voices and spirits are woven and reflected upon these pages. Additionally, there were inspirational books, passages, references and quotes which contributed substantially to the imagination and citation. Gratitude is abundant for these authors, publications and information sources:

1. *Propertius, The Poems*, translated by W. G. Shepherd,
2. *The Romans – Life and Customs*, by E. Guhl & W. Koner,
3. *In Search of Ancient Rome*, by Claude Moatti,
4. *Rome, A Cultural, Visual and Personal History*, by Robert Hughes,
5. *Caesar and Christ*, by Will Durant,
6. *Ancient Rome*, by Nigel Rodgers,
7. and readily retrievable and ever-resourceful *National Geographic*.

J.A. McKenna
International Day of Non-Violence
October 2, 2022

We shall not cease from exploration
And the end of all our exploring
Will be to arrive where we started
And know the place for the first time

— T.S. ELIOT

CHAPTER I

T HE END.

It was a certain end – *exitus* – my end, her end, our end, though who would have predicted it with the glistening rays, a gift from the sun gods stretching and bouncing off the azure waters of the Mediterranean in the South of France, pleasing our exposed brows and radiating warmth on our tongues as we talked the hours away?

Here was a finality, a defeated moment in the long timeline of man's search for that elusive sense of purpose, contentment and the ultimate prize, peace. Smoke, fire and dirty water, the soiled and bloodied clothing, the stench of dust and taste of salty perspiration found on the soiled cheeks and chins of everyone kissed in the wake of the explosion – this I remembered as the end, hardly aware of the emerging beginning. This, my rapid race and chariot chase, came in a surprising and welcomed presentation, steering me on a circuitous course to a distant victory encircled by defeats.

At that end I heard her gentle voice in the cacophony of the madness, a flash of our last visit in the café just the day before. It was there she held my finger and guided it with her own, a captivating shine of lavender nail polish dancing off her forefinger, counterclockwise, making an impressive indentation upon her neatly folded linen centered on the table. The base of the wine glass could not have created a more perfect impression.

"If you trace it right, then you have drawn it as it was meant to be, a great and nearly perfect circle," she shared in soft tones as if confessing, a rite of revelation whispered in hushed confidence.

Cloelia Hilaire held her tilted head at an angle juxtaposed with mine as we gazed down at the marble-white napkin at the Taverna Una, our favorite of the many charming bistros and drinking holes we frequented in the whirling, countless afternoons in the midst of the French tempest and social circus that is Cannes.

"You see? If you form your circle just right, like so, no one should tell where it begins and where it ends," Cloe decreed. "This is true of life, too, yes Toby?" she rhetorically hinted, the corners of her mischievous lips turned upward in seductive inquiry, begging for engagement and response.

There was the usual tease with an extra tinge and blend of love, wisdom, sex appeal, passion, joy, optimism, hope and faith all wrapped in one shining twinkle in her eyes, accentuated in the inescapable tilt of her head, like the tilt of our lonely planet, the very tilt of time invested and exhausted together, then separated, knocked from the axis, atilt, traced in a gentle stroke of expertise upon a café napkin, a near-perfect circle of harmony that could deliver world peace if we all could just follow its impression and direction, offered by Cloe for anyone watching or eavesdropping. There, on the linen that had carpeted her glasses of chardonnay, we admired a fading circle realized in a dipped index finger into final sips of evaporating wine and time.

This was the farewell, a sacramental blessing unto a passing, the arriving like a fiery comet into a departing, an innocent birth and beginning into a murderous ending.

Cloe Hilaire caught me and taught me, Tobias Nathan Tyrone, as well as any great mystic could, a cosmic, welcoming vortex of surrender. She was one of those souls that intersects your life as a masterful thief, if the gods bless it so, stealing your playbook and reading it back to you – a well-meaning, benevolent, life-experienced gypsy who has nicked the sonnets and scriptures from the heavens, appointed by the angels to serve as astrologer to share in amusement your anticipated foibles and follies in adopted and well-earned joy. She could read my palm and temperature, steady the heartbeat and take the pulse with instinct and desire. Intuitive, demure and vulnerable, an old soul with childlike enthusiasm, Cloe shared generously her spins on the ancient Mediterranean coast, fresh with ideas if not replete with awareness of pending catastrophe and doom. The very air we breathed was full of concern and conflicting carelessness, an inertia and energy these sands knew well, the balance that keeps the ebb and flow, a compulsion of construction followed by destruction and back again. This was ever the recurring theme, the timeless story told and retold along these ancient shores. Soon, it would claim Cloe in its most recent turn and churn.

It was four years before when Cloe drew me instantly when I saw her sitting alone in the Rotonde marketplace, perched on a high stool behind a reception desk handling the parade of delegates, the ceaseless traffic of clients, some genuine, most feigning business interest, passersby attracted by her friendliness and posture and the magnetic axis of the tilted head. She worked the biannual media marketplaces with proper detachment as we flocked by the thousands to this crossroads in Provence, littering her shores with mostly forgettable television programming and disposable miles of film. Guarding her natural beauty, a dark olive complexion draping a mix of Dutch and Indonesian roots, Cloe kept a healthy and austere skepticism which proved handy when an onlooker came too close, misread the rehearsed lines or exhibited unwanted sexual approaches. She had a contagious smile fairly fixed on a square jawline, and a strong brow and sharp nose that could be caught at a distance which separated her from the crowd, bracketed by silky, black-straight hair, shoulder length, parted right side to left that danced on shoulders in each enthusiastic convulsion of her giggle. She emitted kindness and friendship with direct eye contact, freely spilling the ready and available laughter both loud and unapologetic. One felt naturally at ease with Cloe however far one had traveled to be here, welcomed and warmed, hosted and served, free and awakened, happy and hungry, wistful and young. Thus, I naturally gravitated to dine, drink and smoke with her wherever our spontaneous spirits would take us. Our friendship grew in bounds of confidence and loyalty over the seasons as she shared her wide view of arts, politics and love with me, secured in the deep, loyal and generous life blossoming in the commitment to her husband, Philippe, a playwright based in nearby Nice. Cloe's years on the French coast gave her the air of a seasoned ambassador along this coaxing harbor. She seemed to know everybody, and those she did not would soon in time know her. She kept tabs on each sprouting and trending spot in Cannes. There wasn't a street, shop or restaurant unfamiliar to her. Her critiques and recommendations were well-tested and supremely trusted by colleagues, clients and friends, and she was widely sought for suggestions and scoops.

Raised in Amsterdam, Cloe was called to the Riviera when she was seventeen, finding the enticing, rolling hills of Provence magically familiar and genetically inclined to her sunny essence and light disposition. The very perfume in its breezy air entered her lungs and pores and she never looked north again. The home of her childhood was a cloudy, dark memory of buried hopes and dismissed dreams, walled-in expectations surrounding a fortress of emotion, unspoken love and empty days of misunderstanding, if not silence, between her three half-sisters and a stern, sad and damaged mother. There was a father somewhere in Indonesia she never met, one single, fading image of him barely visible in a two-by-two-inch yellowed photo, he in full-military attire, stoic in a permanent blank gaze aimed at an opposite and equally blank wall in the lonely living room of her youth. There for what seemed would be an eternity the stony cold soldier kept watch from a rarely visited mantelpiece. Why he had such stately presence or formal position in their home she never could know, for within the small frame behind the fragile and brittle glass stared a stranger.

This coldness she had put behind her, preferring sunshine and buoyancy somewhere, and that somewhere was to be found on a path south until the last hurdles of the high hills of the Midi descended and greeted the harbor of Cannes, a conquest all her own. She always chose patios and terraces over walls and halls, windows over doors, skies over turf and tundra, theatrical movement over static monotony. If she could rule, she often said, then may she as a queen of peace, reigning in laughter to drown the soldiers' bellows, boasts and cries, where no echoes of a mysteriously muted father in starched uniform could ever be heard above the boisterous and bountiful cackle from her happy throne.

But war, man's perpetual war, had now visited Cannes again in all its raw reality, unlike the fictional exploits and romantic images we plastered and pilfered in this multimedia marketplace, exploiting and propagating simple amusements at conferences and festivals, ad nauseum, until cinema and screen, horror and history become blurred by the confused senses. Our long line of tragedy in real time is documented in innumerable films, videos and programs, peppered between ceaseless, aggressive and militant advertising, until we hardly distinguish between the prophets and profits. So who were the seers and gypsies on that fateful day? Despite our myopia and imagination, no fiction properly braced us for what was to come.

The rapturous violence that killed you, Cloe, on an otherwise cloudless, crystal-clear, azure-blue afternoon, left me with a yearning I had never known existed, and Cannes was broken to its core. The imperfect world that chased to kiss you reached back but missed you. The cafes transformed to chapels, candles flickering upon the altars, their napkins moistened and crumpled by tears and soot, a deafening silence enveloping the air except for the occasional clank of an empty coffee cup against its useless saucer, the waiters making white noise to interrupt an impossible inner quiet.

No words were found in those horrid hours of suspended belief, followed by cacophony and chaos. Words cannot compete with entities, forms, shapes and art, the colors created when skies opened in a spew of murderous red, pink, silver and black. A million words cannot define a single, perfect circle. The Romans, in their neighborly influence next door, delivered the most widely used alphabet on the planet, still in use today, but it was impotent to communicate what needed to be expressed, far too logical, rational and pragmatic in its imperial applications to explain the inexplicable.

And who to blame when the wheels of hate and anger fall off the chariot carts of our journey and roll into the halls and rooms where babes sleep and innocents dine? Who to scream to, whom to run toward, whom to cry for and upon?

I was not alone in this cataclysmic questioning, targeted into an angry sky in puzzlement and awe-spun wonder, as the great poet Ovid did on the great cause of it all. The legendary Roman lyricist handed me a line from beyond to consider. Perhaps, indeed, this was all *carmen et error* – a poem and a mistake. I tapped the centuries of spirits who pondered the same question, and as my moon came, my moon went, where my sun rose, alas it must set. Cloe lived, then Cloe died. How she lived resided now in the mystery dust of the cosmos and elements, like song, like scent, aromatic lavender, dashed within the perfumed, rolling dales of Grasse, like the bouquet of sweet-fermented grapes on a summer eve on the small terrace of Cloe's warm and inviting seasonal apartment along a back alleyway behind the Hotel Martinez, nestled between the ancient, calm and calling sea to the south and the bustling commercial enterprises running the length of Rue d'Antibes.

Who to blame, indeed? I blamed me, followed by an endless condemnation of every shattered spirit and soiled soul that crossed my path that afternoon and in the subsequent, hazy and foggy days that were to come. I blamed faceless strangers walking aimlessly along the Croisette, heads lowered in personal loss, defeated, broken and betrayed. I blamed the merchants in the open markets carrying on in determined resilience, stacking tomatoes, melons and towers of grapes as if the goddess of orchards, Pomona, directed them so. I blamed the sad-eyed Moroccans smoking shared and passed cigarettes, unemployed, loitering, directionless and exiled. I blamed princes and paupers, hustlers and thieves, every carnival character crossing the meandering, lost paths of my mind. I blamed politicos, sycophants and bureaucrats occupying every color of the stereophonic spectrum, bouncing vile and vitriol in harmonic hysteria on platforms above the harbor, microphones and lighting equipment providing proficient staging for the circus to arrive. The show must go on, and in terms most perplexing, it had only just begun.

Shamelessly, unceremoniously and suspiciously I blamed flower girls holding court on corners and generations of French morticians, adorned in Rolex watches with cellphones and earpieces accessorizing fresh-pressed black suits. Joining my expanding list of the disdained were priests and mullahs, contractors and soldiers, cooks, bartenders, dancers, bookies, waitresses and the working women-of-the-night occupying the avenues and alleyways from the Croisette to the train station. Making the honor were hoteliers and yachtsmen, miners and oilers, charlatans and muses, and every damned profession and lifestyle and cursed thread in the economic weave that put Cloe in the lethal trap, the black widow's web of our time spun into the marketplace destined to blow. Cloe, decent, kind and joyful, wise and gifted, ready and willing, open and offering, taken and stolen, sacrificed in the rite, leaving mercilessly a betrothed love, Philippe, to stumble along the concrete sidewalks on a scalded shoreline for answers, and me to stare down all of humanity as they passed him by, another stranger staring in fixed shock.

This was part of the mounting cost and larger toll. Cloe, motionless and mute in the basement of the Rotonde, presented lifeless under her collapsed countertop. Several days passed before estimates of all of the lost could be calculated. Identification had begun in a makeshift morgue inside the Hotel Splendid, the bodies placed and cataloged in the ghastly fleet of refrigerated truck trailers surrounding the Rotonde. Cloe and I once strolled the Splendid's lobby looking at black-and-white World War II photographs after drinking generous carafes of red wine to wash down scrumptious plates of steak tartare on Rue Saint-Antoine. The pictures showed expressionless Nazis guarding the entrance and occupying its opulent corridors, a rewarding duty with obvious benefits reflected in their opportunistic eyes. It was a good post for these fortunate German soldiers, all things considered, for combat and conflict were seldom encountered on the resort coast compared to the massacres to the north and in various bloody corners of the planet, pelted and blitzed by bullets, mortars, bombs and grenades. The quarters here were fine and comfortable. In uniforms well creased and starched, the wine flowed, fine cheeses and freshly baked breads were passed in abundance, a gentle, clean breeze blew constant onto Aryan faces most afternoons as the other world ravaged on in battle, be it across the sea they faced or the land of rearranged borders at their backs.

Cloe was placed on her back somewhere on the fourth floor of the hotel sharing crowded quarters with the numerous dead. It was cramped and cold, no one to provide friendly strokes on her temples as I used to do, rubbing in circles "to get the cruel world out," we would decree in laughter at the end of another Rotonde-fueled day. No matter the trivial nature of self-imposed stress, I counted on her to shake the heaviness from the heart and administer a healthy and proper dose of levity, sealed in the circuitry of mutually applied temple massages.

I felt I would never drink again. Thirst had escaped me. The desire to enjoy the robust and rich grapes had vanished into a gray and putrid cloud above the Rotonde. I was dry, beyond sober, drunk in a new and harsh reality below the decibel level where one might hear a toast, deaf to the clink of crystal wine glasses, as too much glass had shattered the senses. Shards were everywhere, the Riviera sun careening them at certain angles and delivering unwanted, paradoxical beauty, an austere aurora as they glistened, sparkled and littered the sandy perimeter of the Rotonde. But in the Hotel Splendid plentiful pieces at the victims' sides did not glisten, blasted into their dulled, soiled and blood-splattered state, miniscule blades of glass sprinkled among the dead in the dark.

I would soon learn cuts and abrasions, trespassers, violators of the flesh, ran in parallel streaks along Cloe's bare arms in curious tracks up her exposed neck, down again like thick purple lines on a Van Gogh canvas, accenting her fine, bronze and muscle-toned calves. They left blemishes and pock marks in various hues, faint streaks of black-cherry dried blood, and a tragic, almost theatrical residue of makeup providing a shadow on the delicate, sweet face, her displayed corpse a bodily itinerary of wounds, a map of the curious journey finished, a child in Amsterdam to a victim in Cannes.

Who would wash Cloe on that dirtiest of days, violated in our new-found, blemished and polluted selves? She was always so certain and self-reliant, presentable, free and liberated in natural beauty, offered daily in her greeting of the mornings and validated in evenings bidding goodbye to the diminishing sun, a yield to her rising and elusive moon. But she was laid there silently in the antiseptic air, stored in clinical macabre inside the Hotel Splendid, incapable of making herself formal in her final goodbye. Still, I envisaged her radiant and worthy of a royal farewell, a salute to a fallen goddess robbed of years, assassinated upon her Rotonde throne. We could not save you and then we begged you to save us – we, your hapless centurions longing in stoic gazes toward our Isis –the goddess who reigned in splendor across this sea so long ago, intoxicating and illuminating in glorious light with promises of salvation, possessing Roman soldiers aligned in royal reverence.

My senses and vantage point blurred, I did not wish to see Cloe's eyes come the time I may see her. I had hoped to find them eternally closed in a tranquil peace she earned, deserved and divined. I wanted her dancing amidst the constellations we gazed upon over the horizon, beyond the isles of Marguerite and Honorat and twinkling in the delight, pondering the ultimate knowing. I wanted her beckoning me, tugging my shirt tails and plucking my cosmic harp in sweet melodies echoing from Vienna, Nice and Milan to London, New York to Brussels, Paris and Hong Kong, an opera that splits the night and intercepts madness, the buzz from city to city and village to village on this lonely, disturbed, frightened and frazzled planet, dizzy and drowsy in weightless flight and balanced upon the Milky Way, swirling in random circles like two trapeze artists under the Big Top in a slow dance or a delightfully dangerous high-wire act with Orion, or rather a lonely waltz with Leo and a tumbling tango with the mischievous Archer, the voyeur extraordinaire, watching in repose for his moment to intercede.

Save that last dance for me some night when ankles are spree and free to dance again, when feet are cleansed of blood and mud, some liberated night in the raise of a fragrant glass of sweet Riesling to the nose and lips and saying absolutely nothing in return, mirrored smiles sharing secrets of the universal all-knowing, the nebulous omnipotent, twirling and spinning until dizzy in stardust, counterclockwise and colliding in a blinding burst of the supernova into a cataclysmic collapse of the cosmos, Ovid as angel and ghost scrolling the account in a sacred chronicle and rhyming in harmonic verses of Cloe.

The flow of spilled blood stained every thought of wine and dance. I was not thirsty yet parched in the drought stealing my spit, a sandstorm burning my eyes. I was tired, so very, very tired, an exhaustion I knew not possible. Sleep called, and to awaken the next day required a mustering of all courage to face the broken, shattered coastline again, the pathetically altered and repurposed hotel, the tainted and polluted shore of myths surrounded by swiftly slipping hopes and rapidly fading dreams. There was no resting in peace today for the living. The Archer himself wept at arrows gone astray, missing their mark, the aim turned lame. I wished to dream and float as the Archer once did in a sky that escaped me. I envied Cloe in my mixed state of longing and belonging, equally here and nowhere. The target on her back brought a knowing I could not grasp.

That last conversation with Cloe rung between my ears and crushed like a weight of tomes on my sternum, recollecting the books we read and shared and the several yet digested on our waiting list, placed in anticipation on distant shelves for our tomorrows – Henry Miller to Bruce Chatwin, Arthur Rimbaud to Anais Nin – so much unread and too much unsaid.

"Tobias Tyrone, I now know you more," Cloe informed one breezy and revealing afternoon. "It's in your name, you do know, yes? Tobias is a holy traveler, a knight, a noble one, searching. Tobias, who drives out demons, like the one that plagued Sarah. Will you drive out mine, Toby?"

"You possess no demons," I countered. "But you may be one, temptress!"

"You are mean and foolish, and I am innocent!"

"Indeed. And I have read up on you as well. Cloe ... Cloe, comes from Cloelia, the legendary Roman who bravely rode her horse across the River Tiber, escaping a barrage of arrows while liberating her beloved, oppressed and exploited youth. Her heroism freed scores of Roman hostages and ushered in a new peace. Cloe is known to be attractive, yes – very charming and seductive! Warm, engaging, she loves company, especially men – for it is with the other sex she finds her friends, lovers and associates. Her natural comfort zone. She is reserved, suspicious, even cautious with women. Cloe is a subtle leader, the best of leaders, she draws in and convinces, influences and moves others whether they recognize it or not. You know very well you did this to me!"

She smiled, and in a silent pose cued me to continue.

"Cloe loves freedom, yearns to travel, adventurous, a dreamer, yet absurdly practical with her feet on the ground, punctual and business-like when it calls. She is, essentially, of the clouds but at home on Earth," I generously offered. "Nearly perfect, I would say, nearly, nearly perfect."

"Anything else? More, more," she pled with a teasing call of her index finger.

"Well, behind the lightness, sweetness and smiles, she likes her power, too. It gives her the liberation she requires. No path is really direct – she meanders over mountains, needs her roundabouts, not the straight-aways. She is adventurous and irresistible. And, with a good dose of beauty and personal charm, she attracts us to her center, to bear extra witness. How's that?"

The playful exchanges opened doors, glimpses into the life she shared with her husband, the quiet, creative and prolific playwright Philippe Hilaire, and the blossoming plans they had to open a small inn and bistro for artists in the foothills near Arles. She had already succeeded via several scouting trips in locating a real estate gem, discovering the majestic property of her dreams where she would live out her decades. It was not far from the restored and ancient Roman amphitheater whose remains are sturdy enough to host and entertain today's throngs. Once the capital of the province of Gaul, the entertainment there was once very brutal, gladiators facing off against wild African beasts or dueling to the death. Applying an early use of practical perfumery, the Romans scented the fountains of Arles with lavender to mask an overpowering stench of death. Cloe had other transformative plans for the purple shrub flowers, her own brand of lavender candles to be lit as laughter flowed in visits to the waters of Arles.

They would not permit me to the fourth floor to see Cloe. In the chaos, while a cluster of loved ones herded on the front steps, officials from various branches of law enforcement and government authorities from several nations encircled the Rotonde and Hotel Splendid barking conflicting if not contradicting orders from megaphones in various languages. A queue was established for loved ones who had confirmation of their deceased. They used stanchions from across the street where red-carpet film premieres and black-tie affairs were held in preceding days. Local children swung on the ropes with indifference and no one seemed inclined to stop them. Playful laughter from the little ones added to a disturbing excitement and euphoria in the toxic air. Could the children be blamed? Perhaps they possessed some magical, genetic secret to carry on, their chuckles and giggles in circular chases through the palpable darkness and stark reality reminders and indications of youthful resilience. I watched and longed for such antidotes. Perhaps such is spared, justly and solely, for the truly innocent.

The circus had come to town, epic, unprecedented and monumental. Every imaginable news outlet was represented, Al Jazeera, BBC, CNN, popular and notable newscasters placed and positioned under blinding lamps, the hum of generators and media vans drowning out the steady sound of the natural shore. Microphones were shoved in tear-soaked faces, those frantic in the queue, invading personal and sacred spaces of the despondent, demanding answers, truth and reason as if such could be found. People shouted horrific insults at each other, aware of a global audience glued and drawn if not entranced and entertained. "Kill the terrorists! Shame on France! No justice, no peace! Down with the imperialists!"

Woven between the angry insults were calls for the broken, missing and lost, distraught individuals carrying pictures in the pleas. "I want my baby! Where is my daughter? Has anyone seen my husband?"

After two more days of such madness with painfully few answers, the authorities cleared everyone from the avenues surrounding the Rotonde. Cannes Harbor was closed off and the heliports were blocked providing access strictly for emergency personnel. In fear of a possible second attack the village of Cannes was sealed from every direction by military troops as an eerie sense of a city under siege took hold. This was now an official war zone inaccessible to the general public, encircled and occupied by the armed and frazzled, the zombies and the dead. I waited with the frantic others in various hotel lobbies and on street corners for four more dreadful days, displaced and herded when man is confronted with such large-scale, collective shock. A community of well-dressed refugees we had become.

Still, no political, militant or terrorist organization had claimed responsibility. Responsibility – what a charged and misapplied word to such acts. This only added to the psychotic nature that permeated the salty air along the Croisette. Here the broken souls in anguish and unabashed mourning strolled aimlessly past towering action-thriller movie posters, comical-sized cologne billboards and mammoth automobile advertisements draping the expansive reception tents on the empty sand, remnants, left-overs and leave-behinds from business conducted and soirees and parties held just the prior week.

Cloe, I knew you were gone. I felt you depart the instant I heard the unspeakable roar and crash from three-hundred meters away, across the avenue and narrow parkland situated between me and the ornate entryway of the Rotonde. This was followed by several other crashes, the subsequent collapse of mortar, stone and steel, balconies and terraces – half of the great towering façade that once welcomed the film and television industry to this pearl of convening, the cinema showplace by the sea, man's toast to his projected self, his bow to his inflated, redundant and recorded ego – plummeting in gravel and ash into the swallowing sands of the ancient shore.

There, most of it fell, loud and swift in a pulsating puff of gray powder accented in columns of black, pink and orange smoke. Thirty seconds and it was gone in a pyroclastic flow, as if Vulcan himself, the Roman god of fire, visited with his swift and lethal intent exhaling his plume of burning vapor in a heat of immeasurable degree, gaseous, metallic and stony in nauseating blows of dioxide and monoxide. Thirty eternal seconds gave way to bizarre silence. Our entire journey, the centuries of creativity from pictographs on Loire Valley's cave walls to the tedious streaming of digital content on cellular devices, brought into shameful focus in a moment of narcissistic, violent and deadly hyper-expression.

My feet vibrated in the seismic shockwave, bouncing in a physical anomaly lifting me a few inches from the trembling terrain. How high were you thrown, Cloe? As I stared at the pyre, the critically impaired and dying Rotonde, I estimated hundreds inside to be vaporized, though I only had images of you flashing in my pulsating skull. Had your entire, mortal being vanished, or did fate grace us miraculously with the gift to find you in the flesh, however bloodied and broken? Were we reduced so speedily in the calculus of fate, measuring fortune and misfortune in a new math, redefining gratitude and blessing? Were we so quickly on-notice to bargain away our sense of luck, fairness, justice? To be presented a body are we strangely more content than those only finding a shoe, a ring, a tooth? In my trance I muttered within myself a knowledge you had died. My feet back on the rumbling ground I readily bargained with fate, wanting to see your body in a selfish need to say goodbye, when you had already bid farewell along with numerous, unknown brothers and sisters, the familiar and the stranger, in that thick pyre of smoke spilling from the urn that was the Rotonde, chemically transformed, ashes to ashes in the ascension to the heavens to join the saints and gods, prophets and poets, the legions of angels on watch asking of the Maestro, shall we dance, play or go astray today?

Cloe, was there a split moment when you had complete and cosmic understanding of your terrestrial departure? Did you know fear in all its cruel manifestation? Did you seek impossible shelter for you or others? Did you find solidarity with dying strangers? Or was there cruel and teasing hope, fleeting, gained then lost? Did you call for someone, anyone, Philippe, your mother, me? Was love sadly absent then gloriously present? Did the gods abandon for a moment then appear, to guide and protect you, forever?

I did not cry for some time, several days at least. I wore a blank gaze, the expressionless face worn by the battle weary, citizen-warriors in the halls and streets when life delivered a poisonous dose, betraying joyous journeys once schemed and planned. I adopted new colors and earned the soldier's stripes. I was dirty, interior to exterior. I did not shower and had stopped eating.

Leagues of the lost, the mourners and the desperate, made circles around the small plazas of Cannes awaiting instructions or miracles. Hostility met grief. Harmless tribes turned to unpredictable mobs on the once-gentle shore as hours and days passed with explosive stench ever-wafting into nostrils and lungs. The mounting presence of law enforcement and news media only heightened anxieties. Juvenal wrote satirically two thousand years ago about his Roman brethren and descending city, *the ropes are heaved, down come the statues, axes demolish their chariot-wheels, the unoffending... and now the fire roars up in the furnace, now flames hiss under the bellows.* Do we, those on the other side of the yellow crime tape hissing under the bellows, have a bank, a reservoir of tears stored and dammed, at-the-ready to guard us in self-discipline? What happens when such levees break? I had many such sober moments to consider but I shut them off in foggy retreat and thoughts of Cloe. Why a grief directed solely on Cloe? My heart knew she was gone but my soul argued for equity, a share of affection for all lost. But for those several, impossible days the absence was consumed, concentrated and consolidated in the essence of one close and dearly held casualty.

I never kissed you, Cloe. You were married, composed and secured in a uniquely respectful and understood bond, a committed life-partner and companion I got to know over ample servings of coffee and wine. I never met Philippe Hilaire but you provided detailed description, physical to character. I looked for him in the sad faces among the broken masses in those dizzying days. He was roughly my age, about forty, tall and fit. He was a jogger on the beaches and hillsides of Nice, swam in long laps in the waters along the calm shoreline at sunrise and practiced yoga which you had convinced him to try in recent months. He had long, shoulder-length sandy hair, occasionally pinned back in a tail, and kept a short, well-groomed and permanent bronze beard, a stylish five-day shadow of stubble on a face accentuated with round, golden-framed eyeglasses, adding more than an air of taste and intelligence. He dressed sharply, was artistic, a producer and director of live theater having recently opened a three-month run at a large playhouse in Nice which was gaining international acclaim and attention. The production was called *Eden Revisited* and you were happy for him, Cloe, the reviews coming in strong and positive. He was on the cusp of signing a major production contract to bring the play to a few major cities, including Paris and London. You had contributed your talents in the design of the stage and the choice of wardrobe. He was strong-willed but gentle, a public figure but a private, shy soul. You loved him for who he was, yet wished more for him, including a long run in a larger production, and now the dream was within reach as was the country prize, the creative real-estate enterprise in Arles. He could be removed, detached, even cold at times due to uncertainty in his pursuits, but he was certain in his adoration and commitment to you.

While gaining substantial momentum, I was discouraged to see *Eden Revisited*. Cloe had created an unspoken, mutual understanding that did not permit the intersecting of our circles. The boundaries were harmless, implicit and unchallenged. We respected the line and did not cross it, like yellow crime tape. There would be no interfering with the emotional zones. Unsaid and intuitively shared, Philippe and I simply accepted the demarcation and obeyed. In time I knew we would cross paths. It was innocent and destined, and I was sure it would happen by circumstance or chance, by invitation or fate, when proper rooms opened for the Mediterranean air to breathe and bless, simultaneously and cooperatively, an intersection to our separate lives.

Eden Revisited was his sixth major play in a director's role in the past two years alone. Cloe said, with a resigned and less-than-genuine chuckle, directing is the rightful profession for Philippe as he was most at ease, dramatically, "on the power side of life." In directing he had control, authority, the right and privilege to discipline others and, if required, himself. Cloe wondered if he got the most of out of his actors who were intimidated more than inspired, pushed rather than led.

"Philippe is half German. What can we expect?" Cloe pondered in resignation.

The play was written by a retired Greek Orthodox priest. It was set on a desolate, self-sustainable isle with a dozen inhabitants who, while choosing an existence free of modern communications, got wind of Germany's occupation of Greece in World War II through an Italian newspaper washed ashore in a sealed bottle. There ensues a struggle among the twelve as to how to best go about living their designed, agreed-upon isolation with the knowledge of the world's trials. Half feel called to know more, to respond to the imperiled human race they have escaped, a noble combination to take action tempered with a palpable dose of guilt. The others argue for a continuance in their committed journey of sanctuary and bliss, for the troubling news from the mainland only validated their initial instincts to retreat from morbid madness, the rabid race and chaotic, bloody circus playing out on the continent. It is a dramatic musical posing the questions of the ages – to know or not to know? To be or not to be? The apple or the hemlock? On stage or stage side? The ringmaster, gladiator, clown or spectator?

Cloe never disclosed how the play ended.

"You can witness it for yourself, someday distant, if you dare. See it by yourself and take it in, fully. And sit toward the rear," she suggested seriously. "It is haunting and too scary in the front."

The gallery is not closed. The opera is not over. The symphony calls for crescendo. The circus tents are yet to be collapsed and folded. Another act commences, more striking and disturbing than before. A world's audience sits on edge, atilt, anticipating and excited as children swing and play, their gentle free laughter drowned only by the uglier side of exhilaration, the barking and howling in darkened delight. Attention, we have discovered, requires extreme measure in such competing and catastrophic times. Attention, dearest and lost Cloe, has been gained. Everywhere the people lined up for a free ticket to the spectacle, the luckiest or bloodiest ones closest to the danger, several deep on the curve of the Circus Maximus where the view is the greatest, as the scent of lavender permeates and poses as an imposter in the asphyxiating and ashen air.

The sprint on this chaotic and compelling track was far from its destined finish line. Indeed, it had just begun.

CHAPTER II

AMONG THE 623 dead and missing were over twenty young visitors, children of press agents and media executives perhaps in the Rotonde for their first and, fatefully, final time.

Ambulances and coroner vans did not suffice. The mortal demand was too high. Specially rigged refrigerated trailers and unmarked white freight trucks surrounded the Hotel Splendid to store and transport the dead. Military aircraft from various nations were dispatched to take their fallen sons and daughters home. United Nations transport vehicles waited in queue as huddled vessels in Cannes Harbor bobbed on standby to accept the scores of the unidentified and unrecognizable, or discourage any unforeseen troubles splashing in the nasty crime's wake.

It was at the makeshift admittance station I learned Philippe had placed my name on the manifest of next-of-kin and family visitors permitting access to Cloe, an act of nobility, humanity and kindness not lost on me. Civility was resuming and restoring the shattered city as hostility gave way to a gradual if not hard-earned acceptance, evident on worn faces of broken loved ones hovering and roaming throughout the city ushering in a welcomed calm and resignation compared to the maddening hysteria of the prior week. In the air remained a pall of palpable sadness, the unspoken, still and unmasked qualities of French resilience, the ready pivot and lean for bouquets of wine and wafting lavender which in an instant could turn to wide and wanton depression not seen in France since the Second World War. In moments most needed, spontaneous and thoughtful acts of respect and gentleness prevailed.

In this spiral and spin I wanted to be at Cloe's side. Philippe's generous gesture made it possible. She had been moved from the Hotel Spendid, one of many sorrowful details in a final journey her husband had to mitigate. Philippe had left a note for me. In the coming days Cloe would be cremated, her ashes kept in an urn until a private sprinkling into the Mediterranean off Pointe de l'Illette.

On the other side of a portable glass partition in freezing quarters Cloe laid on the bottom of stainless-steel body slabs stacked in one of the frigid freight trucks adjacent to the destroyed Rotonde. I was escorted by a medical examiner and a French guardsman. The examiner read from her report clamped to a clipboard, an earpiece tucked in her left ear and a radio buckled at the hip. She seemed too young for such duty, I thought, but she matured before my eyes, her yellow latex-gloved hand flipping pages in search of Cloe's gurney number and other dismal details. She read aloud sharing no eye contact with me, describing in clinical terms the extent of the lethal injuries. While visible, external wounds were limited, bruises and scratches to her arms and forehead, Cloe did lose her right hand just above the wrist, kept under wraps and gauze. This would have caused severe hemorrhaging in the final agonizing minutes, moments I spent staring at the Rotonde from three-hundred-meters distant, the chasm which stood between my survival and Cloe's demise.

It is believed the blast had thrown her a substantial distance in a common direction with scores of other unfortunate souls, as she was located among a disturbing number of bodies found clustered against a fully intact back corner of The Bunker, the below-ground, windowless exhibit floor in the basement of the Rotonde. The concussion from the explosion, as well as several grave internal injuries, were proven to be deadly to nearly everyone in The Bunker. In short, I was told, we can ascertain with some relief and certainty Cloe perished quickly.

Cloe was on her back as the examiner led me to her side. She lowered a plastic cover revealing the face, neck and shoulders. The woman stopped there, and taking a few paces back, left me alone with my deceased friend. I leaned in close to examine her, not in fear but puzzling anticipation, a personal, content and grateful reencounter with my lovely friend.

I uttered for anyone to hear, including myself, "I'm here, sweetness."

For a split second I thought a small smile began to form across Cloe's pale face, a cosmic return of comfort.

"I'm sorry, sweetie. I'm so sorry. I'm sorry," I whispered between salty sobs.

She looked beautiful, peaceful, resigned. There were pocked blood marks on her forehead below her delicate hairline, and a few faint scratches running along her collarbone. Her hair was fine and fragrant, groomed, pleasing to my touch as always. I ran my fingers through Cloe's soft, shoulder-length mane.

"God keep you, sweetness. God forgives us," I whispered in a repetitive act of yearning reconciliation.

Was I apologizing for the mad behavior of the entire world, expressing a guilt owned by the entire human race, or myself? Did she hear me, and if so, would you forgive us all, Cloe?

Your expression was boldly stoic, as if knowing in your eternal sleep all that was now clearly lost on us, the stirring and sobbing. What is this secret, Cloe? If you had the clues, the code, the elusive answers, could you have found a way to share it with me in my selfish, lost and curious state?

I was feeling utterly alone. I wanted the patient and silent medical examiner, standing fixed and attentive, to leave us alone. It would be best if all these other deceased souls could have been readily brought to their respective final resting places, too. Perhaps if I was left truly alone with you, Cloe, the magic that was our bond could have materialized and spun a blinding halo around you and me, and for one immeasurable moment we could share innocent laughter again, transported in time to our favorite café or, alas, in this cold, macabre cubicle on display, granted a final, lasting and appreciative farewell.

But Cloe could not perform her magic, horizontal on stage in front of humanity, authorities and officials with radios and earpieces, the press, the satellite dishes and cameras, the generators and clipboards, the living and the dead disrupting her peace. We needed to be left to ourselves, but the bloody world was busy spilling the gory details, interruptions and distractions stealing the day, with timekeepers and young attendants clasping clipboards having sorry jobs to perform.

I was glad your right hand went messing, Cloe. They don't deserve to take all of you, and that right hand should be left evaporated into the cosmos with Capricorn, Leo and the Archer. May it never be found. Its separated atoms had been shot into the atmosphere above the hills of Provence, a reagent into the infinite horizons bracketing the Mediterranean. May it clench a defiant fist then point its index finger skyward to the heavens, grip a glass of wine or caress a cup of cappuccino, cut tiny morsels of succulent chocolate raspberry tarts after tasty bites of steak tartare. May it trace a circle, a fine and radiant orb illuminated in every color of God's pluming aurora, perfect, so very perfect, eternally revolving in its orbit, that the loyal legions of amused angels could never tell where it begins or ends.

I bent down closer until my breath, dry and belabored, stirred in circles of vapor like a tempest, a swirling *pneuma*, a hurricane of our own making, a cyclone of thought and love blowing upon your closed eyelids and mapping the years spent smiling at those who had crossed your poetic path, strangers, courtiers, me. Closer I lowered. Closer, until I touched the lips where rhythmic words once flowed freely. Now, my lips to your lips, Cloe – a first to a final – an affectionate end from an imperfect beginning.

I was famished for you. A hungry man is dangerous with his stomach empty, the soul craving. I was hungry for answers, and there were none in sight – only Cloe, silent and still – perhaps the only one here possessing what I needed to know. The levee had broken, the heart's chambers left hollowed and arid. I was dry and tired leaving you, Cloe, with a fuller love I had not known. This was your final gift to me, vacating rooms carrying any last airs of vengeance. You would never call for it. Nevertheless, questions continued to mount, mainly the biggest, for it is always the biggest: why? Why, Cloe? The answer was not to be found in shattered Cannes.

Those back home in America were aware I had survived. Within an hour of the catastrophic combustion I had reached my mother and employer in Los Angeles to share the haphazard turns of fate. I had left the Rotonde twenty minutes before the explosion to take a pleasurable stroll a few quaint blocks away to the renowned chocolatier, Jacque Cousine. It had become a tradition of sorts starting with my first visit to Cannes. What had begun as a few fresh trays of regionally grown grapes and strawberries dipped into vats of pearl white and decadent dark chocolate as an afternoon treat for my colleagues grew to plentiful packages of boxed chocolate gems distributed joyfully and generously within a wider circle of friends in The Bunker to mark in sweetened delight the close of each market. Such delivery guaranteed buoyant reactions, and thus the chocolate tradition grew. Cloe, of course, was a regular recipient as were friends from Singapore, a family three generations deep in the business of documentary film production. Four of the Singaporeans were now dead.

Chocolate boxes would be brought to Charles and Vinny, my amusing business pals from California and steady drinking companions on the road. They were spared. Marge, a veteran of the cinema circuit who served as my mentor on my first escapade to Cannes, always lit up whenever I brought her favorite treat, cocoa-glazed tangerine wedges. Marge survived the initial blast but passed away four days later having never regained consciousness. Charles delivered the sad details over medicinal pints of Harp and Guinness at Morrison's Pub in the old city center of Cannes where we met each day to drown the bubbling and troubling thoughts and sorrows. It was increasingly common to say nothing at all, tipping the pints with blank stares fixed on Morrison's walls, adorned with quotes, maxims and philosophic nuggets spun from wiser men in years of yore.

Charles was anxious and not well. Overweight and diabetic, he had not been sleeping, a sudden insomniac like the rest of us with a disturbing numbness in the left shoulder running down the length of his arm, and now awakening each dawn with a stinging, unnerving chest pain. Yvonne, a French woman he had been chasing, dined with him the night before the blast after a coastal run to the romantic port of Antibes. She was listed as missing. Charles, never having found true love, was ready to fully give-it-the-go and lovely Yvonne was responding in kind. We expressed condolences to each other and emptied our glasses in rapid succession. Words failing and nowhere in particular to go, the natural option was to stay and imbibe, round after uncounted round.

I told Charles how the visit to chocolatier Jacque saved my life. Significance had collided with the trivial, thus a journey for chocolate was rewarded with survival. I felt fortunate and foolish. My escape was void of heroics, a single act of sweet intentions translating into bought time. However, I accepted a curious comfort knowing my fate was loosely tied to performing an act of kindness. Charles and I managed a faint chuckle at this as he caressed his gut in rebuttal. It was hardly kindness to add pounds to his inflating torso over the years.

I replayed the fateful steps over and over again in my dizzy head.

From the chocolate shop I walked back toward the Rotonde, then paused at the Eglise Notre-Dame de Bon Voyage, a large stone church I visited whenever in Cannes. It is noted Napoleon stopped here to pray on his infamous escape route from Elba to Paris. It was noon, the bells tolling as I approached. Here I held a last and fleeting memory of my innocent, sun-drenched days in Cannes, spent upright and content right on these concrete steps, whimsically toting bags of chocolate in the moments before the terror. Obliged, having missed Mass the Sunday prior, I stopped as the wayfaring French emperor had for a brief prayer. I was struck by a sad, attractive but disheveled young woman, seated and stirring all alone in the rear of the mammoth church, hyper-ventilating in muffled breath with both fists at the mouth filtering as best she could her panting sobs. The typical, constant and happy bustle was just a few meters outside, vendors, merchants, students, conference attendees and elderly pedestrians with little dogs on leashes, but here in the church, crumpled in a pew, wept a single and despondent soul capturing my attention. I recognized her. She had spilled from the front of a slow-moving delivery truck ten minutes or so prior, just around the corner from the church on a narrow path near the chocolatier. She could have severely injured herself for it was quite a leap, from the bench-seat in a high cab on the passenger side over the truck's footing and down to the curb. But she was agile enough to maneuver the leap, and abruptly tumbled until she came to a stop on one knee some twenty feet from the truck, which hesitated for a few seconds before speeding off, making a dangerous right-hand swing past pedestrians before vanishing into the clusters of Cannes. She had been shouting something unintelligible, perhaps in Russian, unclear as it was. She rose startled, frightened, scared, a panic and distress most troubling to witness, a distorted, frantic and fixed stare in her eyes, as if lost in everything but focusing on nothing. She was flailing both arms in hysteria, purring lowly to herself in fluctuating mumbles, now in English with a Russian accent, and before I could consider what to do had run around the corner and out of sight.

Appearing again, she trembled in the back row of the cold-stone church, rocking in the pew as a dozen others paid no mind in the dark, each locked in silent prayer near the altar as the troubled girl and I remained at the rear.

"No, no, no. Don't. No, no. Please. Don't. Don't do it. No, no, no," she repeated between sniffles and convulsing sobs.

I slowly approached nodding affirmatively and slowly, extending my free hand.

"Are you okay? Can I help you, young lady? Can I call someone for you? The police?"

She murmured in lower tones but provided what I interpreted as an opening in the positive nod of her head. I pulled out one of my business cards and extended it toward her in a gesture of invitation. She extended her palm and accepted it.

"Do you have a cell phone?"

She nodded.

"Call the police if you need to, and they can help you. Maybe they can direct you to a doctor or hospital, okay?"

Her head had bent lower toward her knees with eyes closed.

"Or you can contact me. I can help, too. I know a lot of good people here. Don't be afraid, okay?"

In tremors she waved me away, and where Napoleon prayed for salvation I left a broken soul alone in anguish, then exited into streaming sunlight with the harmony of Cannes buzzing on its streets as far as one could sense. At the bottom of the church steps I stopped in full stride. A black and red leaflet, covered in ominous, obscene and ugly symbols, was so provocative I could not help but pick it up. It was out of place, foreign, a departure from the typical litter, the postcards and paraphernalia that saturated the sidewalks of Cannes at market time. Still, demonstrative if not incendiary political literature was not uncommon across the French landscape, particularly around election seasons.

The tattered girl exited a few paces behind me. She stood at the top of the steps, locked eyes with mine, the leaflet clutched in my left hand and bags of chocolate gripped in the right. Her flailing now rose in pitch and tone.

"No, no, no! I'm sorry. Don't! Please!"

Her Eastern European accent was strong but the words came through clear in amplified English.

"Serious! Serious! They are serious! Oh, God! No, no, no! Please, please, please," she exhaled in cries echoing against the stone walls as scores of passersby kept their gait. Two tourists, women with satchels and cameras in tow, stopped for a picture in front of the church. They asked if I would take one of them, missing the hysteria and cues of the moment. I looked up at the girl, then back to the tourists, English or perhaps Scottish travelers, sharply dressed in summer attire, adorned in floral dresses and designer sunglasses. I motioned them away with a wave of the leaflet and a negative nod of my head. I retreated up the steps toward the girl and placed the bags of chocolate down near her feet.

Then – a blast – a deafening roar!

My legs bent as if turned to rubber, followed by a mysterious bounce from the concrete ground lifting my feet from the surface in a series of bizarre pulses. The roar was coming from the south by the shore, the location of the Rotonde. Could it have been some sort of miserable, action-film promotion from one of the exhibiting production companies? Or had a cruise ship blown a tremendous engine? Whatever its origin, the sheer volume and concussion was too mammoth to be normal. I stood frozen in the sight of instantaneous pyres of black smoke followed by secondary crashes, lesser booms, different shades of rising smoke, oranges and pinks blending with the black. This was followed by a few moments of eerie silence and a churning clamor, then drowning screams rising from the paths, alleyways and streets of the town. The howls were feminine and masculine, piercing and guttural, a chaotic chorus of the old and the young. All of Cannes was responding on cue to the presenting horror. People homed in a frenzied pace as if called by instinct or trained to the source. Some collectively began to trot that turned to a mobbed sprint. Others, such as me, were lost in a centripetal spin, dumbfounded, moving in tight circles, neither retreating nor joining legions listing toward the explosion. These brief yet interminable moments locked us in tight but wobbling ellipses, rotating our odd orbits as the Earth tilted from its axis.

I remained for indeterminant minutes before a force spun me from the fog. Everyone was disbursing by reflex. The girl had vanished. A quick pace took over, my clouded mind obeyed the restless legs that raced in long strides in the direction of the Rotonde. As I rounded the last corner to face the historic convention hall and its familiar dome I knew at first glance my presence was fruitless.

Cloe is gone. I swallowed the truth as a rusty dust began to enter my nostrils and evaporate the moisture of my sinuses. The Rotonde was destroyed, engulfed in dramatic fire. Unconsciously I had managed to maintain in the grip of my hand the leaflet, stuffing it into the back pocket of my slacks. Strangely, I took mental account the chocolates had been left behind at Eglise Notre-Dame. Days of delicious deliveries were over, forever. Hundreds must be dead, I surmised.

Life is fragile and no one immune from consequence, circumstantial, accidental or destined. For everyone who exited the building minutes before there must have been a poor, unfortunate soul who had made the fateful decision to enter. There was nothing those of us on the outside could do. There was a flood of broken and panicked survivors to the rear, nearest the water's edge, but no one was coming out of the burning black horror show that was once the main entrance. Flames were rolling in, tumbling wheels of fire, recurring and innumerable from the base to the upper cascading terraces, as rubble fell in regular, cataclysmic crashes. Smoke, in a most-foul flavor, polluted the once peaceful and fragrant Riviera air.

I shook my head as I watched it all go down, layers of floors and walls, tons of cement, beams of steel cooperating in the latest imperial fall. I knew by instinct this was no accident, but a bombing. I stood paralyzed in resigned philosophy, pondering the point and purpose in a blender of swirling thoughts as the smoke thickened, helplessly observing as the incineration of the hall entombed Cloe.

Alas, within the framing came focus, the rehearsing, reckoning and recording of conquest over the centuries, scripted in Cannes where mass media met mass hysteria. Here I stood where Romans trekked, Nazis marched and Hollywood played. But the Roman she-wolf, the ever-loyal, watchful protector called upon by the god Mars, the *soter*, savior of founders Romulus and Remus, the sons of Mars and the vestal virgin Rhea, could not be expected to parlay her powers across the French border. Cannes was innocently exposed and hopelessly vulnerable, the palace absent of her guards and centurions. Now I solemnly saluted to all I built in my trite years within this grandeur, everything I gave and chased in my run in this arena, choices taking me into that building, christened as a palace itself, the playground of the privileged and royal – we the self-appointed princes and kings, czars and queens – so very important, powerful and perfumed, not to mention civil, structured, wistful and worthy, fortunate and free, until all afire.

Once the palace falls, fiction to non-fiction, the genres are blurred. We now faced one complete and stark end. Violence sells and violence is bought today, and behold, the cost! In the final transaction, violence takes the day, just as it took the better part of the twentieth century and countless other periods in the bloody round-robin turns of tumult over millennia. The welcomed pauses of tranquility and prosperity are only pocks on the constant landscape we continue to sketch for ourselves, marked and scarred by gunpowder and projectile, conceived in the eternal power grab, founded in the hostile take-over, accentuated in the recent blast and heist of what once was Cloe, six-hundred-plus more, and me. Pompei and Vesuvius have nothing on Cannes and country today. There will come a time when we wish to reside perilously and purposely on the crest of Mother Earth's volcanoes, for nothing else but to admire and respect her potency and beauty, free of intent, malice or design, absent of contrived murder and destruction, the natural blasts that rewind and remind man of nature's mighty firepower. *Contra virum*, the volcano boils to create. From her placenta spills magma to land and life, ash to nutrient and seed. We are alone on this planet possessing a singular, sadistic thought to destroy for the sake of destroying, to kill for the simple drive of killing, to ignite the fuse of death when the majestic matchstick of life can be lit all around us. If we claim to be exceptional it is because, Eden to Cannes, we are, bragging and boasting of our choices as all the walls come tumbling down.

In the recycle we return to remove and salvage, pillage and dispose, staging for the next dramatic act of destruction. A damaged man idle in his spirituality is the most dangerous creature in the known universe. Our infantile, ego-driven minds know but two paths when left to our own devices – art or arms. Every artist will one day meet his nemesis. Am I the artist or his nemesis?

Be one an architect, teacher, musician or painter, the man with a buck to make, property to usurp or an ax to grind trails not far behind. Only the target is left to be determined. Indeed, in time, the aim is taken, lecherous if not arbitrary, the stakes rising higher, higher and higher. So it is in Cannes one heard the incessant echo of the prophetic poet Virgil, warning *graviora manent* – heavier things are to come.

Today, Rotonde, you made your turn, along with 623 lives, souls and spirits in the rubble and dust. We do not take pity on palaces, nor project pain on the children. We mourn for the adults and weep for ourselves and, in dire preparation, brace for the next, and next, and next thing to come. I hear you, Virgil. Remind us to give up all fairytale notions of the learned and matured, embrace the sound tales and valuable trials of youth, where benevolence, heroism and morality reign. We feign in our claim to be artists and profiteers at the same time. This is the new and malignant addiction, compounding our contradictions to new lows. The artist storms the palace armed in craft and imagination, influenced and entrapped by the menacing merchant. In ancient Rome, the palace rose majestically, towering in its magnificence high above the great oval of the Circus Maximus, impossibly imposing upon the Palatine Hill. Emperor Domitian had it built to impenetrable, imperial specification, motivated in paranoid reclusion. Subsequent Caesars occupied it for their various desires, the lavish reception halls, vaults and baths secured within elaborate walls of the finest marble. The opulent fortification could not protect Domitian, however, who found himself on the receiving end of an assassin inside the faux protection of his chiseled chambers. In his palace death was decreed, an emperor doomed by his own trajectory. This is the final chapter of the palaces. The architect weeps as the emperor dies. It is a billion deaths before the gods cede and remind Domitian, Nero, Napoleon and Cloe, their earthly domain spouts burning magma at whomever they choose to subject or afflict. The volcano obeys as its bloody guts flow, Vesuvius salutes and Pompei documents, while scores of observers sculpted in ash, muted in clay, frozen in moments and for all time, lay their claim to a place in the race, a race that presses on and on, and on and on – as it does, track to track, gun to gun, its mortal finish line drawn indistinguishably from its innocent start.

Profiteers, meet your artists, and then chase these artists toward the masses, over and over tiptoeing and traipsing through hoops of time in wider and wider concentric circles in the cosmic spin, the recurring whirl of construction to destruction and back again, a sprint from a start to the finish, the perpetual rerun, clockwise to counterclockwise until the whole world's economy and its racket of moneychangers is dizzyingly spent and exhausted but its consumers refueled and fed for the next charge.

So it's you, money, who cause our life's afflictions, Propertius the poet concluded. *For you we go death's journey prematurely. You proffer callously food to man's vice: The seeds of anxiety spring from your source.*

This is what I witnessed from the sidelines, our grand circus on perpetual tour. As I looked unto the charring pyre of death's dust I did not know which one I had become, profiteer or artist, but my bent was on the former, more the marketer surrounding myself in the illusion of creator. But I managed to kiss Cloe farewell in the artistry of the unfolding drama, warm lips to cold, creating a perplexing new outlook and gait. I walked more upright in my mourning. At mid-day on doomsday the true artist, Cloe, died. When all the obituaries, memorials and tributes were set to fuse, Cloe's was scorched deep beneath the embers of departed industry executives. Such rank is nonsense if not relative. History is written but truth is the breath, the exhalation. Cloe was a queen, royal incarnate. She was a goddess, crowned in the stars where the heavens eagerly await her divine destiny, reigning in the charms and proximity of Venus, blowing kisses and dancing in revolution across the Milky Way, where our microscopic efforts and silly skirmishes are hardly resonant in a powder puff, deafened by the flutes, harps and oboes in the orchestras erupting with the blinding supernovas, where Cloe takes notice, amused.

Let the obituaries serve as mortal record. The infinite universe keeps its own score. Cloe skips and prances in time in her hora, victorious after this cheat and defeat. May she in company with the emperors and kings gain due affirmation as she strolls in her garden of lavender and vines. *For as the mutation and dissolution of bodies make room for other bodies doomed to die, so the souls that are removed into the air, after life's existence, are transmuted and diffused,* Marcus Aurelius says from a nearby throne. *Pass, then, through this little space of time comfortably to nature, and end thy journeys in content, just as an olive falls when it is ripe, blessing the nature that produced it, and thanking the tree on which it grew.*

The office attempted to reach me over those incomprehensible and insane days. Beyond leaving a brief message informing them I was okay, I had not been in touch with my Los Angeles colleagues. Tinseltown could be Jupiter as far as I was concerned. It was in the happenchance sighting of a friendly colleague at a pharmacy by the Cannes train station as I was purchasing a toothbrush and razor that I was told it is best I check in with the head office.

It seemed a lifetime had passed since the last exchange with my boss. It was on the eve of this trip, and the conversation with my superior was glib. He spoke for an hour about his investment in a condominium development in Florida. Despite his inflated salary he could not balance his happiness, suffering everyone with his drumbeat complaints, being hopelessly bombarded by taxes and the drive of his financial adviser to make more solid investments. The cost of his daughter's private education, aromatherapy for a squadron of felines and two new Jaguar coupes covered in a carport in Pacific Palisades only contributed to his obsessions and concerns.

Still, he managed to wish me a passing "good luck" with expectation I would return with a healthy lump of increased sales at this year's market. If we had not discussed contracts, budgets, transactions and expense accounts there would be painfully little to share between us.

I found an internet cafe with a decent WiFi connection and logged on, a reluctant link across nine time zones. It being six o'clock in the evening in Cannes, my boss would have been arriving in the Los Angeles office about this time. If he wasn't on his computer then he was drinking black coffee, unsweetened, delivered by the personnel director and sharing gossip to start the day, idle jabber about the trite exploits of movie-industry executives or the personal, hapless lives of his subordinates. I was a regular source of such exchange, not helping my case with open yet friendly flirtations made to attractive ladies roaming the floors of the high-rise office tower high above the Wilshire Boulevard corridor. I was, candidly, good at my work – very good some would say – and I found the duties came naturally if not easily. Having surpassed sales goals every year, I attributed such to my style, an effort to remain courteous, affable, kind and generous. I trusted clients instinctively, warmly and fairly. I gave my effort and was attentive to their needs, interests and lives. I offered my heart and emitted soft mirth. This did not keep me immune from judgment, pettiness and the occasional raised eyebrow or coldness from the home office, where high-strung anxiety and pressure were preferred over a calm and light disposition. For my bent toward the latter, my boss elevated his scrutiny, suspicion and jealousy, and it swirled like toxic clouds between us for years

Here, a week since the bombing, a lack of such concerns streamed from my soul into a brief composition of an e-mail, a direct and economical choice of words flowing from veins in the temples through tendons of the wrists then outward to the flexing digits making a harmony of taps, a symphony of spirit upon the accommodating plastic keyboard.

"Still in Cannes, " I wrote unambiguously. "You all know the depth of what happened here by now. Nothing can compare to being on the frontlines as witness. Exhausted. Exhausted. I will be taking some time under the obvious circumstances."

I pressed the send-button.

Immediately a reply popped onto the screen.

"Cannes??? Returning when?" launched the interrogation.

"Haven't decided yet. Matters have taken a significant and sobering turn, " I retorted.

"NOT a good answer. Be specific," the emperor commanded.

I hesitated to respond, calculating the appropriate and strategic words. I sensed the full scope, the limits, the emptiness and absence of context in this medium and certainly at this moment, and I recognized more profoundly than before the utter void of empathy radiating from the other side of this screen. Unable to digest the tone I no longer related to the language. Sirens and screams, weeping and whispering were the synchronized sounds in my head and, in the best of interruptions, hymns of mourning and sentimental songs filled the vacuum in my heart for Cloe.

I did not care to be strategic. I had grown tired of analysis, gamesmanship and dueling. Competition and jousting over the trivial and mundane had no place here. My fuse shortened, an explosion seemed apparent around every corner, ignited in a look, a glance, a stare or a word. My boss had given me all I needed, words that pounded and bruised my heart, and for the rest of my days will remain a crystallization of humanity divided in universes apart.

"How were sales?" his next email crossed.

I stared at these three words to fully absorb. My knees moved toward one another and while my legs danced in restless, anxious quivers, I felt steam rise from my chest to the sinuses, into my ears and overheating the temples. My eyes burned with infuriating focus, the pupils swelling, a steaming film coating my lids. Bold were the three words appearing ever-larger on the screen.

"How were sales?"

Incredulous, I sat silent and alone in unspoken thought. Perhaps, dear boss, you should ask how was the food? How is the weather? How is the shopping along Rue d'Antibes?

Sarcasm won out as my epiglottis loosened. I replied in words that would serve as this job's epitaph.

"Sales were grand," I replied. "And thank you, though profits were mildly interrupted by a bothersome bang. I hereby surrender and resign. May you be comforted soon in your dealings in the deep south of Florida. My plans call for remaining in the dear South of France."

I logged out and exited the café, having quit my job and perhaps ending a career over the internet. The very beauty, irony and absurdity of it all. Nearly two decades in the business brought to a steaming climax in the push of a button. The immediacy was breathtaking and liberating, a sure and sudden clemency, an amnesty providing immediate rush.

There was so much to do, but where does one start? Flashes of Rome appeared. I would walk across the River Tiber near the ancient castile, taking in the vibrant vistas looking east. I had looked west long enough. Every free man deserves the right to make a turn and take in a different view. It was my turn. Unemployed but occupied, I was instantly void of a conventional timetable, an itinerant in search of paths and purpose. I was exhausted and refreshed. The nearest shop I could find provided essentials. I holstered a journal and a dozen pens, then reloaded my system with fresh, ripened Bartlett pears, bananas and grapes. Nourished and nomadic, I stood upright as I marched into the avenues of gravely injured Cannes, fragile but free. I went next to an open-air bar, vacant with its empty tables and absent of clatter and song and took a stool with a view to the sea. A few servers stood and chatted with the bartender who kindly acknowledged my patience. As a cool salty breeze braised my brow I watched the new and old Cannes sway from my stationary position. Cannes! Cannes! Cannes and the whole wide bloody world would pass by for six hours from that spot. I got mortally and willfully drunk, proclaiming warped freedom and declaring intoxicated independence, martial lawlessness and inebriated emancipation. As evening crept in so did the return of mourning for Cloe. In stumbling stroll I made way to the hotel alone and said goodnight to yesterday, and the yesterday of me.

The following day I caught up with Charles and Vinny at Felix's on the Croissette for pizza, quatra fromage with fresh anchovies. It was the first real meal I enjoyed in a week. Showered, shaven and hung over, I was briefed on rumors flying related to the horrific crime. Apparently, there had been a shift in theory from malevolent Algerian malcontents, extremists holed up on the Riviera, despondent, angry and alienated along racial, cultural and political lines, to an organized terror cell emanating from Lebanon and perhaps fed by Hezbollah. Conspiracies were aplenty and leads followed haphazardly if not recklessly, spilling in the streets and prodded by the press. Though travel was greatly impacted with heightened security measures, flights out of Nice increased and many were America-bound again. Charles and Vinny scheduled their departure for early the next morning and, with masterful encouragement and salesmanship, put on a heavy sales pitch that I ought join them.

Charles and Vinny were accustomed to my aloofness and periodic detachment, the possession of a healthy aversion to cellphones and skepticism of ceaseless technological fads and trends embraced by the hyperactive communications of the day, steered in no small degree by those in our business, money flowing and feeding the digital mania. Yet, more perplexed were they at my lack of awareness on the latest information, for I was the regular, ready source, the steady consumer and supplier of news flashes and story splashes across the world, their headline junky extraordinaire. They were surprised then offended by my short appreciation of the plight of travelers, as well as my general dismissal of the breaking headlines, founded on rumor, speculation and conspiracy. I told them I had no need for such awareness. I had done my internal homework and research. Recusing, I had already embraced an understanding of events, summed up to the best of my necessary comprehension to all that had transpired, and now was closer to my conclusion of what had to be done next. A short-term plan of action was in effect. Having a reasonable grip on what we were facing, I had an innate anticipation of what was about to become. This was news I could swallow. The rest was circulated, dramatic details for the voyeurs, pundits and emotionally disaffected or distant.

"Have you a clue what we're up against here, Toby?" Vinny poked.

"Have you?" I retorted sharply.

"Yes, I do. But now I hear you've quit. What's that, Toby? You're done? At a time like this? I don't get it. I don't know, Toby. Just seems reckless, irresponsible, stupid."

"Reckless. Irresponsible. Reckless. Irresponsible," I muttered his words softly back to Vinny, with a gentle if not condescending grin. "Yeah, that sounds like me. The new me. I like it well enough. Care to join me?"

The jousting ended swiftly in awkward silence. We finished the pizza and took another walk past the destruction zone, our fallen *comitium*. Charles and Vinny talked about the potential resurrection of the Rotonde, a variety of rebuilding schemes already in circulation spun by event planners, organizers and promoters. The dead were not yet buried as profiteers checked the market's pulse. They waxed on about the next proposed expo, scheduled in six months, and speculated on the mitigating factors involved in the selection of an alternative tradeshow site.

Caveat venditor. Seller beware, dear brethren Charles and Vinny.

I remained quiet in the drone of the misplaced banter. Vinny repeated he was sorry about Cloe, recalling how nice she was and what a terrible shame she did not make it. He was holding onto the edges as our friendship was collapsing in real time before our eyes like the upper terraces of the Rotonde. He lectured how we must all move on, as these are just the rules of engagement, of life itself, the signs of our times and ways of the world. I disagreed. I am not resigned to such rules of life. These are the rules of death, defeat and destruction. Vinny omitted an important qualifier – this is a chosen life with the emphasis on chosen, a frantic rush in the race, the hyperactive and manic pace of days where such a human-altering sequence of violence can be nonchalantly gripped in one week's time until our myopic media blinded with attention-deficit disorder steer and stumble into the next horror show, the subsequent bloody, broken, soul-killing episode brought to us in brilliant, familiar hues of red before fading to black.

The times determine choices. It was a quick and reckless decision on their part to stay the course, in my view, and I would not be on their plane back to America in the morning in a supersonic sequel I no longer heard, the alternative steady booms of change holding court in my head. Their journey back was a return to a certain death. I could see the assassins lying in wait. The scoundrels on horseback or glued to the desk, phantoms with sidearms or cavaliers at the podium, united in a pact making us feel mite and small. Look around and it is easy to be dismissed in the masses, diluted in the incessant blender. We are pruned each moment we are plugged into anonymity. It turns and reduces our very spirits to generic ingredients, additives, colorings and dyes, a grand disguise, then whirl! We are spun, pulverized, minced into dizziness, so confused we hardly notice being swallowed down in the daily chug. We are a faded memory when the emperor burps. We satisfy and nourish him but only for a while, for in due time his bloodthirst resurfaces and addicted to the hemlock and potions he bellies up and consumes us again. He curses our absence and seeks damnation from the gods, lashing at our expense. Dependent on us each morning, he grows weary of us each eve. The next day the ritual repeats, and as we lay exhausted, spent and used we are consumed all over again.

Vinny was choosing a death and I saw it in his empty eyes. His heart, always guarded, was now hardened, cold like the watered-down concrete encircling the Rotonde. His focus on surviving was killing him, a distortion that could blast away the entire human race in the flick of a fuse. Hope still had its chance in the warm and vulnerable Charles who would carry the loss of his fallen French love with him to California.

"How will you survive out here, Toby?" Charles mustered enough courage to ask. "You know, financially ... how long?"

I was lighter in my explanation to the sad and weakened Charles. I will simply listen to my soul, I assured him solemnly, and it was telling me to stay in Europe. I was light on cash, but I did have a decent line of credit. The nudge to remain was convincing and so I would heed. In my casual decision and carefree demeanor I sensed the fracture of our trio, musketeers who had shared these streets and multiple adventures through many cycles, across continents and time zones, season to marketed season over two decades in the turning of our Roman calendars. My decision was final and beyond reproach.

They were sad for me and themselves. Pulled to go back they shared the seduction to stay, if only for a little while. The pulling would win.

Rationale would beat romance. Security would preempt the search. I prepared to be labeled a betrayer – *et tu Brutus* – as the musketeers anticipated mutiny. Somewhere in their hearts, I trusted, they must have seen me as a valiant if not defiant charioteer, a noble pilgrim or reluctant pirate fighting in their stead for an experience and truth they may never know. I was not enslaved in this action. I was *libertus*, a freed slave, welcoming my manumission moment.

Our appetites returning and farewells nearing, we had a late dinner at Al Charq, delicious lamb shawarma and stuffed grape leaves chased down with copious bottles of cold Lebanese beer, and I picked up the tab. Charles offered me cash to carry me over should I need it but I declined the kind gesture. Vinny stood expressionless, hands in the pockets of his chic French-designed windbreaker.

"Friends are friends, but we should be clear on money issues," the familiar businessman said. "Otherwise, it will divide us. It always goes that way," he warned himself more than me, before offering a personal loan on the condition I sign a promissory note. This, too, was summarily refused.

Vinny conveniently forgot the countless acts of generosity I bestowed upon him in the restaurants, pubs and clubs, country to country and market to market over the years. I could not harbor anger over Vinny, only mild disappointment. He was often the lead jester, the life of the party and master storyteller, a welcomed clown providing timely and proper doses of comic relief, but he was also a businessman, though his timing here was abysmal. On the promissory note he was not joking and in the rejecting of his offer I was rejecting him, not by word but in a glance.

Solo, I went off to the Cat Corner, a risqué, damp and dark drinking hole a few blocks west into the back alleyways of the Old Harbor. I drank a half-dozen shots of German Bitter Truth liqueur between several bottles of Kronenbourg 1664 lager. I was drunk in the new independence, an American becoming quickly alone in my critically injured and adopted France, declaring freedom from all I once was and accepting an amnesty for what I may become.

At the bar I pulled out my return boarding pass which was no longer needed. I defaced it properly composing a short poem upon it, inspired by an awakening in the darkness and armed with a pocketbook of poetry by Propertius, the diehard romantic and idealist. My poems flowed and ran to moist coasters and pink napkins, each completed piece stuffed into my sports coat and pants. Day was breaking and the black horizon turned to deep magenta. It was time to leave the Cat Corner in search of a real farewell to two souls in retreat. The world had lost order, and one could feel its compulsions, its warring drumbeats and rising pulses, either onward into bloody conflict or backward to comforts of shallow amusement, menial, trivial tasks and continual, gradual and frightful abandonment of civility and citizenry or, more likely, a curious combination of all. Yearning for a higher order, a constancy of maturity and leadership to wash upon the shore, one could witness a wave of trite and frivolous distraction, the pull to fill one's gut, distract the senses and curb carnal appetites. It was grabbing everybody just as it took hold in the Roman tumble and stumble on the way to the fall. *Time was when their prebiscite elected Generals, Heads of State, commanders and legions; but now they've pulled in their horns; only two things concern them; panem et circenes* – bread and circuses – the poet Juvenal prophesied, referring to the limited wants and descending desires of the populace.

As dawn broke I found myself in front of the Grand Hotel where Charles and Vinny were awaiting transport to the Nice airport. The noble knights guided me to Charles' room where he still had the reservation for the better part of the morn. Teetering and tilting on my wobbling axis, I fell over two end tables and broke the base of a lamp. Laughter erupted and echoed into the quiet and still of the new Cannes light. It was our first authentic laughter in days. A ceramic golfer adorned the coffee table, a clumsy character in olive green drab with jet-black saucer eyes. I grabbed it in haste, snapped off his happy, pasty head and in one delightful swoop tossed it expertly through the narrow opening of the sliding glass window. The decapitated golfer's noggin sailed over the balcony railing where it arced out of sight, a descent of four stories, and after a few, long seconds of heightened anticipation climaxed in a terrific crash and seismic smash onto the silent street below. More bellowed laughter followed and filled the room. At this the curtain closed and I passed out on the couch. The good knights departed to resume old roles, to tiptoe upon perilous high-wire acts awaiting them, masked in duties to compete and complete tedious tasks left undone. I was the exposed imposter, having lived an empty and hollow falsehood far too long, yearning for love in sight and out of reach, on the horizon and at my fingertips, performing roles to a fixed audience, their applause insincere and its rewards phony and fleeting.

Snapping his ceramic head and tossing his foolish grin, he was me and I was him – a man of clay molded into a fragile caricature of himself – his forced grin shattered in the dark and dank backstage of the fading night, until he joined in sweet slumber the world of the desperate dreamer. But who was the imperial, reigning clown of clowns now? Who stole his own final act? Who was victor, the triumphant, pathetic, vandalizing and broke, intoxicated and despondent, unemployed and unashamed, mourning and missing, lost and losing, man of broken, battered and shattered clay now?

CHAPTER III

I MADE my rounds and took care of essentials. Arranged was for my residence in Beverly Glen to be subleased to a friend, an artist who had long admired the charming, wooded Southern California cottage nestled among the eucalyptus and pine perched within view of the Century City towers, where Charles and Vinny performed their movie-industry magic dance among the hungry, desperate, lonely and obsessed, those drunk on the intoxicants the industry serves and the public consumes, dose after mind-numbing dose. Now and then the business dug deep enough into its capacities developing and delivering treasures and masterpieces to stir our spirits, educate our minds, stimulate our sentiments and uplift our hearts. I was most proud of the proof, the shows, documentaries and motion pictures which would stand the test of time and provide sound record of stellar talents reaching for our higher selves. But more times than not the content was empty, regurgitated junk, easy and effortless, the quick turn of profit feeding trained appetites, produced and distributed in a fixed model of mindless, mediocre fare.

In Roman times the banal form of entertainment, secondary only to the dramatic races to be had at the circuses, were endless episodes of silly farces, companies of juvenile jesters and pantomimes taming adolescent cravings with colorful and lavish displays in the special effects of their day. Compared to classic Greek theater-goers, Roman audiences were considered simpletons, less educated and poorly equipped intellectually, inclined and led to basic entertainment and light amusement versus serious, cerebral stimulation. Suetonius offers the account of one ambitious, acrobatic performer bent on pleasing the carnal Nero and satisfying the salivating appetite of the Roman crowd by attempting a dangerous and daring reproduction of Icarus. Solar bound by hubris and a jealousy of the winged, Icarus attempted to touch the stars and sun, but the use of wax as a seal for his feathers was hardly the brightest idea. Coming ever closer to the searing heat, the wax melts and he crashes back to Earth where all mortals must die. The Roman stuntman's reenactment was no more effective and flopping back to our planet at the feet of Nero he splattered the shocked emperor in a jettison of blood. Vinny, Charles and the ringmasters of Hollywood could not have done better.

The bougainvillea in the Beverly Glen garden, left unattended, carpeted the exterior of my cottage in fine, feathery flowers, a pillow of pink and white camouflage where the tucked and hidden abode stood behind expansive mansions and fortresses of the neighbors. My friend would be happy there. She made plans to paint the interior walls in shades of bold violets and purples. What may have seemed a shock a few weeks before now was met with no objection. Besides, the absentee landlord who resided in luxurious *suburbium* in the San Fernando Valley would never know nor care so long as rent was paid, fully and promptly month after passing month. Across a span of six years I had never had a verbal exchange or visit with the owner, the Valley to Beverly Glen separated by a chasm bridged only by monthly remittance and a postage stamp.

Accounts were settled. Outstanding credit card debts were balanced and the auto insurance canceled. My artist-friend could awaken the tired Mercedes coupe, hibernating in the carport, its keys in the kitchen cabinet on a hook above my Corona Petit cigar box and Cabo San Lucas tequila shot glasses. If she declined, then the Mercedes could gather layers of bougainvillea flower dust until my distant return, should I return.

I had not been in automobiles in two weeks, adapting freely of them. Liberation on many fronts was sinking in, transportation on foot the primary mode. In daily walks, one at mid-morning and the other at dusk, my favorite time of day, I became increasingly annoyed at the loud, aggressive and polluting noisemakers peeling and scarring the ground in rubber and soot. Europeans have amplified the global cacophony in the introduction of thousands of Vespas on the Cote d'Azur, high-RPM motorbikes all-the-rage, capable of awakening and startling an entire, sleeping French village from several kilometers distant. The piercing frequency is part of the draw, the young, hormonal males in late-night dramatics informing the world of their eminent presence. Indeed, they have arrived in perpetual motion, starting and departing in grinding, ear-piercing circuitry. They circle, circle and circle until everyone in their orbit is forced to take notice. They are compelled and combustible, exerting and whining in every thrust until the engine and they are one. Testosterone fuels the revolutions of the tiny, Napoleonic machine until the whole of southern France is awoken and sucked into the vibrating vortex. Young maidens and mademoiselles in little hamlets unleash the couriers in rehearsal, spinning the desperate and desiring on lonely after lonely quest, dispatching them from the very villages that stole their desires then captivated the compulsions, strangled the loins and pulsated the crotches in the noisy, sexual pangs and pursuits upon the throbbing and bobbing chariots of our times, steered by amateur gladiators in search of some undefined finish line.

The combustible engine and the firearm rank among the most destructive inventions in history, both predicated on mechanical explosion. The Rotonde received a lethal combination of both. I was surrendering my grip on the auto and, as for gunpowder, I never understood the appeal or addiction, its prolific attachment to our cultural psyche. It certainly was propagated and ubiquitous in the selling of films. Everything I once held as vital was put into existential question. Rapid and reactionary change was firing. I could taste it in the air, as fine as gunpowder and putrid as sulfur. Rules, regulations, penalties and prices were to be exacted on local and macro levels. Law enforcement was drooling. Soldiers, attentive and erect, stood armed and aimed. Jets revved overhead in elliptical exercises, roared in regular revolutions in a drown of the ceding Vespas. The Roman poet Horace could be heard in the distance, refusing to accept this reactionary inertia, the new laws serving as replacements for old morals. *Alas! The same of our scars and crimes, and of brothers slain! What have we of this hard generation shrunk from? What iniquity have we left untouched?*

In chorus could be heard the soft voice of St. Jerome as it reverberated in the pulsing chambers of my head. *It's the end of the world. The city that once subjugated the universe has fallen its turn.*

Rome and Cannes, sister citizenries now in the deposition, unsteady, anxious and terrified, Christians and pagans alike.

In the convulsion I purchased a three-month Eurail train pass and a waistband wallet at a travel shop off Rue Louis Blanc near Cannes Harbor. Plans were fluid, the rail pass symbolic, a pledge to myself and a ticket and license to roam. This suited my stirring spirit, a mounting restlessness rising from the chaos of Cannes. For the next several days I would wander the towns and villages in the lush green, golden and rocky hills of Provence, a sentimental journey afoot, a farewell to an environment I had known and a world swiftly disappearing in each step and turn.

This bounce in the step returned me to the outdoor market held on the grounds of the multi-tiered parking structure in Old Cannes near the train station. There I purchased a leather rucksack, two scarves, three white t-shirts, khaki shorts and parachute pants and a comfortable pair of walking shoes.

I headed east on Rue du General Ferrie to Cloe's apartment house. I stared at nameplates adjacent to doorbells and read her name, penned in her own hand several years ago, Cloe Hilaire, a button I had pressed countless times in pursuit of late-night wine, fine cheese and caring company. I placed my index finger upon it but did not apply pressure. I kept it there for a minute, smiling with pleasant thoughts and memories of Cloe joyfully answering my call through the intercom, a spirited welcome amplified from the electronic box into the avenue and loud enough to drown the annoying Vespas.

"Come up, Tobias! Vino awaits you. *Carpe vinum!*"

Now she was but an echo in the concrete canyon. I heard her bouncing off the high, adjacent apartment houses, her spirit electrifying the air and charging my senses.

I often arrived with her favorite wine in hand, Riesling in a paper sack, perhaps a blooming bouquet of lavender or a seasonal plant for the terrace, or fresh-baked French bread and tapenade, tomatoes, olives and grapes, birdseed or a book, all accompaniments for the repast to come.

I stepped away from the building's entrance and strolled along its side on the gravel driveway making my way to the back. I looked up to the terrace, level three, and there as orphans sadly waiting and wilting were her potted plants and flowers, struggling for sunlight and water and the caress of their caretaker, her birdfeeder swaying on the overhang gently in rhythm and cadence with the warm Riviera breeze. While obstructed from an ocean view by taller buildings to the south, from her perch one could taste the tempting sea a few hundred meters distant.

Many an evening we conversed on the small balcony, greeting and feeding the visiting birds as we listened to her latest and favorite musical find, typically songs from England or America. Her steady and supportive love, Philippe, working late into the night in Nice, kept a studio near the playhouse. Any threat to their bond was countered in the sharing of his talent. As I would read from a book recently discovered in the English Book Shop on Rue Bivouac Napoleon, near the chocolatier, Cloe enthusiastically recited lines from one of Philippe's plays. Interrupting each other with our take on such, seated cross-legged on cushions, we shared position and place with the plants and vases, tulips, daisies and roses. Cloe would share her sketches. She liked to draw horses roaming free in the fields, and mischievously etched a few onto the walls above the interior entrance to the terrace. The balcony was tiny with no chairs, and when nights grew late we'd retire to the floor just inside the sliding-glass door, the hours drifting and passing, the Mediterranean changing colors as the night sky turned a collage of seductive deep blue, purple and black. A world below and beyond spun in its orbit around us as freedom rung in the chiming bells high above Le Suquet.

She never suggested and I never moved to spend the night at her side or in her bed, though on the occasion when wine flowed generously I swore I heard the seductive voice of Eve murmuring in conversation with the Roman goddess Pomona, each with tempting, ripe-red apples in hand.

Occasionally Cloe would not answer the doorbell. I would throw pebbles from the gravel driveway against the glass door. She charmingly took her time and proceeded to talk to me from above until granting, as an empress to her patron, the formal entrance, a designed delay and penalty for the casting of stones her way. Dangling her Riesling ultimately permitted passage – *in vino veritas.*

Now in bittersweet blue and somber reflection I picked a few pebbles up and held them loosely until they fell like crumbs from my palms to her arid and empty driveway. I was a trespasser here, a stranger, a ghost on a haunting journey. A curious older woman appeared on the second-floor terrace just beneath Cloe's and offered a sad and parting wave. She knew why this stranger was gazing longingly to the heavens above her, as though Cloe, not I, was transmitting the sorrowful goodbye from above, reclined alone upon her cushion on an empty veranda, beyond approach in her mourning Cannes.

A hummingbird danced solitary and thirsty. Unfamiliar with wilting tulips, drooping daisies and orphaned roses, he moved side to side, up then down, then unnaturally in whipping circles, keening in the soft breeze. He, too, must say his goodbye, just as the dear, elderly neighbor below must. The three of us were in this together, and as I locked on the kind woman's gaze it was understood she already had. We shared a half smile in my final turn to depart. My heels rotated in a grind of the gravel, pulverizing small pebbles into the ancient dust, and I headed back to the avenue.

I walked around the corner in a return to Al Charq where Charles, Vinny and I shared our last supper. Cloe and I frequented the Lebanese restaurant, too, where guests are welcomed to help themselves to wine on the shelves or beer in the coolers, as lamb or chicken is shaved from the succulent spit. I stood at its open-aired entrance as one of the young men asked graciously if I would like my usual, extra lamb meat double-wrapped in toasted pita and heavy on tahini sauce. I quietly declined in a half wave and walked on, around another corner alongside the Hotel Martinez, my home away from America and Beverly Glen. Here I had stayed countless weeks across the span of my career, year after passing year, where at its glorious entrance rows of adoring fans and gawkers would hold court behind guarded rails to simply catch a glimpse of a rising, shooting or fading star. I smiled in a quick summation of light and joyous days spent on the inside of the rails. Then my feet instinctively steered me to the shuttered doors of La Chunga, our late-night cabaret drinking hole where we once put back strong, cheap and bottomless bottles of liqueur, stood on teetering stools and sang off-key in drunken chorus until the rising sun peeked through on the aqua horizon.

At the shore I stood entranced at Le Plage du Martinez, where on its sidewalk several years prior my fresh and frenetic friend Cloe ran into my arms as she barreled out of control, weaving like a maniac on new rollerblades between scores of nonchalant pedestrians walking unfazed dogs. Her fancy for skating had begun a few days before. She raced rapidly and impressively but had yet to master the art of stopping. She rammed into me face to face, toppling a mint chocolate chip ice cream cone down the length of my white polo shirt. Grabbing my shoulders to keep balance she started laughing until she cried, unsuccessfully applying my napkin up and down my torso, smearing gooey green and black streaks into a masterpiece, a Van Gogh on wheels, my cotton shirt serving as her canvas.

I looked west toward the site of the Rotonde and the imposing cliffs of Le Suquet, formidable as ever with its clocktower anchoring the Old Port of Cannes, a two-kilometer trek I had completed scores of times. Upon the snake path to its summit Cloe and I often hiked, a steep endeavor rewarded with lunch and wine on its western crest or an early evening respite in one of the many inviting restaurants in the delightful descent of Rue Saint-Antoine.

Smoke still smoldered above the demolition zone of the Rotonde. Boats and yachts typically hugging its perimeter were clustered like patient gypsies a few hundred meters out to sea. For a moment I considered walking the Croisette for a final and deeper gaze into the building's tomb. One look westward and I thought better of it, the islands of Marguerite and Honorat in the greater distance stealing my attention.

It was a ferry ride we'd taken to Ile Sainte-Marguerite a few seasons ago, a picnic lunch of freshly caught sea bass smothered in capers, lemon, garlic and saffron, and a tour of the old fortress stirring the senses and haunting my memory. There the infamous prisoner, the Man in the Iron Mask, was detained centuries ago, and it was at Fort Royal on one bright Sunday afternoon Cloe and I peered into the cell of the immortalized inmate before making passage to the mysterious and serene abbey on Ile Honorat, where a monastic community has kept their peace since the fifth century. One island held a man for his imagination, the other housed men for sanctification.

If it be so no man is an island, then may it be true no man is fully free. That is, as long as he is fodder for his angry, competitive and unevolved soul, he is willfully imprisoned and discovers, often at his own peril, the greater cost for self-imposed exile and isolation. When the ferry makes shore do we return as prisoners or saints? Are we passengers on the revolving and redundant merry-go-round, blended dizzy, bemused but confused like perpetual riders on the carousel anchored upon Cannes' waiting bank? To be fishers of men bearing the better news seems the higher calling. But who among us need calm the sleeping Mediterranean today, placid as glass yet concealing a hidden, turbulent current below which offers then teases and topples man's fleeting hopes and dreams, century after bloody century? What is it about your calling, ancient and seductive Mediterranean? This sea and your arresting isles hoard stories of the ages, grinding pebbles in the erosion of history, reducing your cliffs and coastlines to grainy sand, fine as gunpowder wedged between our weathered and water-logged toes. Your sea floor is littered with the flotsam, the evidence and debris of our ceramic urns, vats, bounties of gold, tossed and scattered, spilled and sunken with the cannon and vessels, christened by the gods, merchants and marauders, pirates and kings pursuing riches on other shores, the eternal quest for gain, status, more, more and more, until so heavy in the hoard they sink with their submerged dreams, the tears of a billion ancient navigators and passengers filling the salty, bottomless basin. Yes, Mediterranean, you win. You always win. Cannot we tell by the latest graveyard funneling its cremation, the talcum of bone and ash of the Rotonde into your belly?

I am not a saint. I am more the monk provided the missal or the Man in the Iron Mask granted a key. I am an empty vessel aimlessly afloat on the sacred sea, aging and cracking as the sun kisses and drifts in a

Mediterranean neither angry nor sad. Pity has no place here. Empathy is something to be found on faraway shores, perhaps across the ample Atlantic and its beckoning *novae terrae*. Maybe Columbus and Napoleon departed from here, be it in propelled ambition or imposed retreat, simply in search of somebody who cared.

The Mediterranean coaxes us into gentle, everlasting sleep in her womb at Gibraltar, giving birth to implode or endure, explode or explore. She simply is, and in our existential stare-down we recognize each other. She rocks familiar, like the towering clock high upon her cliffs counting the passing of the minutes and millenia, taking her arbitrary toll, as her minutes pass to hours in the fleeting minutes to measured hours, churning years into ages, spraying her sands through our fingers century after passing century for anyone left counting or consoling.

The time had come. I had swallowed all needed to be absorbed here. I waived down a taxi and left Cannes for the dry, parched and rising rambles to the north, deep into the flowing labyrinth and hills of Provence. It was mid-afternoon in the thick of June. The sun felt good on my exposed neck and brow. My watch was tucked in the rucksack, replaced by a brown and ivory-beaded bracelet purchased from a roadside artisan in the charming village of Grasse, nestled in the bosom of the world's perfume industry. Fields of every color elevated and heightened my senses. Here, classic perfumeries bottle nature's glorious fragrances in an alchemic magic trick to camouflage our sweaty and soiled selves.

The famous French chemist Rene-Maurice Gattefosse planted his immortal name in these fields, bringing aromatic production to new heights. In his lab he discovered the essential virtues of lavender by accident and injury. Having burned his palm badly he sought the nearest remedy, submerging his seared hand in a tub of lavender oil. Healing commenced immediately, relieving the pain and, in short order, leaving very little residual scarring. He took his experiences to heart, introducing and experimenting the medicinal qualities of lavender on the injured, ill and poisoned troops of World War I, then campaigned on behalf of lavender farmers suffering under harsh labor conditions establishing a growers' cooperative for the industry. The father of aromatherapy, Gattefosse left a sweet scent to follow, and I was readily upon his path.

We plant, cultivate and compound flowers to disguise our natural, odorous layers, a delightful game we play with nature and ourselves, chasing away scents in every secretion of our perspiring glands. A handsome price can be paid for such deceit but sweet deceit it is, and here in Grasse was planted a memory of Cloe, friends and I swathing and sampling cologne, perfume and oils under our begging nostrils when the world once smelled so good.

I sweated from the long walk, choosing not to impose on the theater playing out in the perfumeries and legions of the latest sniffers. I stayed on cobbled paths and strolled Grasse's fields, into golden, eye-popping red, purple and emerald orchards until an appetite blossomed. I found plums and bananas, strong French cheese and a freshly baked baguette. I ate half, sharing the remainder with gathering birds in a shaded plaza where three water fountains flowed from stone walls into cool, rocky bowls. I pulled out my pad and wrote a poem about the pigeons whose meal was disrupted by one lone, aggressive black crow. I titled it *Fair Competition*, a stanza peeled: "Wings taunted and tattered never anticipated the scorch, Should not the widow recognize her flock? Perched stares the raven, hard and black, Comes, like cloud, steals as night, Yet raven meets wrath, In a soft chirp at sunrise."

From Grasse I made my way to St. Paul de Vence where watercolor paintings, sketches and drawings, jewelry and pastels, olive oils and wines collide in a colony of artists and businessmen. The products were grossly expensive in a village spotless in its display of dueling galleries. Overnight tourists in bright and bold clothes peered window to window and door to door, credit cards drawn and flashed. No one was painting but everyone was selling and shopping. The walk was welcomed but I was feeling cheated, clumsily clean in my own perspiration. My skin burned but I absorbed the pain and price willingly. What is such suffering compared to Van Gogh's amputated ear and Cloe's torn hand?

I leaned against a shaded stone wall and dozed into a blissful afternoon nap. Rest was calling and here it was cool, a breeze on my brow similar to afternoons I knew before, a lifetime before the Rotonde blast ushered in an end. Is it an end or just a continuum? How could I feel stone-cold comfort against this wall while others lay on steel-cold gurneys far below? Survival and endurance are utterly random. Though alone in this contemplation, images of friends and lost ones flashed in the fragrant air. They whispered as I peered through the olive trees, swaying, dancing and weaving in the waltz of my sorrow. These orchards shaded and tempered sadness over decades, centuries, and now provided perch for birds wanting to be fed. Music from a far-off accordion bounced off the chambers of my heart into a whirlpool of yesterdays until it alerted me to the moment, a delightful melody calling me to stand up straight and dance.

Who shall join me? Partners in crime or defiance, a great dance circle, enter for a spin on the glorious hora. I am. I am. I am … alive. This is my obligation, to continue living and noticing, to bear witness, all that was, all that could and ought to be, as the accordion shares the gift and promise of harmony and friendly birds keep warm company, the angry, black crow up and gone until all that is present are the survivors and the hungry seeking shade and rations.

I wrote four lines of another poem when the notion terminated suddenly, two screaming Vespas spoiling the concentration. For the first time in two weeks I openly cursed and it mattered to no one as nobody was listening. Only I heard the reverberations of my profanity. I watched with guilt as innocent birds scattered down the narrow path. A short thirty seconds later they reappeared, returning to the same spot at my feet. The pigeons were obese, out of shape, lazy and overfed. I, too, felt vagrant and idle. Dirtier in each passing kilometer beyond St. Paul de Vence, a weight was falling in each stride, salty sweat pouring from sun-burned temples, down a reddened brow and along the nape of the neck into electric currents of the spine. I tasted sodium on my lips. Several birds followed my descent down the stony streets to the dales in the distance as I spread breadcrumbs at my heels. Some were more fit than me. I could tire quickly and lose stamina. If something suddenly rips their sky they exit in unison and on cue, spreading their wings into forgiving flight, faster, higher, out of sight and danger before their brave and bold return.

Will I escape this time? Am I the proper distance, the safe kilometers away to not be trapped, crushed or condemned? How lucky can one man be? How many spins on the wheel and tempts of the fates? You were supposed to soar above me, Cloe. I find no pleasure in the taunting birds, following, stalking, haunting and reminding me. Who was lucky and who was stronger? Who was spared, and who got speared? Who gets fed at the feet? Who hunts and who gets hunted? Who wants wings and who has wings? Icarus flew until the wax melted in a whiff of lavender, crashing to the earth where the crow watches and Cloe crumbled, into the sands of Provence and the dust at my feet.

Nature struts in confidence. She is consistent and fair. The Mediterranean, once again, splashes victorious. Provence, evergreen and sweetly scented, enduring and erect high above her shores, survives in peaceful peaks. Undisturbed in her cocky, colored and fragrant fields, she is immortalized in the museums and minds for all time by Van Gogh en route to his violent demise. We plant, harvest and make battle with you but in the end the stark truth resurfaces and all the showers, shampoos, oils and perfumes cannot wash away or sanitize our sins. We continue to stink, overeat, imbibe and indulge, homicide the lasting linger.

Napoleon and ancestors, retreat, retreat. Elba or Saint Helena await us all, the odor of the exiled, the decaying, the neglected and the lonely, the imprisoned and the oppressed, dirty and orphaned, traipse like stubborn troubadours with accordions and paint brushes in tow, wandering and wistful, swords rusting dull and leather boots wearing thin, the Mediterranean breeze providing direction and propulsion at their backs.

Consider, I did, the birds of the Grasse fields. I considered lilies radiant on Provence's terraces. I considered Van Gogh, Rimbaud, Whitman and Chatwin. I considered the boomeranged arc of beauty to tragedy, and tragedy to beauty and back again, and thought of the innocent spring that gave way to a ruptured summer, the last fall yielding to a bitter winter, season after perpetual season, every century that led me here and pointed me, ultimately, to Rome. The route would be circuitous and spontaneous, hardly direct by intent.

The fine, fortuitous phantom of Jean-Jacque Ampere joined me on the path, the appreciated historian providing his timeless reminder, that following pleasure comes a much-misunderstood melancholy. His voice carried across the fragrant countryside and drifted as a cool and corroborating confidant.

He traced me as I made my way to Biot. If not Arles, it was in Biot that Cloe had dreamed of living out her years with Philippe. She had never felt such charm as could be captured in Biot. I came to adore the very way she uttered its name, impossibly released without a warm smile and sparkle in the eyes in each poetic enunciation. How nearly perfect the village's name rolled off her tongue, spiritually, economically – its four little letters usurped, such as her name, Cloe, tugging her wayward hopes to a permanent place in her heart where her eternal home calls, be it in elusive, broken or displaced dreams – Biot.

Ampere relayed, his words rippling like the skipping of flat stones across the fooling, placid Mediterranean below, east to the ruins of Rome in a ping and current arcing back to shattered remains on the Riviera, until they ground with the scattered shards in our lives. *Whoever has no more ties in his life should come to live in Rome; there, he will find for company, a land that will inspire his reflections, walks that will always tell him something. The stones he walks over will speak to him, and the dust that the wind will raise under his feet will contain some human greatness.*

CHAPTER IV

T HE QUAINTNESS and beauty in such a peaceful village as Biot did not compute in my spiritual calculus. It required violence and atrocity in the total, accurate sum. War and hostility challenge life's fundamental outlook. Such was evident as I multiplied my thoughts before surrendering in the rental of a Peugeot sports car, gripping its manual stick shift and departing Provence in a crossing of the open and expansive French countryside northwesterly into the Vezere Valley of Dordogne.

I stopped for a few days in Les Eyzies where the first members of Homo sapiens to settle Europe started exhibiting their genius and talents nearly 50,000 years ago. They were astonishing cave artists, creating here the Great Ceiling of Rouffignac, friezes and engravings of mammoths, horses, deer and woolly rhinos cut into soft clay-limestone walls, hidden until the past few centuries. At Cap Blanc are the famous bas-reliefs of horses where archaeologists discovered the carefully and respectfully buried remains of a young woman who may have been the artist herself. The intention of these once-hidden masterpieces remains a mystery but scientists believe spirituality could be at the core, a creative ritual and attempt to connect with other realms through artistic expression. Cloe would appreciate this theory and share joy in knowing these sophisticated works were produced by full-time artists wholly supported and patronized by the clan with ample supplies of craft tools, food, clothing and shelter. These early artists had their Medicis, but caravans of later man desecrated the grounds with graffiti in the nineteenth century, such that the great cavern at Rouffignac had to be fully restored. But it was the Lascaux cave that stole my soul even though it was a replica, too, an imposter. The original was discovered in 1940 as France was distracted by a second World War and contains over 600 paintings. With human traffic threatening the environment of this artwork, in 1963 it was closed to the public and my eyes got to see its exact reproduction. It should be no surprise that our prehistoric, masterful and artistic brothers and sisters chose the Dordogne's Vezere Valley. They had good taste and, predicting our passions to ruin a good thing, hid it for thousands of years.

Traversing several hundred kilometers in the overnight hours beneath an early June moon, fortified by espresso and heavily caffeinated chocolate, I was fully alert anticipating the next stop. I entered the village of St. Marie d'Eglise on the Normandy coast on an early, foggy dawn.

A comfortable and hospitable inn awaited in the center of the small hamlet. It was here paratroopers had dropped into the fury from exploding skies, rendezvousing in the pre-dawn hours of June 6, 1944, D-Day, to take out key Nazi defenses and installations and secure the higher ground. In their wake came the advancement of tens of thousands of anxious, storming Allied troops onto the beaches below.

Operation Overlord was executed here, the single largest amphibious invasion ever ensued in history, the full, bloody measure of man's ability and affinity to settle his scores, army against army, tribe versus tribe.

I found it difficult to channel or harness the horror on such a gentle and tranquil overcast morn that once these villages, their paths, fields, bridges and shores, were littered by the bits and pieces of human flesh, scattered and shredded in the debris, ripped from planes, trucks and landing craft, tossed among helmets, rifles and the torn nylon of parachute nets, as dissected boats bobbed and the bloody beaches yielded in a flotilla of fallen bodies.

One more nearly complete, great and epic cycle of gains and losses spiraling into the skies and slamming into the shores, beachhead to beachhead, contributed to the immeasurable toll paid high and mighty on history's ledger, the latest aggressor and occupier barricaded and formidable, the English Channel in its scopes and all of Europe at its back.

I gathered myself at dawn to pace Omaha Beach at the approximate hour the invasion had taken place decades before, passing hedgerows, farmhouses and bakeries to the ghostly shore, not another mortal soul in sight. Here, on these stones and sands and upward to the bluffs, the young men flooded in by the legion, the deafening, mind-splitting roar and unfathomable fury raining down, heavy-artillery machine guns greeting their arrival as bells foretold a hell that was to reign for several eternal hours and subsequent, dismal days on Normandy soil.

I entered the thick, concrete-casted Nazi pillboxes, so fortified they remain affixed in the turf today, their permanent sights set on the sea, their prey entombed en masse on the rise.

Reliance on a single method of attack or defense is futile, for man continually innovates and employs instruments of war by steady investment in an ever-evolving circuit of weaponry. Had not Julius Caesar himself won the day against fortified Avaricum, wresting it from the Gauls with the clever *onager*, the Roman precursor of the cannon? The emperor's ox-drawn catapult pelted the enemy into a pulp or the humiliation of an imposed surrender by a hailstorm of lead and stone. In Normandy I imagined Nazi soldiers ordered to stubbornly and insanely man the concrete fortresses, trained to shower indiscriminately by machine gun-fire rows of young, flooding Allied strangers, American, Canadian and British boys through cleverly placed viewing holes, mass execution par excellence. The pillboxes were death chambers of the Third Reich, judge, jury and executioner conceived and concentrated in foot-thick concrete. As fog and smoke blended in the morning mist, the Allied lads appeared in waves, thousands at a time in the rush to judgment.

In another period or time the Normandy shores may have served as prime real estate with their majestic English Channel view, ideal for resorts or retreats for the aspiring, vacationing and retiring. Instead, history records it as another position on the planet where man committed mass homicide in a systemic shooting gallery, a slaughterhouse of epic and predictable proportion, planned, measured, calculated and executed, folly and fortune on each side of the equation, from Genesis to Revelation, Cain to Abel, Caesar to Rommel, and Masada to Normandy.

I sat on Omaha Beach beneath its infamous bluff. On these sands, bloodied, wounded and shell-shocked soldiers assembled during the butchery, standing-room only with a front-row seat to man's latest confounding confrontation with himself. How high the cliff must have seemed, an interminable distance of destiny, hell and heaven in the balance, a purgatory over the rise. How distant must have felt their neighborhoods, homes and farms in America, Canada and England, or Germany, Austria and Poland, massive graveyards on the bluff above destined to be their resting place soon enough.

The ocean's spray mixed with the perspiration surfacing on my forehead. It flowed like salty creeks around the bends of my cheeks and nape of the neck, soaking my shirt in a cling to the ribs. I leaned my back to the bluff, struggling to grasp this puzzling desire, the magnetic tug and pull that placed me here.

My library back home was substantial, a fair and adequate supply of world history, volumes lined for posterity on lonely shelves, their chapters unfolding our long story of politics, philosophy and biography. My knowledge of D-Day, while hardly complete, was comprehensive enough. But nothing harbored the heart for being on site, racing as my heels traced the trail of dimples in the sand as the gusts of salty sea air penetrated the nostrils, taxing the lungs and watering the eyes. Senses must be exposed to be fully stirred. I blended in the Normandy mist, shaken and sobered in a steady sweat.

War doesn't fit here, any more than it belongs anywhere. Our natural landscapes are pure, intensely majestic, too dramatically unspoiled to accept this desecration and defamation, the litter and graffiti we dispose upon her terrain. Will natural parks, beautiful architecture, the caves of Dordogne, Van Gogh and Michelangelo mark our time here, or shall concrete pillboxes, rusting barricades and decaying headstones be our lasting, prevailing scar?

I made the obligatory visit to the manicured graveyard above but it was the beach below that continued to beckon. There is the real cemetery, where streams of blood are expertly absorbed and purified. The churning, turning, regurgitating sea does as she wills and in her own time. Our echoing poet Propertius spoke in soft and experienced tone. *Nature has smoothed the main to ambush greed: It can hardly be that you win through even once. Triumphant vessels broke up on Capharean rocks, Shipwrecked Greece was drawn down by a mighty tide. Ulysses wept at the overboard piecemeal loss of his crew, Against the sea his ingrained craftiness lacked its power.* Though polluted and poisoned, vandalized and victimized in the depths and currents of her waters, she floats and gloats in interminable triumph. In the cycle she will wash away the very pillboxes planted here, her winds and whirls, stinging salts and ceaseless tides will erode all we have laid here, and the volumes of yellowing D-Day tomes in libraries, universities, bookstores and museums, and those gathering dust in abandoned Beverly Glen, will be reduced to data, statistics and a few glorified and elevated figures, arbitrarily anointed on the shifting sands of time, adrift in fading fondness or molding markers by the roadside, where they share sacred or forgotten space with Alexander, Sherman, Midas, Zeus, Cromwell, Poseidon, Augustus, Cleopatra and Herod, on and on and on, in trite contests of popularity, perpetuating myths of immortality gained by fleeting glory, figures into footnotes where all scores are kept on the fledgling ledger of history, where they argue their place and position among the redundant and dead, their company among the repetitive, boasting and boring. Their field is crowded with kings and countesses, jesters and generals, their marble monuments to themselves hardly a fair fight against nature's patience, her army of sun and saltwater, storm surges and tsunamis. No one beats or defeats her, silent and still she may seem in her subtle demand to be heard. But heard she will be. The wise turn to her song. Poets, dancers and comedians in desperate pleas beg for the stir of our souls and imaginations. They dance in the great hora with forgotten and discarded giants, yesterday's heroes turned to history's dead. They rest in peace or remain restless by war beneath stoic mimes, frozen in time in concrete blocks and cold columns of marble, shadowed by the statues who are locked in a gaze, where no one is watching or bothering to ask anymore, if we dare to duel or care to dance.

The beaches have weathered other battles, innumerable bloody encounters of Normans and Britons, French and Moors, and no doubt they shall bear witness again. With Nazis in Cannes, why not Poles in Normandy, and Americans, Canadians and Britons in Sainte-Mere-Eglise? Only the negotiations and terms change. The French Republic during imperial times, in an eighteenth-century armistice, demanded of Rome twenty-two million francs, control and occupation of the Citadel at Ancona, a hundred pictures, statues and specially selected manuscripts as well as the popular bust of Brutus, a specific wish list. Across the European continent, in raid after ceaseless raid, geniuses and artisans left homeless and adrift, under-appreciated and unhappy about hometowns that had neglected them during periods of strife, simply let go of their masterpieces, a priceless litter of legacy in the wake of a grand exodus. Attila the Hun exacted a perplexing price, too. Regardless of his reputation, "the scourge of God" could be surprisingly gracious. Storming toward defenseless Rome, he and the disarming Pope Leo met in peaceful negotiation inside the holiness' tent, the outcome being Attila reversing northward over the Alps never sacking the prize of Rome. Exchange for such mercy required but a detailed supply of pepper and silk. The pope obliged and Italy lived to dine and dance another day. So it is, the music plays and marauders march on, christened by appointed nobles and blessed by knights, led by commanders and steered by czars, a debris field of mortar shells and masterpieces strewn across the landscape. Alas, it wages on in the fodder of the common, fathers and mothers, brothers and sisters, sons and daughters, elders and the youth, called upon when Hitler seeks more than the Sudetenland and Attila desires more than pepper and silk. The common are steady and ready, consistent and true, apprehensive but anticipating the next call to engage, to aim, shoot, drop or blast, away and away and away. Occasionally is called the bluff beneath the bluff. But at regular stages we quite simply fail, led to our sad and sorry surrender. When to tally the total and draw the final line in the slipping sand? Germany in an opt of surrender in 1944 versus 1945 would have quelled unimaginable suffering. A simple hoist of the white banner would be a welcomed sight against a backdrop of blistering red and black, signifying the chaos is complete in a deafening and glorious ceasefire. May negotiations and concessions commence! Well-read Rommel, how could your library elude you? Could you not recall the Carthaginian ship in the surrender of the Second Punic War was adorned *with white wool and branches of olive,* as Livy, the ancient Roman chronicler described? Did not Tacitus tell of white flags on display in the surrender of Vittellian forces at the Second Battle of Cremona? Surrender requires more than facing reality. It expects sincerity. In our time the Hague and Geneva Conventions moved to codify and standardize surrender's deployment, forbidding armies to deceitfully wave the white flag in phony gestures, ambush the real ploy.

Homicide taught is homicide learned, sanitized only in the burn of the sun and sanctified exquisitely in the evaporation of sea to sky. Mother Nature forgives and forgets in the incessant slap and crash of every wave, currents cleansing all that came before, tossing as she will in our desire and by our compliance, whether we be visitors or vacationers, maniacs or murderers. Intentions ebb and flow, season to changing season, century after passing century, cliff to sand, blood to mud, rain to river, river to sea, and back again, the currents in a polar dance on the axis, until overheated Mother Nature, perspiring and evaporating, drenching and drying, absorbs all we shout with a gentle whisper, a simple, fading hush in her gentle breeze. It says, "I was here," something we all wish to utter, in pain or in vain. It can be heard and felt like a vibration at the feet, a muffle beneath the louder, incessant collision of sea to sand, over and over and over again – always here, right here – kissing then blowing everything away like all those plans I once held firm in the palm of my hand but a few weeks before and a lifetime ago, before a blast rocked my shore and shot my sweet friend into her sky.

Strolling the Normandy cemetery amongst the scent of manure and cows roaming the adjacent pastures, I was physically bent in sorrow, pacing row after endless row of Operation Overlord dead, many killed out of the gates in the first moments of battle, sprinting for something profoundly outside themselves into the rich, fertilized and manicured soil in a race with history, destiny and time.

Tobias Nathan Tyrone, choose a tombstone and a place to rest.

That was me in the dirt beneath enameled crosses. There was me in eternal sleep under chiseled stars of David. Then could be heard the ghosts of everyone who ever lived, loitering or lost in aimless wanderings in a circle in the cemetery, humming in the affirmative over and over and over again, in chorus with kings and captains nodding in approval, pacing silently and stoically in the ellipse, round and around, counterclockwise to the breeze.

I was a voyeur, violating the sacred space of more noble spirits, this time on the deep-green grasses of Normandy as a phantom of myself. I stood in unworthy and undignified guard, my soiled shoes caked in its coagulated mud as the words of the fifteenth-century surveyor Poggio Bracciolini's contemplation on the antiquities etched their way onto the marble before my eyes – *the wheel of fortune has accomplished her revolution, and the sacred ground is again disguised with thorns and brambles ... This spectacle of the world, how it is fallen! ... The path of victory is obliterated by vines, and the benches of the senators are concealed by a dunghill.*

Medics would recall of D-Day most of the dying cried for their mothers, a return to the safe womb, innocents unto innocents before the fall and fatal fumes of gunpowder and exhaust, firearms and combustible engines, and the peer of unknown assassins in pillboxes took aim at the arriving Higgins landing craft, severing the umbilical cord.

What nationality was the assassin that stole Cloe from her mother? What ideology possessed me, if any, and where might my assassin wait in earnest?

The gaming and gambling rolls on, a hypnotic whirl on the great wheel, war the ultimate bad bet, its ante exponentially raised higher and higher. Our roulette wheels revolve from underground parlors and shabby saloons to the posh clubs of Cannes and the Grand Casino of Monte Carlo. Each of us steps up to the wheel and takes a spin, a turn upon the Circus Maximus.

Most of us take our chances gradually, conservatively, carefully, until the odds change, circumstances and directions recalculated, the centrifugal forces stronger than the tilting will power. Ultimately, even pacifists among us will reach for the rifle. Undertakers are perpetually occupied, their artistry, make-up and performances fine-tuned and nearly flawless. War stimulates the machinery and economy. It makes magicians out of morticians and fools of all. It was for thoughts such as these the Roman literary geniuses, Ovid, Propertius and Tibullus, paid handsomely and painfully. Deemed most dangerous in their persuasive anti-militarism, they bravely put forth influential odes dedicated to love, minimizing the propagated glory of war. This threatened and countered the incessant recruitment of young lovers being hustled into the armed ranks, just as the poets were stealing their hearts. Tibullus chuckled in sarcasm and pity watching youth march to their deaths rather than trek to their loves. In the June breeze high atop the Normandy bluff Tibullus could be heard once again, longing for Saturn where in the age, *there were no armies, no hatred, and no war ... there was no war when men drank from wooden cups ... give me but love, and let others go to war... the hero is he whom, when his children have been begotten, old age overtakes in his humble cottage. He follows his sheep, his son follows the lambs.*

We are running out of marble. Artists are commissioned to carve monuments out of shrinking and sinking quarries. The erosion is artistic and agnostic on each side of the Channel, Normandy to Dover, the quarry to the cemetery ground into tiny pebbles and granules of sand. They find their way along the arches and soles of my feet, the familiar powder of Omaha Beach to Cloe's driveway.

The sniper is a most foul specimen, in hiding or on the run. Cast in a contract with himself, willingly, intently and expertly he terminates life. Better should the gods strike one dead readily and naturally than be in the crosshairs of the sniper's scope. He who can coldly perform such an act is already dead, and to die at the hands of the dead perpetuates the cycle, creating generations of maniacal murderers and monsters. The sniper joins the viper, the cobra and the asp, projecting the lethal dose from a calculated distance then scurrying into the underbrush for others to consider cause or guilt.

In the passing of the ages, the most sophisticated and well-financed armies in the world train and groom farmers and shopkeepers, mechanics and clerks to be their silent assassins. On each and every side of the inexhaustible manufacturing is a re-engineering of man's nature, morphing him into a cold and bitter killer, planting him into the ground or recycling him into society as a roaming replica and sorry imposter of his former self. He can be found dancing and ducking from the fog into shadows of his own purgatory, a veneer of his higher potential, damaged and diminished and hardly recognizable.

It is a recurring D-Day every day for such veterans. Beware of surviving as the slithering viper. For such, the hard time on the parched earth is a long and tortuous death waltz, circuitous, circling him regularly back to what he once did with trained precision, his sharp eye forever stuck in the socket of his scope.

Rattled and stirred I opted to forgo the war museums, my mission completed and the soul justly spent. Additionally, I elected sobriety, choosing a nine-hour trek though the villages of Normandy in a fast of fresh fruit and copious liters of distilled water. Poetry was flowing, four, eight, ten poems in a sitting, against a stone wall, in a bistro or in full stride, pen to pad.

Sustenance was easy. I was spending little and eating less, truffles, walnuts and pears, with ample enough put aside for however many days I thought this journey could have in store. I headed east to explore the Somme where my grandfather suffered and died in World War I. His story was spotty. There was little record of his experience and even fewer personal accounts passed on to his daughter, my mother. Something compelled me to his resting place. From there I could forge on to Rome before any thoughts of a return to America would take hold.

What was this burning call to battlefields pocking the French countryside? Would such roads truly lead to Rome? I thought of the Appian Way, the 350-mile path across the Roman peninsula canopied in lush fauna and foliage, olive, pine and cypress trees providing *memento mori*, a reminder of death in all its healthy contemplation and stark finality. Traveling its route would mean a regular view of the funerary structures, the walls, temples and urns of the dead outside the city placed purpose-fully for those in motion to weigh in on one's mortality.

I could not afford paralyzing contemplation to derail or deny the quest. Yet death, organized, immediate and violent, planned and orchestrated, funded and deliberate, was of wholesale interest to me, and it was in full consent I wore all of it. It draped me, a cloak, a dark and heavy quilt providing comfort, as if by carrying the weight its well-kept secrets would unleash healing powers, a mysterious peace, the ulti-mate paradox in my unsteady state. This subtle pull and tug brought a troubling thrill and acceptable danger. I was aware of its tentacles, the curious capacity for it to grab hold in its lethal lesson – *memento mori*.

The laws of motion, each move requiring a move however risky the inertia, became my driving force. I had to be careful, more cautious than reckless Icarus, and not permit this preoccupation to steer faulty senses, a construct of my own flight where all colorful instincts yield to the compelling gray and black. Shades of my new outlook could paint the entire sky dark, capable of blending in the trolling ranks of assas-sins chasing assassins, killers dodging killers. The challenging trick was to look the assassin in the eye and recognize myself, disarming and destroying the worst of our capacities in kind. Disciplined toward light meant a full recognition of the dark.

Historical images of contrast flashed like photographs as I swiftly marched into the graveyards of the Somme, a daisy in the muzzle of a National Guardsman's rifle, the pope holding compassionate court with his accused assassin, a brave, lone and anonymous citizen standing unarmed and erect before a tank in Tiananmen Square.

We are hardly noble and brave huddled in dark shadows of a fortified pillbox. We are mortal sell-outs. We have cheated. We arm ourselves and disarm nothing. All the radiant colors of the French countryside escape us. We are destined for the black holes hiding in the recesses, behind the beautiful, bursting supernovas of time and space where an ultimate judg-ment awaits us all, where Virgil and Ovid hold court and sing their odes harmonically with the angels. We will be held to account for every grave we dug behind us and each innocent soul we willingly interred.

My grandfather, young and handsome, a first-generation American boy of hearty Irish farm stock was one of twelve children. His clan in the Catskill Mountains of New York anxiously hung on the hope of his return from the war, and awaiting was a wife and three children, the youngest a two-month-old tot, a little and happy girl with golden hair and widely open aqua-green eyes, my mother.

He was gassed on the Western Front, a putrid, sulfuric-mustard fog searing his young and athletic lungs making each inhalation a merciless gasp for life. The early twentieth-century had concocted another murderous method in the ever-clever arsenal. The poison burned lips, tongues and nasal passages and set the esophagus and airways afire, rendering clutched bayonets, heavy rifles and other artillery obsolete, useless appendages when one only asks for oxygen.

Here beneath the rolling greens of the Somme Valley he was buried with thousands of his brethren, a century before his roaming grandson came to breathe freely and deeply above him, marked by the eternal and unanswered question – why? Historians spar and scholars argue, baffled at the cause, rationale and surely hefty cost of WWI, one meant to end all others.

My grandfather was James. A few years ago a shoebox on a high shelf in the Catskills was discovered, containing military records and revealing correspondence between James' father, my great-grandfather, and the U.S. Army in the weeks after learning of his son's demise. A generous and gentle soul, the aging merchant ran his general store in the mountains with the same spirit and sense of service as his beloved pastor who resided next door. He was asking the military's leadership if it would be possible to have his son's body brought home to rest in the family plot of Elka Park in the Catskills, a slope nestled in the hemlock and pine with a commanding view of the ancient mountain range and its crests, where heavy gusts blow through the treetops with such regular ease and might they take the breath away. But such a request could not be granted. His boy had died in one of the muddy trenches of the Somme and was buried without pause or favor among mass casualties. It was simply practical protocol under such dire circumstances that he sleep eternally in the valley across the Atlantic and thousands of miles from familiar Elka Park.

My great-grandfather responded to the reply with all the dignity and integrity to be mustered. "Very well," he wrote in long hand. "Please see to it my son receives a proper marker. I will never see it, but may it be said my beloved son James was once here and gave so much to our lives. For this I would be most grateful."

With meticulous assistance from the cemetery staff I found James' marker. How could I have been in France dozens of times before and not taken the proper time to pay this visit and respect? I found you, Grandfather James. Indeed, you were once here, just as great grandfather decreed.

Here in this sweeping, green and peaceful valley fertilized in the fortified French earth by thousands of young lives, death trenches absorbed and transformed trained killers into mud, once coaxed, armed then led to evaporate in clouds of mustard gas, never to realize their futures where grandchildren can stand over departed kin in silence, each keeping guard secrets and dreams lost and found.

Stop them, please! Don't. Don't do it. I beg you, stop, the mysterious, broken girl said in the moments before the blast. She made me shake at the grave in the Somme as she did in the back pew of the church in Cannes, a shared shiver down our spines to the tips of our toes, grinding in rotations above whatever remains.

By cheating you, James, they cheated me. The whole human family, robbed, cheated and spoiled, bearing witness to the slaughter in the most beautiful places. Lured away in our most vulnerable and aspirational years we are fixed to fly and share the sky with free birds over the Somme Valley absent of trenches, alongside gulls on the Normandy shore void of pillboxes. But armed we are disarmed, knighted to be condemned, lifted to be left – on beachheads, valleys and the dust of the Rotonde. The horn plays taps until the accordion takes turns in a call to the center of the circus.

While Cloe danced the hora with James, I do imagine they heard my cries.

Cover, Cloe, cover! Duck, Grandpa, duck!

I sought you but I was decades late. Punctuality is an elusive virtue and history forgives not the habitual truant. Time provides what it may but fate cares not for the clock.

Please, no. Don't do it! They are serious. Stop them, please, the dirty, desperate girl warned, but she was late, too.

Chocolates? The girl? Grandpa. Why? The church? Napoleon, the hero, the commander, retreat? Is it safe on the bluff? Is my gas mask on? The Catskill Mountains, will I return? My wife. My kids. I'm sorry. These guys are serious. Stop them. Ceramic golfers, headless in flight, Charles and Vinny, drunk in laughter, Riesling and olives, shawarma and ice cream and rollerblades. Ovid, in harmony, returns to the womb ...

It burns, momma. It burns ...

I left the Somme staggered but upright and pressed swiftly east, crossing into Germany and south to Munich in a single day to the hub of history's most organized and mobilized horror show, a front-row seat to where two World Wars were fueled and foisted upon the human race.

I stood alone in the hollows of the enormous cavity of the Munich stadium constructed for the 1936 Olympics where healthy competition among nations consisted of innocent bouts of running, leaping and jumping, the sharpest objects amongst the athletes a javelin, as the games commenced in a wretched, screeching voice bellowed from the hosting Fuhrer and a blast of cannons startling hundreds of liberated doves overhead, splattering athletes below with their evacuated excrement. He would reveal his other games soon enough, a dance in Paris and upon the graves of millions in the human race, his design and redrawn finish line being a maniacal final solution.

To the Dachau concentration camp in the gentle suburbs, a mere 17 kilometers away, I bore witness to this intention, a purification of the race, a dagger into the construct and heart of the Olympics. As self-declared winners in a deadly duel, groomed and well-trained men raised their palms in a sea of swastikas, red, black and gray dominating the earth and sky in orchestrated terror, a signature salute of wholesale evil in full rehearsal and compliance. The trains rolled in and the soldiers marched on, transporting the enslaved and doomed from territories near and distant, a cargo of helpless humanity, Jews, Catholics, the Roma and the afflicted. Family heirlooms, jewelry and precious metals were systematically confiscated, gold yanked from the jaws of precious life. The gas was dispelled again. Torture chambers, macabre medical experiments and mass murder reigned in the sweet green suburbs bisected by gates, barbed wire and barracks, fumigated by canisters of Zyklon B inserted meticulously and deceitfully into showerheads, an entire apparatus of genocidal circuitry staged by swelling ranks of posers and imposters.

I took respite beneath a tree in the green of a placid, peaceful park and wept for an hour, considering power tilted in obscene rotation, the monumental loss of potential to galvanize supreme authority toward a unified betterment of man, but spun on the Axis with grotesque, vile and unchecked inertia. Munich and Berlin, how had you lost direction and view? Had you not read history's back pages? Poggio Bracciolini offered from his fallen Roman vantage point all that was at stake, where past is prologue. *The hill of the Capitol, on which we sit, was formerly the head of the Roman Empire, the Citadel of the earth, the terror of kings; illustrated by the footsteps of so many triumphs, enriched with the spoils and tributes of so many nations.*

I saw Nuremburg where man rebounded as he ought, putting to trial and account the madness unleashed though justice be late. The entire human race was on trial. It was found not guilty by reason of gross insanity. A few survived to cleanse our sins. Others committed suicide in retreat, cheaters to the end. In this race whole nations unfairly played and the entire planet paid.

In its aftermath through decades of debris, the heavens sighed and the armies regrouped. The atom was split and commanders boasted and toasted. The people slipped into a heavy, deep fog, followed by habit and retreat into a long, cold slumber, its ever-present nightmare looming and repeating. A bomb exploded on the Riviera, a minor alarm, an aftershock of disruption considering heavier consequences. We turned and spun, rushed and reached for another plush pillow, then welcomed in time the soft afternoon doze. In horizontal Germany I was foreign in a vertical stance, afoot and alone.

I returned the Peugeot vehicle and reached for my train pass, rolling steady to Regensburg deep in the lush of Bavaria. The city beat steady, confidently and peacefully, history in its blood, Roman ruins in the spine. It conjured the full cycle of man on the move, armed and poised. The Huns, Turks, Teutons, Crusaders – they had little on the Romans. Such consistent, certain and deliberate architecture and material are unmistakable implants on the premises. The use of the versatile and adhesive construction material, *caementicum*, a strong soup made from volcanic ash, lime and water with fragments of stone or brick mixed in for strength and color, was evident and applied generously by the Romans in Regensburg. The cement made an immeasurable contribution to construction here and throughout the Western world, making possible the great Roman arches, domes and vaults. The concoction liberated the architects, such as Vitruvius, from the confines of gravity. Aesthetics had their place, but so did practical functionality and purpose. The buildings must be delightful but firm. Where else but Germany could this be applied firmer or heard louder? One could smell Italy from the breezes in Regensburg, a virtual colliding of the skies between Berlin and Rome.

But in his pleasure and measure Hitler would have turned the Roman bricks and mortar to dust, only retaining triumphal arches with images of his own. The Romans haunted him, his envy of their expertise, gallantry, expansion and usurpation a constant compulsion. His fascist compatriot Mussolini would have continued an imperial path for posterity in a different direction. For Benito, the propagation of Roman power and prowess was pre-ordained, its grandeur to be flexed from its origins through modern war, Caesar to himself. "Rome must appear in all its splendor," the clench-fisted orator proclaimed. "Immense, ordered and as powerful as it was at the time of the first empire, that of Augustus." In twisted revolution he would simultaneously widen Rome's piazzas and boulevards and build a modern army, all the while turning civilization back to the imperial glory of two thousand years ago, requiring a literal digging-up of the past. "Buried but not dead," Mussolini decreed of Rome. Posing as a champion of peace and harmony with divine power, he commissioned a statue of himself as Augustus. But the glory would be fleeting much as it was for Cola di Rienzo, the fourteenth-century populist and defender of the people and friend of Petrarch, who wiled away his days in imagination staring at the littered marble and ruins, admiring the inscriptions with undying appreciation for the nobility of the senators and magistrates. Cola, too, could mesmerize the masses with his emotional, patriotic passions, stirring Roman crowds on the very spot where Cicero and the Caesars did the same. But in each turn of power on the track of temptation is the seduction of tyranny. Cola would be killed in a frenetic turn of popularity, his mangled body dragged through the city for three days, receiving blow after blow and a barrage of stones at the hands of his people, then dismembered and torched. Mussolini, in escape but not retreat, dodging but not surrendering, concocted a run toward the Italian Alps and the lure of neutral Switzerland, only to be headed off by impassioned publicans in pursuit. Shot, his corpse was dragged and hung upside down in a Milan piazza above a service station, hardly a heroic ending, where the people took turns beating his flesh to a pulp before incinerating him into the heap of history's ashes.

Competition yields to the noble and the lethal. In posterity, losers pose as winners, Nero and the Third Reich to the Olympics, Dachau to a Milanese service station. Contemporary, violent whims of hubris require amnesia, but the record stands. I was reassured of this by the German archaeologist, theologian and humanist Joachim Winckelmann, who while living in Rome and employed as librarian, pointedly professed *the only means by which we may attain greatness, and if it be possible, to be inimitable, is to imitate the ancients.* But villains and tyrants conspire against the scholar and artist as well. Winckelmann himself would know this intimately, dying at the hands of an unidentified assassin in 1768.

I considered Prague and Berlin but resistance prevailed. I stayed in Regensburg for two weeks for reasons unquestioned. It was calm, communal, and one might dare declare, a pinnacle of peace. I walked daily for hours and regularly past the Roman ruins. I wondered if the quaint German town, for all its tranquil demeanor, may have been relatively free of various horrid atrocities of two World Wars. Did the Romans, in ruin and shadow, as influential ghosts, aid in a larger, unspoken conspiracy of understanding? In the grand continuum, the circle and cycle of competition, the transparency and respect of power, was Regensburg by obedience and compliance, Roman to German, spared the fate? Were the Regensburg faithful granted reprieve by the ruins, or did the ruins stand as a testament to resilience of the faithful? Something puzzling had happened here, history weathering and rotting side by side with the formidable. All roads lead to Rome, it is written, and apparently so was mine. Regensburg into Czech territory seemed to be a natural gateway. I followed its call into the Karlovy Vary region, melding in the mosaic of its mountains, passages and parks.

Over the Czech border I crossed with its dizzying degree of natural beauty stopping me in my tracks. I stumbled upon the charm of Plzen, and though I could have most naturally indulged in its fine, indigenous ale, being the birthplace of Pilsner lager, I did not. I was intoxicated reading Roman poetry and my poems were flowing like the crystal streams of Bohemia. The blood still boiled but not as swift. I spent more days in one place, choosing hamlets such as Cheb, five, six, seven days at a time. I washed my clothes in Marianske Lazne, the first laundering in a month and discovering a boarding room in a medieval manor house I settled in for a week. I attended Mass, my first appearance in a church since Eglise Notre-Dame de Bon Voyage in Cannes, where I lit a candle for Cloe. Peace was setting the new pace.

On one most timely and auspicious stroll I stopped to write on a small iron bench as the sun danced off the multiple shades of green and rock strata of silver shrouding the Singing Fountain, a circular pool presented imperfectly but impressively with its stone sculpture of flowers adorned in perplexing, polished steel. It was there I met a truant traveler whom, in the dropping of her white handkerchief at my feet as she strolled past, I hailed for attention. In her smile she expressed gratitude, placed the cloth into her palm and turned to leave. Then, she spun and in a single motion asked what I was writing, her impressive English accented in glorious Italian.

"A poem, an ode to women," I surrendered. "I guess, perhaps, I am writing to you."

"Hmm? Do you know much of our kind?" she poked, an inviting and curious smirk on her face.

"Enough, I suppose. Enough to know my kind owes yours a very, very big apology."

"Is that so?" her voice rose in surprise and volume. "Do share. Apologize!"

She boldly took a seat next to mine and launching an entertaining exchange, we chatted for a good hour – art, poetry, the power of myth in storytelling and the known and unknown qualities of a good, daily walk. It led to coffee the following morning and a casual stroll in the parklands of the Socha Goetheho.

Tutela Sasso, a human-rights attorney, was born and raised in the quaint Italian town of Todi north of Rome, her father the famed architect Mateo Sasso. In her late 30s we shared similar age. She was of medium height, lean, athletic and toned, her taut and tanned biceps bare and both wrists adorned in loops, several sizes, shapes and colors of jangling bracelets. Golden hair streaked of bronze in the bright sunlight, tied back in a long mane exposing high cheek bones, a small, sharp nose and a disarming smile framed in full lips. Her ivory skirt was draped at the waste, and a peach sweater tied loosely at the hips seemed to sway joyfully in her gait, two companions out for a dance in the park.

Returning the long and pleasurable way from a recent conference in Bonn, addressing the pressing legal challenges to human rights around the globe, it had consumed her energy, months of work investing in research and preparing presentations. She was on a quest of her own in Bohemia but not retreat. The conference became an extended summit, ten days of dignitaries, activists and advocates tackling everything from multilateral conflict resolution to international courts and tribunals, drug cartels to global pandemics, African debt relief to climate change, deforestation to human trafficking. Tutela's expertise and contribution focused on the direct effects on the populations impacted, and the most practical and creative methods, long term, to correct the course. Pitching the development of a creative global peace project, she was meeting in Bonn to secure international partnerships. Recently, she had the honor of being named an official Italian liaison to the United Nations in pursuit of the Sustainable Development Goals, the ambitious agenda to positively turn the course of the people and planet by the year 2030.

"A simple mandate, Tutela" I said sarcastically.

"We Italians still believe in miracles. Don't you? Something tells me you do. You must. How else can one comprehend the works of Ovid, the Sistene Chapel, Toby? Create, Toby, we must create. Creativity is key! Beyond all the white papers, research and proposals, there are creative answers to every problem."

"I can't argue with you there. I wouldn't argue with you there."

"I believe in romantic solutions, Toby."

Romantic solutions – Tutela's words in confident and calm enunciation – rang like song in my heart and ushered in a welcomed, pleasant pause. For each playful, cynical or critical position I took, she returned an optimistic, reasonable and helpful retort. I was struck by her natural beauty, the tandem bounce of her skirt and hair as she shared a complex thought, entranced by the sincere and determined passion of her work. This was a woman out to heal if not reshape our world.

One could be easily amused by her light spirit but Tutela was far too intellectual to be dismissed as a simpleton, an aloof utopian, her head high in Bohemian clouds. I saw intuitively and immediately the considerable drive in her purpose. It held conviction, truth. She meant business but was all heart. Furthermore, she was an artist as much as an attorney. She sketched beautiful images of people, always from the neck up, only the faces. She used color, not the typical black and charcoal shades, sharing several with me between recitations of the Roman poets.

"We have enough landscape artists, the en plein impressionists as they say," Tutela imparted. "They have their place. Me, I am attracted to people, and where they reveal themselves the most, of course, between the forehead and the chin. Everything you need to know is there. What can I say? I am partial to the elderly, too. I love their lines. It is the map of their lives. The itinerary. Sometimes, in those lines, I can see where they've been."

Tutela did not press to read my poetry. She said if and when I was willing and ready to offer, that would be the proper time to receive. So

it was that I eked out one of my works for her ears. She was generous in her art, willing to share sketches in hasty order, readily in reach
tucked in her denim tote bag, yanked at the mere suggestion. Her
drawings tended to be small and detailed, no more than five-by-eight
inches, scores of them filling sketchpads lining the compartments of her
satchel. She carried them everywhere, a walking exhibit, adding three
or four to the catalog daily. Indeed, and just as she said, not a subject
drawn below the clavicle, a fair distribution of female and male imagery,
leaning more to individuals over 60, many eyeball to eyeball and a few
in profile. It was a talent she possessed for her own delight and, while
clearly works worthy of gallery or market display, she never sold a piece
but frequently gave them away to the most eager of her subjects.

I was deeply interested in her career and motivation. Tutela studied
in Bologna, disciplined in both law and art. In her freshman year her
spirit was infused, she emphasized with glee, in a thunderous concert by
an American rock star visiting her country, Bruce Springsteen. The artist's bellow and call for an authentic and stronger sense of country and
home spoke to her. Other Americans would provide amplified influence
in her bent for peace and harmony, consuming books and journals by
spiritual movers and social-justice shakers. She could recite passages of
Martin Luther King Jr.'s *Letter from a Birmingham Jail* and Henry David
Thoreau's *Civil Disobedience*. She had also studied the classics, admired
Socrates and vicariously traveled the journeys of Homer. Her heroes
were plentiful, antiquity to contemporary, Ovid, Aurelius, Voltaire and
Thoreau, Tubman, Angelou, Lennon and Bono. Absorbing the trials of
Jesus and the saints through the American Civil Rights Movement, she
was resolved to pursue a profession as an attorney, a lawyer with a very
high bar. Peace, she concluded, is the reward of justice. By upholding
the latter you are guaranteeing the former. This was the epicenter of
Tutela's thinking.

"Wait until you hear of my dream project. The birth of the *Somnium*,
Toby. It is coming," she announced teasingly.

Tutela held my arm as we jaunted, a kind and welcomed gesture considering we had just met. Romans are liberated in their expression, well
versed over time and experience. She was on her first respite in two

years and taking her time heading south to Italy. We spent another week in Marianske Lazne gathering for coffee and strolls in the morning, dining and talks in the park at dusk. She informed me of her latest and largest passion, leading a staff working tirelessly in Rome, the "dreamcatchers" as she referred to them, building the foundation of a swiftly moving initiative. Announced at the Bonn conference, it would develop a consortium of globally recognized leaders, artists and faith leaders working diligently within their creative professions and disciplines advocating peaceful and humanitarian solutions to global conflicts and challenges. The model called for professional and renowned players in the arts to serve as inspirational influencers to world decision-makers by example and creative deed, woven in proven grassroots activism, values held by common practitioners crossing national, political and economic boundaries to connect in a most-innovative environment. A beautiful building would be constructed, a center where dreams and visions would guide and shape new decisions and novel solutions for humanity and the planet. It would be called the *Somnium*.

"I believe in dreams, Tutela," I shared. "Out of my recent nightmare, I get this. Build it, Tutela. Build it."

She met my supportive remark with a gentle tap to the top of my head with her open palm.

"I will have the *Somnium* fashioned in the spirit of my father, and of Vespasian and his Temple of Peace," Tutela instructed, referring to the ancient Roman convening hall of ornamental opulence with its rich library, where those assembled indulged in *all that men were curious about*.

I smiled in approval if not guarded enthusiasm.

"I know you better than you think, American movie guy. You want to see this world at peace, too. Admit it. Be a dreamcatcher, Toby. It is an easier step than you may imagine."

"Fair enough. Tell me how, Tutela. I don't think I have fully lost the will to dream," I prompted with a smile.

"You want simple. I will give you simple, dear Toby. One of your poems could do it, my friend. One beautiful, heartfelt, soulful stanza at a time."

With that she said she was headed to Switzerland and onward to Rome where an eager staff awaited developments and designs. Would I join her? I was headed in that direction all along, but never anticipated such company.

Plentiful and rich in spirit is the path shared by those pulled to Rome, the pilgrims who have crossed the Alps into Italy laying claim along the way or in search of joy, understanding, purpose and that altogether elusive prize, divine peace and wisdom, awaiting on the other side. When navigators were crossing the seas in the sixteenth century in search of treasures and new worlds, the *novae terrae*, it was the artists and scholars, the curious and compelled, pointing their way toward Rome. This period of the great walkers took scrupulous notes on Rome's works and wonders, the Seven Hills, the temples, statues, columns, bridges and aqueducts, the palaces, theaters and ruins – to the Palatine Hill, the center of political and social life and the Forum and its historic marketplace – to the Capitoline and the sedimentary elements of its foundation, the minerals and gems adorning its presence, alabaster, onyx and serpentine in antique colors of yellows, greens and reds. These explorers circled in an orbit of restoring and recording Rome for what it was, the intersection of the past and future. The noted archaeologist of the time, Pirro Ligorio, advocated for its undisturbed and unearthed structures to remain as they were. But other intentions were in play as the Roman soil was stripped. *As the columns and other parts were revealed, I saw something that I could not have imagined: Most of the building's ornaments were sold as though in a cattle market... the epitaphs were lost through ignorance and ill-will ... when I cannot say any more about it, I weep,* Ligorio chronicled at the Arch of Augustus.

Like Ligorio, urgency propelled my pilgrimage, to observe and bear witness before it was too late, a mysterious omen all its own, as if minutes could not be wasted now that the decision and destination were clear, and Tutela Sasso had me locked at the elbow with sights and dreams set on Rome, a stronger tug than the one which launched this journey.

The poet Propertius provided affirmation. *Or if my girl intends to travel far by sea, I'll follow: one breeze shall move two faithful ones, one shore will lull us both and one tree shades us, and we both will drink at one spring.* The one breeze moving us would require a stop in Switzerland before a cross of the towering peaks of the Alps.

"How are you traveling?" I inquired.

"By train, of course, a good way. Then on foot, the true way."

I met her at the train station on the chosen day at eight o'clock in the morning. We spoke of Diogenes, Horace, Whitman and the Beatles. Nourished with fresh pears, grapes, coffee and pastry, we boarded the first car. Its only occupants, we bound for the Swiss Alps and Interlaken, the land between the lakes.

CHAPTER V

TUTELA RESTED her head on my shoulder as our train crossed the Swiss border. It was mid-afternoon and from the window I was taken by the majesty and beauty of the landscape in all its alpine splendor. The sky was a hue of blue I had never seen before, hints of silky purple blending in lofty lavender, as if one could taste its creaminess simply by extending the tongue out the train's window and licking the cool breeze. The groves clung to mountainsides in the warm summer sun. Our train hugged the valleys and glens in concert with the curves of a raging river below and, as Tutela slowly opened her eyes she smiled up at me taking a bar of Swiss chocolate from the waste pocket of her overcoat. She broke off a square for me and another for herself. She raised it to my mouth and I took it in, resting the succulent tablet on my tongue as my eyes locked on hers, a salty and savory sweetness exploding the senses. My palate was awoken as the train climbed higher, reaching for the upper Swiss cascade. Heaven was near. Was not hell only yesterday? Chocolate. Chocolate. Rich memories of the innocent sharing of chocolate in Cannes appeared and passed in the rapid turns on the rails.

To be at the foot of the Alps was to share good company with pilgrims of yore, restless souls on similar quests for adventure, redemption or love, or perhaps some contrived and benevolent combination of each. Several centuries ago they came by the hundreds of thousands, circling at the base before making the challenging trek over the summit, their sharpened drive focused on eternal Rome. With the Einsiedeln itinerary in hand their routes and sites were foretold with great anticipation, like mine, as Tutela's, in heightened excitement and steadfast resolve. As the determined pedestrians graced themselves before the long journey, they would drink from the famous fountain of fourteen spouts, refreshing their unquenchable souls and stubborn spirits. They considered Rome the center of the world and more than two million alone made their way into the city in the year 1300. The itinerary included a map depicting Rome as a perfect circle.

Tutela and I, while following their lead and dream, hardly shared their hardships as we climbed in cozy comfort. The mountains began to chill the train's cabin. I draped my coat over both of us and we reclined in the hum and turns on the tracks. As her fingers combed through my hair Tutela whispered a request into my ear.

"Tell me about your father," she softly instructed. Her inquiry was direct, an attorney taking her client to task.

"Here? Now?"

"Is it a sticking point?"

"Not at all," I rebutted, followed by a moment of acceptable silence.

"You would have liked him, Tutela. He would have adored you."

I surprised myself in my readiness to reveal. I had not spoken of my father in some time. He died twelve years prior following a brief and aggressive illness complicated by a poor diagnosis and two botched surgeries. I had let go of my disappointment, bitterness and frustration, the medical mishaps and incompetence which had contributed to his rapid and painful demise. He had helped me in his mortal transition in the final weeks, exhibiting courage and dignity of a fading, noble knight whose time had come at the intersection of fight and surrender.

I remembered the afternoon he got the official read and measure of his condition, a fallen warrior and tired sage learning of the terminal nature of the disease, an aggressive cancer on its boastful victory lap wrenching its latest prize.

My mother was softly weeping in the kitchen, slicing potatoes and rocking slowly on her arches, a stare stuck on the task, her hands in a will and discipline all their own.

"Go see your father," was her hushed directive. "You need to have a talk with your father."

He was resting in his bed alone in his underwear, a crossword puzzle on his lap, the nightstand lamp dim but sufficient enough, reading glasses dipped and strategically perched low and balanced upon his bold Irish nose. Was there a more resigned or content man still alive?

I stood bedside as he said in calm resignation that he had led a good life, the news is what it is, and he had no regrets.

"We'll need to just deal with this, kiddo," he said with reassurance. "We'll all manage."

"I'm so sorry, Dad. I'm very, very sorry."

"Thank you, Toby. Now see to your mother. This is going to be hard on your mother."

The magnanimous moment was settled quickly and in gentle informality. I had clumsily interrupted the calm and serenity, his concentration on a crossword puzzle, for he was already making plans to process the death sentence in his own time.

The immediate task was to solve the puzzle, his charming innocence taking on this delightful, daily challenge. Seriously ill, he was a spiritually healthy horse. He was weakened yet steady, resigned but resilient. At his natural core he was a fixer, healer and problem solver. Calm and deliberate, a mechanic and tactician, he was not a scholar of letters. Yet, he was the truest of scholars, perpetually curious, learning and yearning, a stack of history books, biographies and newspapers serving as ready reference within reach on his bookcase, nightstand and mammoth desk. He was a student of life, contemplative and selfless.

Caesars, surrounded by men of medicine and title in all their splendor, had nothing on this man in his underwear. The emperors and magistrates misdiagnose, misjudge and send innocent souls to early graves. Efficient and loyal accomplices surround the condemned and afflicted with obscene medical bills, legal waivers and ever-present insurance documents. Invoices and policies were organized dutifully and meticulously on my father's desk to be tended to after the crossword puzzle and before a brief nap, then the monumental effort to digest a dinner in the hour his large family rendezvoused and rallied.

"I love you" should have been said at that moment but it was not, as if the utterance would usher in a more rapid demise. It would be some time before I learned to express this. Still, he knew. I knew he knew. It was in my eyes as I nodded to him then turned to leave the man with his thoughts, newspaper and puzzle. Why use words when the room, the hearts, the whole universe shouts what is clear? He had lived a good life, indeed. The gentle servant had said it himself. Now began preparations for the next journey, more beautiful than the last, a final battle to be waged and a peace to be won on his terms.

I am fine but the bones are brittle.

I am fine. The meals cannot be kept down.

I am fine. The bills must be paid.

I am fine. The doctor is not in.

He gave it one more valiant push. He turned his cheek to laser-focused physicians armed in invoices and syringes and accepted the blasts of radiation and onslaught of chemicals. The poison and toxins reduced the once robust, stocky and formidable figure to a frail, exhausted and pale image of himself. He tried to have a few productive days near the end, fixing a door frame, grocery shopping or replacing lightbulbs in the stark hallways he now paced alone late in the night. It was in the final days of that summer when I saw him pull up on a sunny Saturday from a grocery errand and for a fleeting moment felt reassured, pleased by the sight he was having a decent and mobile day, until he leapt from the driver's door and expelled a spray of fluorescent vomit into the street. It would be the last of countless grocery runs he had made to nourish his insatiable clan over the course of many decades. Some days later he tried gallantly to join us for the six-o'clock dinner ritual but excused himself, getting sick in the kitchen sink, then returning to his rightful place at the head of the table apologizing for most likely ruining our appetites. I watched as Mom's eyes welled, a fork in one hand never meeting her plate, a white napkin clutched in her other palm, disarmed and surrendered.

Miracles come in many forms. Somehow he managed in the final weeks to buy a refrigerator and had it delivered with his expert guidance up a daunting flight of stairs to a struggling family a few miles away from our neighborhood. They lived in a run-down apartment house on the second story abutting the alleyway behind the catholic church. On another Saturday he brought soil, fertilizer and plugs of St. Augustine grass from his lawn to a neighbor hoping for a miraculous rebirth of his grass after several failed attempts. He spent two hours helping the man freshly and successfully resod the turf. His Samaritan kindness and instincts knew no bounds.

Then, in that September I came for a visit but found a vacant house. Neighbors arrived to ask how my father was doing since the accident that morning. What accident?

An ambulance had taken him away just before noon, my mother at his side holding him at the elbow. Something was uttered about a fall in the upstairs bedroom.

In an effort to dress himself, my father had tried to put on his pants, but he got tripped up in a pant leg and fallen forward and, too weak to adequately brace the fall, his forehead caught the floor first. With bones brittle and the muscles atrophied, the head took the brunt. He suffered broken vertebrae at the base of the neck. The mighty tree of our lives had fallen.

A weekend of agony followed, a legion of physicians nowhere to be found over the Labor Day holiday. The oncologist was attending a fund-raiser. The blood doctor was on vacation. The pain specialist was simply not returning calls. For three days and nights the family kept vigil, shifting his tortured body side to side, up and down, higher to lower and back again on his hospital bed as he directed the moves and begged for relief from the unceasing pain. He had two specific requests directed strongly to the staff, a stronger dose of pain killer and a regular cigarette.

Such was granted, not by physicians or hospital administrators, but in the defiance and merciful measures of the head nurse. She had just joined the staff the week prior. Incensed by what she was witnessing she defied standard operating procedures and the absent chain of command and managed to approve a morphine drip to flow into my father's broken body. Furthermore, she had a makeshift sign made, a message of compassion and due caution, "Please make sure the oxygen tank is shut off when Mr. Tyrone is smoking." My father referred to her as his Angel of Mercy.

He had also reversed his position on euthanasia from his death bed. I overheard him the evening before as my mother stroked his tired, damp head of fully white hair, making slow and deliberate circles upon his scalp as he stared distantly out the window from the fourth floor into a small cluster of pine treetops facing the western horizon. He muttered if there was the strength, he'd will his battered self toward an open window and make the leap.

"Honey," he professed to my mother. "They wouldn't put a dog through this."

Sunday afternoon I visited at the base of his bed. His bare feet exposed, I caressed his toes as we talked over small matters.

"Thank you for coming in, Toby," were his last words to me. He was an eternally giving spirit even in the pain, consistent at the end as he was from the beginning, a full circle with an imperfect close, triumphant in gratitude.

With morphine increased he managed a delicate drift into the silent Sunday night, surrendering in the early dawn of Labor Day. How altogether fitting he should pass on this day, a man who worked for others his entire life. I got the phone call at five o'clock in the morning. I had been sleeping on his pillow back at our grand family base, cradling his presence in the upstairs master bedroom. It was the only real home I had ever known, a place entrenched in sentimental charms and memories and a property with my father's fingerprints all over it, the cemented base of the Roman pillars on the front porch, the bronze-varnished front door which never was locked and welcomed all, the wooden slats placed in the upper-floor windows preventing his children when they were little from a perilous tumble in their romping.

The ring of the phone brought immediate alertness and split my slumber, anticipating the message to come. I walked to Dad's desk in the dark and lifted the receiver.

"Dad is at peace," one of my older brothers calmly reported.

Down the hall it was my turn to inform another brother sleeping in the corner bedroom, the one we once shared for years, its windows facing the backyard and alleyway out toward the basketball court where much of our formative, sun-drenched years of youth played out, our father within comfortable earshot toiling in the garage or under the hood of a car in the driveway on countless, warm weekends when the sun never seemed to set on our happy lives.

I sat at my brother's bedside in the dark and lowered my head to impart the exact words just solemnly spoken to me.

"Dad is at peace," the words fell. "Dad is at peace."

I wept for the first time in my adult life there on my brother's chest. He rubbed the crown of my head with his palm.

"It's okay," he whispered assuredly to himself and me. "It's all going to be okay."

"We were lucky, right?"

"The luckiest."

"We had the best father, didn't we?"

"The best," my brother cemented.

The moveable and elusive Irish luck, it was sprinkling its pleasing and puzzling dust on Labor Day, most certain. Sitting up I caught a glowing round orb just above the crest of the garage shining baby-blue effervescence through the trees. A September moon never appeared so large, a lone luminous disk in the ancient sky. I quietly rose to leave with the words of my brother in my head, a father gone, a childhood released into serene moonlight in the alleyway and upon the basketball court of our yesterdays. Of course it was going to be okay. He showed how this life can be okay, victim to victor, luck and fortune spinning in opposite rotations on the same wheel, not always our way but our way enough, fortunate enough to be a son of such a man – *gloria filiorum patros* – the glory of sons is their fathers.

He chose cremation and a celebration of his life, funding his funeral in a final act of joy and generosity. A keg of beer and cold cuts satisfied the grieving while sweet roses presented to his wife stood tall and colorful next to the urn, a palmful of his remains then gently sprinkled upon the St. Augustine grass of his backyard lawn. The good emperor departed, he called in the wind for the celebration to commence. Rome itself would have approved, their ancient tradition of the pyre, hot ashes extinguished with milk and wine, the bones collected by mourning relatives tucked as keepsakes in the folds of their robes. If I had my way his remains too would be drizzled in milk and wine, dried with linen, mixed with scents, herbs and a hefty dose of languishing lavender.

Some weeks later we placed the remainder of his ashes into a grave on a peaceful knoll high above town, side by side with his brother. A lone raven perched on a branch above the slope. A calm breeze offered comfort as the crow remained silent in repose and respect. I heard soft Irish keening and the hush of Latin in the final words of farewell – *sit tibi terra levis* – may the earth rest lightly upon you.

Tutela's caramel eyes, slightly swollen in a liberating unleash of tears, fixed on mine as the train meandered higher into the escalating turns of the Swiss Alps. Her grip on my elbow tightened as she tilted to kiss my cheek. Together we looked out the window as pillows of soft white clouds draped the ceiling of the greeting sky, now a bright baby-blue, as Saint Paul's concluding words echoed of the gift of Dad and properly filled a grateful heart – *I have fought the good fight, I have finished the race, I have kept the faith.*

Such could be said of my father's run. But the earlier rotations required sharing, for it was his formative turns which shaped and defined his destiny, and Tutela prodded for details on his start.

My father was born on a dirt kitchen floor in a thatched cottage in central Ireland in the midst of the revolutionary period and interminable struggles for Irish freedom on a remote nineteen-acre farm absent of plumbing and electricity. The farm failing and America calling, his parents packed the three small boys and one little girl onto a horse-drawn wagon with their few belongings and set out from Longford to Cork to board a freighter westward across the Atlantic and a new world awaiting. Normal passage could not be afforded so steerage would have to do.

Glimpsing the Statue of Liberty they arrived at Ellis Island with hordes of others, then on to Brooklyn where hospitable Irish arranged for their new start. The Great Depression stared them in the face and in a tenement house full of Irish immigrants they bore the weight together. His mother housed and fed a regular flow of acquaintances and family from the Old Country. What little they had was always shared. Cooperate, share and count your blessings – this maxim rang in my father's head throughout his youth – and echoed across his lifespan.

His father took a series of menial jobs, city labor he had never known in the Lakelands of rural Ireland. He shoveled coal into the fiery furnaces in the deep dungeons of the mammoth department stores erupting across the boroughs of New York City. His mother made a few dollars in an array of resourceful and helpful services to the steady stream of weary Irish arrivals.

A natural mind for engineering, by eighteen my father had shown an acumen for mechanics. He could repair anything and created impressive, makeshift gadgets, tools and widgets. He had handyman gifts and employed them practically and liberally, always for the betterment of others, offering his trade generously to extended family members, friends and neighbors. He scored high on the college entrance exams in science and mathematics, and a world beyond Brooklyn was in reach.

But the world had other plans for him and millions more. War was to be waged again, but this time mightier and messier than before. My father and his two brothers enlisted at the same time. His younger brother, Joseph, was sent to Michigan to learn aeronautics and manufacture instruments and gyroscopes, the growing field of sophisticated positioning devices essential for optimal air and watercraft navigation. His older brother, Henry, went to the infantry.

His mechanical aptitude thoroughly assessed and appreciated, and with the diagnosis of a minor case of *pes planus*, or flat foot, my father was deployed to provide mechanical support to fleets of aircraft, specifically the B-24 Liberator, the perennial bomber of bombers. He served in faraway places and lands he had only read about and never imagined he would ever see, the coasts of the Carolinas and beaches of Florida, the ports of Cuba and deserts of Utah and California, where the wide-open spaces of the West would capture his curiosity for another time.

It was in the San Bernardino Mountains of Southern California during a test flight serious trouble occurred. Extreme vibration sent his crew tossing and flailing within the fuselage. In the chaos he slammed against the bomb chute causing it to fly open. My father was hurled in a free fall from the doomed plane, instinctively releasing his emergency parachute. As he gently floated downward to a barren and desolate landscape below, he watched helplessly as the teetering and sputtering aircraft spun then slammed into a mountainside, killing the crew of ten. As the lone survivor, he paced in the high desert for three days before a search squad located him making steady, patient strides in large circles in the sands of the burning Mojave around the perimeter of the scorched crash site.

Who wins? Who loses?
Who starts? Who stops?
Who flies? Who falls?
Fate. Luck. Fortune. The spin and the toss.

I often wondered how those three days may have impacted my father's vision and scope across the decades of his remaining life. He rarely mentioned his past, and when he did it was not in detail let alone revelation of deeper thoughts or emotions. This was his private path securely stored, stirring in the sovereignty of secrets, adrift in the hiss like the omnipresence of the Mojave rattlesnake, where a man alone in his elements walks in circles around the coiled dangers in patient measurements and passing moments of precious time. You could catch glimpses of his reflection in the far-away gaze when his warm emerald eyes found a fixed point on a distant horizon, keeping the hidden thoughts deeply and privately to himself.

Three days alone in the desert emboldening his mortal fiber, counting or cursing the fleeting hours in each rotation of the Earth on her ancient axis – could these seventy-two hours have shaped everything else to come? Open sky and distant horizons are dual companions, soaring and descending, sunrise to sunset, two arcs meeting and greeting on the circumference of the same circle where some spin off in the speed and turbulence, and others manage, one way or another, to remain, be it by grand design or the hanging thread of a dangling parachute, the forces with you or against you, centrifugal or centripetal.

Sunrise to sunset. Moon to sun. Burning sand to rain. Water in an oasis of downed men and blood. The elements. The math. The odds.

The engineer. The fixer. The world at war. One lonely, lost and broken airplane. One spin. One exit. One slam. One boom. Once here ... then gone.

But me? Still here?

Peace in the temptation. No war. No surrender.

This victory in the desert.

Only me and the still of the moon. Not me versus nature. Me alone with nature.

Do you look for me? I don't need rescuing. I never asked for you. I never asked for anything.

I am fine. I thirst.

I am fine. I shiver.

I am fine. What about the others?

I am fine. We must find them.

They are dead. All of them. Each one, to have their families informed, in a formal Army visit or by telegram.

Everything will be okay. Too many men aboard.

A basic test-run.

I told them. I told them. A weight displacement issue.

I told them. Too many men, too much equipment. Too much weight.

Something is wrong.

A sputter. A shudder.

Mom, something is wrong. I am lost, Mom.

I am lost in the California desert.

Brooklyn? I miss you, Mom, Dad, the neighborhood.

Have you heard from Henry? Joey? Sister Maggie? Don't worry about me. I am fine.

I don't see a rescue, and I don't want to assemble or fix planes anymore, just so there can be more of this waste. The vicious cycle. The planes keep coming, and the planes keep breaking. They are ordering too many planes, too fast. I told them, Dad. They rush and the push is causing faulty mechanics. The shortcuts are deadly. We should pace production until it is right and safe.

I think we will win this war.

The desert sun is a different kind of heat, Mom.

My face, neck, ears and arms burn. It is a different kind of burn, Mom, not like the summers and sunburns at Coney Island.

If I could close my eyes and wake up in Brooklyn I would, Mom. Should I come home?

Why this and why now, Mom?

I need to keep going here, in large circles, but my eyes are closed.

I think they are coming, Mom. I hear them. I think they see me.

I will wave them down. Here they come – they are near.

Mom, they will catch me crying, but I am crying with thoughts of you, Brooklyn, home.

I want to come home.

I thirst.

I want to go home, Mom, but I don't think they'll let me. There is work for me to finish, this war to win, this war to end.

I promise, Mom ... I promise.

As my father recovered his two brothers faced separate battles. Uncle Joey remained stateside while Uncle Henry got the worst of it. They sent him to North Africa where American boys freshly trained took on the Nazis and Rommel's army, malaria and the blazing Sahara.

After pushing back the Germans from Tunisia, Uncle Henry and the troops crossed the Mediterranean into Sicily. The Germans had fallen for a ruse, expecting the invasion in Greece or Sardinia. This deceit was contrived by intelligence officers who dropped a corpse off the coast of Spain weeks earlier, staging a suicide of an officer possessing top-secret documents, specific plans of an Allied invasion on other shores. The Axis was meant to find him and fall for it, and on cue they did both. The corpse was an unwitting imposter, a tramp who died on the streets of London then adorned in fine officer's clothing, stuffed with the phony plans and dumped in the sea in a final dramatic act.

Successfully moving north into Messina, it was during the diabolical assaults at Monte Cassino where Henry went missing. For days the fighting went on, fierce and intimate, American soldiers eye to eye with the Germans day and night, huddled on the rocky hillsides and nestled tight in abandoned villages among the Roman ruins. They found Henry trapped in a gulch, barricaded beneath mounds of boulders. Nearly his entire platoon killed or injured, he was laying on his back, trembling and muttering with an empty rifle clutched to his chest. His fellow soldiers, unable to safely approach him over the course of a few endless days, threw ammunition, canteens and provisions of food over a barricade of boulders in his direction, and that which didn't reach him he scrambled to fetch, sniper fire tracing his every desperate move.

Henry could not function in combat any longer. North Africa and Italy took their mounting toll. He was sent back to the States where experimental treatments such as electric shock therapy were attempted to ease the nerves and erase his war. He was only 23 when risky attempts were made to put Henry back together again. Another two years passed before the war ended and the brothers were reintegrated back into the Brooklyn neighborhoods where they were readily employed by the New York Fire Department, met their wives and started new families. Drawing upon circles formed in the years before this war, or a lifetime ago, each began again.

Starting over here, anew, one race completed and another begun, maybe it could be drawn right, amended, corrected and clear, one circle lapping delicately but directly over the other, concentric, until no one can tell where one life ends and the other begins.

This race lasted a while for some but severely long for others. Henry's war returned. The voices of fellow soldiers, the sounds of war, the terrors in the night and the shakes at sunrise would revisit, over and over and over again in a recurring hell. Alcohol became a sedative but did not suffice. Henry was now a drunk veteran fighting a personal and perpetual war and, though a very young man, ahead on the track awaited decades of combat, fight and fatigue. A tolerant fire department covered his tracks as much as possible, an understanding and patient wife, soon enough a mother of three, privately pacified a turbulent domestic front. Within a decade the full façade would fall, exposing years of pain, nightmares, violence and addiction shared in the company of several suffering fire firefighters at the station and countless broken souls holding their own in the neighborhood bars – the lonely, forgotten strangers, war veterans lurking late in the night in every public park, empty lot or subway stairwell in

Brooklyn – muttering to no one and in anguish for anyone who would hear, listen or care. Henry became a drifter, taking periodic refuge within the arms of a broken-hearted Irish mother in Flatbush until he was listed as officially disabled by a nation he helped save.

After she died, Henry was rendered homeless, a battered and beaten shell of himself, joining the ranks of thousands of fellow warriors whose hopes and heroics were buried with their youth.

My father spent two decades saving souls with fire hoses and hatchets in hand. He retired from the NYFD as soon as it was practical to receive a proper pension. The job was getting increasingly hazardous, too dangerous for a man with an army of children to care for and feed. Through a friend in the neighborhood he was offered a sales opportunity and, after serious examination, took it, moving our family to California to start anew. He and my mother were raising a clan of their own, a dozen Irish Catholic children, a long-held goal of Mom's to bring a team into the world just as her beloved grandfather had done with the same number in his quaint hamlet of Haines Falls in the Catskill Mountains of New York. Despite the clamor and cluster, they made room for one more soul. Henry was taken off the back alleyways of the Brooklyn bowery and brought west to our new environment in the sunny suburbs of Southern California for a fresh start all his own. His war wasn't over but the weather was nicer.

My father loved and cared for his brother until Henry died in a Los Angeles veterans facility on Father's Day some fifteen years later. The tired soldier had never reunited or had direct contact with his family over this time, though he often spoke of them, especially in melancholic confessionals repeated passionately when intoxicated. Dad reached out to Henry's family in the final year, imploring them to make any amends they could muster, as the man was sinking into a grave and terminal condition. When my father went to make final arrangements at the government hospital in West Los Angeles where from the windows one could view the endless rows of headstones of departed soldiers, an express letter from one of Henry's sons had arrived from New York, sealed and staring at him with his brother's name on it in the hospital's inbox. He sorrowfully had it returned to sender, its contents and sentiments forever a mystery having never made it to a father's dying eyes. Whether expressing love or regret, the message came too late.

The memorial was dignified and solemn if lightly attended, and it was the first and only time I saw my father weep.

"My brother died alone last weekend on Father's Day," Dad declared. "Brooklyn was our circle, and Henry danced, boxed and charmed like no other, around and around, the whole city was his, and he was ours. Yes, Henry died last week, but the Henry I knew died in 1942 on the day he went off to fight in World War II. He may have managed his survival in the decades since, but the Henry we knew never came back."

The decision to retire early from the NYFD and move his large family to California was an utterly and naturally selfless one for my father. At the time Dad was only 45. With twelve children to raise he had dodged serious and fateful episodes in fighting tenement fires, once nearly falling off a ten-story roof. Catching quite accidently his boot around a vent pipe, Irish fortune once more turned lucky, this time around his arch and ankle.

A friend who was expanding a printing-press business on the West Coast offered my father a sales role in the enterprise, one that could turn into a business partnership in the blossoming company. The position seemed promising and renewing enough. He accepted the move, leaving a world of relations behind to provide a fresh start for us. An end of sorts for him was an entirely exciting beginning for the family. If he had any trepidation he disguised it well, fixed was his love and direction, east to west.

For the subsequent twenty-five years in a tedious commute to downtown Los Angeles, the monotony of a traveling salesman, a dutiful servant expected to develop business and drive weekly profits, this became my father's hidden work life, a fifty-hour weekly routine he bore for us Monday through Friday, fifty weeks every year. He took care of his clients, a sincere and honest man incapable of maneuvering or manipulating, cheating, swindling or steering a customer wrong. He worked steady and methodically, built a client base across the expanse of the Pacific Coast, his warm, sincere greetings and consistent check-ins and frequent phone calls, following through on purchase orders, driving on long streatches to their cities and towns, the small, quaint and faraway outposts with single printing presses, shaking their hands and fulfilling their urgent requests for pallets of plates and cases of ink, earned a deep respect and sincere friendship in newspaper publishing circles from Arizona to Washington state. He was as liked as he was fair, and frugality was a necessary if not basic virtue. He dressed professionally but modestly, his wing-tipped shoes resoled countless times, his rack of ties unchanged over the passing years. He packed his lunch of cheese, meatball or tuna sandwiches and kept fortified on coffee and cigarettes throughout the long days. More than two decades in, he could not afford to retire a second time. When the company was bought out they forced his hand, turning over his lengthy and hard-won client base to young and finely dressed ladder climbers in new company cars brandishing fat expense accounts, while requiring my father to meet ever-escalating if not impossible sales quotas. I watched as the new, aggressive and greedy corporate America of the 1980s stripped my father of the last of his workplace pride and trust, yet he never surrendered his deep integrity and dignity. These were not for sale.

I made a home movie for his 70th birthday not long before the terminal diagnosis tempered the joy in our days. His love and charm fully intact, I caught him reclined, as always, just after five in the evening in the hour before supper completing his Los Angeles Times crossword puzzle. I had but a few feet of reel remaining.

"What is your special birthday wish, here, now, at this moment, Dad?" I prompted.

He paused and calculated for only a second, looked up over his reading glasses, one arm of its frame replaced by hanger wire in the latest handy craftsmanship, his gentle green eyes focused directly on the camera lens, and uttered in his comforting voice ever melodious in a lilting Brooklyn accent.

"Peace on Earth," he summed.

Our train stopped at Interlaken an hour or so after I had shared the account with Tutela. We rose together and quietly gathered our belongings then strolled to the hotel, a large, wooden alpine inn just as one would imagine. Complementing the radiant summer colors adorned on its veranda were multiple flags of the world's nations flapping and clapping in the sweet Swiss breeze. Here in Interlaken, between the lakes, we found ourselves between two worlds, the one I had left in a black cloud of Cannes, and the unknown, inviting and colorful one just ahead, Italy on the other side of the spine of the imposing Alps. Switzerland was the appropriate place to rest, the auspicious, neutral intersection on the journey, the right crossroads of days recently spent and those yet to come. Tutela was welcoming the critical anticipation as much I was. We were embracing a landscape providing a buffer of serenity when a roar of NATO fighter jets training and preparing for what may be next ripped and tore the peace in two for a suffering half minute, leaving Tutela and I breathless, motionless, as flocks of traumatized birds scattered in the direction of the lakes. We gripped each other's palms until the last trace of the deafening interceptors left us, and the skies of Interlaken, alone.

We had a light lunch of cheese sandwiches and raisins and split a Swiss chocolate bar and beer, then walked upon a thick-wooded trail encircling the lakes. In a clearing we laid down, shoulder to shoulder, our backs on the lush, grassy turf. With eyes to the skies, the Swiss clouds danced swiftly southward, hugging the peaks and regularly revealing the warm sun, its golden rays streaking between the treetops and upon our faces. Tutela turned to kiss my cheek and I returned it. With no blanket and liberated to desire, we made love in a private, natural grove surrounded by trees then fell into a slumber of sweet alpine bliss, the bird whistle of the occasional Turaco hastening the nap. Tutela's soft inhalations were in rhythm with my exhalations, each breath a *pneuma* of nourishment into the lungs.

We arose to take a picture, but realizing we were free of cameras, phones and all other devices, we captured the memory in our hearts. She drew a sun on my forehead with her finger and I did the same to hers. In a flash I thought of Cloe's finger, tracing the near-perfect circle on a café napkin on a sun-drenched afternoon in Cannes, but here sadness had yielded to something else. I smiled into the clear, glistening, caramel eyes of Tutela until we drifted into another soft and welcomed sleep.

I awakened first and calmly brushed Tutela's brow. As golden rays stirred her eyes open, I kissed her forehead then whispered into her ear.

"Your turn, Tutela. Tell me about your father, love."

She brushed my cheek with her palm and readied her response.

Raised in Todi north of Rome, she instructed, there are countless branches of ancestors and generations of timeless tales traveling through her ancient tree.

"I can start with father, but I have many, many fathers. Which one to share with you, Toby?"

I answered by gesture, placing a gentle, tender kiss upon her preparing lips, and onward she contributed, Mateo, grandfathers and great-grandfathers to the faraway past, a lineage of solid roots and sprouting family branches forming familiar shade for Tutela, a grove of ancestry lining the road to Rome.

"But it is most important you hear of our great Lucius," she insisted, launching into a dream of faraway yesterdays – a somnium of sacred truth – one that would turn, stir and spin the imagination of the past into a tumultuous and timely awakening to the future, to be revealed in all proper mystery on the southern side of the towering Alps.

CHAPTER VI

I T IS the age of Trajan – the beloved emperor, *optimus princeps* – the best ruler. Trajan greatly benefits by the grace, virtue and wisdom of his influential wife Pompei Plotina. By her deep empathy she has gained the love and respect of the Roman citizens, won by many popular actions, among them her influential push for fair taxation. Assuming the ceremonial throne she had turned to face the crowd as she ascended the imperial steps, declaring to her people, "I am with you."

Rome is whirling in a civil and social spiral, a race to rediscover and redefine itself. There at the hub of the mighty city they convene in respect and ritual, hundreds of the citizenry in the Circus Maximus, to bid solemn farewell to their righteous, decent and loyal brother Lucius.

There, centurions, guards, warriors and laborers, joining in a great circle of relatives, friends, politicians and noblemen, high priests and physicians, scholars and philosophers, gather in the grandest stadium and upon its spectacular track, a contest of emotion in a chase with time before high authorities may discover them and disband this controversial assembly of mourners in a most-public setting.

For the scribes and record, it is in the Circus Maximus where Senator Darius and Lucius' loyal friend Marcus arrive in stride together, taking their rightful place on the steps above a swelling crowd, and in the raising of his right hand Darius gestures for silence. In attendance is Lucius' lone surviving kin, his son Tobin.

The senator begins his eulogy of Lucius, placing his palm reverentially on a block of stone and into its noticeable grooves, the dried-mortar impression of the *palmus*, a large man's hand. In dramatic pause Darius steadies his outstretched hand, keeping it in place and solidarity with the molded caementicum.

"Today we bid honorable farewell to our beloved and noble Lucius. My dear friends, may the immortal record reflect Lucius was above all a Roman builder, a skilled worker, a man of labor for all Romans, an example for industrious craftsmen here and throughout the empire. As a younger man he worked the quarries with the physical stamina many of you remember, as do I, with awe. He was tireless, free of fatigue, capable of exerting equitable energy at the highest level from the sun's rise to day's end. Indeed, he grew stronger in the passing of hours under the beating sun, not weaker. His ambition was personally and deeply driven, and he took care of his workers and countrymen around him with all the care, compassion and concern of a father and a brother.

Lucius excelled in directing labor crews, a natural leader, and was justly promoted. He was appointed head foreman across the span of the Roman districts. It was in one of these such crews he supervised the performance of Ciro.

This was a challenging period for our beloved Rome. Progress and plans were pressed to the brink with a growing population in desperate need of the government to lead, support and build roads, walls, bridges, houses and sanitary channels. All of these were important and necessary. We recall how civil disorder was mounting. Poverty was pandemic. Lucius and his workers were intensely aware of your needs. As certain and understandable dissention rose, a parallel movement of compassion and empathy gained momentum. It was in these days our beloved Lucius met Marcus, this noble of Romans here today at my side, and the two began to organize the laborers there in the quarries, there on the streets, there in construction of our buildings.

In the great and perpetual trials for economic justice, Romans saw a growing chasm forming between the greedy, frivolous expeditions of the affluent and powerful and that of our common citizens, avarice taking hold, neglect of the basic needs of the people a most predictable consequence.

Lucius and Marcus made extraordinary efforts, organizing hundreds of teams of public servants to shift their focus to the poorest districts throughout the expanding city. This was courageous and heroic, but risky and dangerous.

They had their Brutus in Ciro who found it personally advantageous to disclose the plans and operations to suspecting, punitive and self-interested Roman rulers. Ciro reported all his knowledge, the very movements of Lucius, to an awaiting and ambitious foe who, admittedly and ashamedly, was me, Darius.

I had wealth. I was a young aristocrat, a man of privilege formally educated in Greece and Cyprus, a staunch protector of the rule of Roman law. It was I who was set on arresting our friends Lucius and Marcus, and Ciro provided the trap. Lucius and Marcus were confined on my orders.

It was in the city prison, by my permission, Flavia was granted access to visit Lucius. Flavia was beautiful, cunning, convincing and persuasive. Posing as Marcus' wife, she met frequently with our dear Lucius. I had no knowledge Flavia was an underground supporter of an ambitious, dangerous and passionate labor conspiracy. Together, this special pact would plan and devise a full network driven and determined on redirecting resources, supplies and basic services to the common Roman people, into the poorest districts and regions, there from the jail, there by the direction of Lucius, and there through the empowerment and dispatch of his loyal Flavia.

Via my source I would learn of the secret network and its clever operations and methods, including the stealing of Roman stockpiles and the unauthorized deployment of labor and services to rather unpleasant, highly impoverished districts.

I, Darius, could be clever as well. I negotiated and authorized the release of Lucius and Marcus, permitting, secretly and unofficially, this freedom to further their subversive activities and risky causes. In return, I negotiated for their support in my senatorial aspirations. Their impressive influence and charismatic leadership would be of great value and benefit to me. Furthermore, I came to wisely share their greater vision of a more just, compassionate and fair distribution of Roman riches.

Good seasons, fair and peaceful, followed in our unspoken understanding and conspiracy. May it be noted our beloved emperor, Trajan, was committed to sincere and genuine reforms as well. We did not ease away from our opulence and egos, constructing palatial residences and monuments to ourselves, but we launched significant projects across greater Rome designed to improve the quality of life for you, for all. A functioning, fair and just Rome was in our sight, however faulty our judgment and methods. We deeply believed in this vision.

It was in these warm and promising days our lovely and loyal Flavia and our true, humble, courageous servant Lucius fell into Venus' trap and design. Their love cemented, they married.

Rome fulfilling its promises, Lucius and Marcus returned the dedication and commitments, faithfully. They accepted honorably the offers to serve the Roman army for a temporary term of duty, in sworn agreement the future would bestow higher appointments for each of them in Roman civil service, a generous pension and the authority to pursue their popular aims for the people.

Our good fortunes continued uninterrupted. I, Darius, arose as your senior senator. The pact was prevailing.

But abroad our legions were spread thin and dangerously unprepared. Too often, in our lack of proper intelligence and supplies, enemies made gains and triumphed. We were gambling, over-confident in our ability to suppress tensions and rising hostilities across the territories. The Roman ego was intoxicated in its arrogance, becoming blind to the troubling political and social reality.

Still, hope was perennial if not eternal, and the gods blessed our brave efforts.

We received glorious news of great victories, the sacking of legions at the Danube in the Dacian wars in Romania. Though deaths and sufferings were great, fate permitted Lucius and Marcus to survive. Enemy forces held them captive where they were detained in horrid slave-labor camps, enslaved in unspeakable conditions. It would be a year before negotiations resulted in their successful release. While Lucius was imprisoned, Flavia gave birth to twin sons, Haloven and Tobin. The headstrong and handsome Tobin is here with us today.

Lucius and Marcus returned to a flourishing Rome but witnessed a shocking flow of corruption and civil disorder among their brethren, legions of fellow Roman soldiers cooperating in the crimes, reaping reward for acts of disgrace and dishonor, disobedience and desecration, traitors of the highest order wreaking havoc and despair across our great city."

SPINA

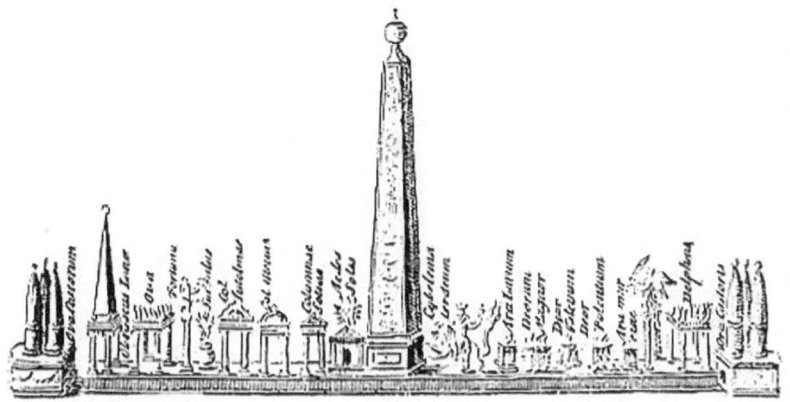

M E T A E

T HE JOYOUS spin of the hora dance started centuries ago in the eastern parts of the Mediterranean, demonstrably in Romania. It is customarily observed with kin, lovers and friends joining hands in a great circle, rotating in rhythm to any readily available instrument, be it accordion, flute, violin or trumpet. The dance flows counterclockwise, a tradition of movement shared by competitive athletes, racers and jockeys making their laps around tracks and ovals all over the globe, from horseracing to NASCAR. Speed measures the success in these races, meticulously kept, recorded and chronicled. The human body and mind rebel against the clock's incessant ticking and direction, thus, by moving in its counter motion not only is there a desperate effort to beat time but in defiance counter its forward, passing motion. The hora dancers are rebellious as well, turning against the expected pains, labors and trials daily life delivers, keeping unmitigated glee at the center. No victory or conquest is declared in the hora, and clearly in contrast to competitive racing, no watch governs duration or line determines the finish.

THEY ARE the Roma, true travelers, the family-centric tribes of East Asian origin, migrating around the Earth and across the centuries

keeping their fascinating mobility and itinerant DNA intact. In more derogatory fashion they are dismissed and marginalized as gypsies.

The "scattered people" are resilient and resourceful since their mass exodus over 1,500 years ago, twelve-million descendants surviving across Eastern, Central and Southern Europe, with pockets of their population sprinkled across every continent on the planet, mostly in the shadows, under the bridges, in rusting trailers and tinker campers, their traditional music, unabashed joy, laughter and solidarity circling their ways and days. They come from a long line of crafty, wayward performers, traders, musicians and artisans. Deceit and deception are mastered for survival. Bulgarian Romani will nod vertically in the negative, horizontally in the affirmative, a curiously confusing and amusing counter-gesture unshared by the "settled world."

The Roma know the sufferings of persecution and discrimination well. Their arrival in Europe, most evident in Romania, was met with abject slavery or worse. The medieval age ushered in mass expulsion and murder of the Romani, forbidding their language, branding by scorching irons, women's ears severed and the children kidnapped. This period was only a precursor for what was to come by way of the Third Reich when Nazis rounded them up en masse into the horrors of the concentration camps, exterminating two million of the traditional wayfarers.

Post-war Europe was hardly sympathetic. In the decades that followed, regular sterilization of the women advanced eugenic thinking in pursuit of the perfect race, which could only be attained by denying or destroying Romani procreation.

In the Piazza del Campidoglio, stoic and formidable on her throne sits Dea Roma, the goddess of Rome, a spear in one hand pointing to the heavens and a globe in the other, symbolizing her protection and dominance over the entire world. She is flanked by the male gods Tiber and Nile, the rivers flowing through her fallen empire. The piazza is located on the ancient grounds of the Roman Senate, subsequently designed and beautified by Michelangelo via papal commission. Dea Roma reminds, expressionlessly, this city was built by conquest and war. She bears masculine and feminine features and carries secrets as well, for as she guards there is perpetual anxiety and concern Roman adversaries and enemies abroad may be lured by her tutelary divinity. However, a bigger secret could be she is not Dea Roma at all but the goddess Minerva, sponsor of the arts, schools, trades and commerce who, while strategically cunning in warfare, is not disposed to violence as much as standing and serving as a subtle, compassionate and determined defender of a creative and peaceful domain. The goddess Roma's role here is one of imposter, a manipulated messenger for the gawkers below, possessing immortal intentions and grand designs for what is best for her people, whether they recognize her or not.

The Romani pass her daily if not casually. Italy remains divided and detached even for the Roma born in the country, the "scattered people" relegated to second-class housing, tin sheds and metallic containers on the outskirts of the city, their citizenry and sense of belonging in a perpetual state of limbo. The well-exercised and worn arches on the resilient Romani remain nimble and mobile, members of the race with destinations unfinished, watched over by a stoic goddess armed, suspicious and unidentified.

IT IS known as the Itinerary of Einsiedeln, a comprehensive, handy and fascinating travel guide made up of eleven sections providing routes from one gate to another inside ninth-century Rome, a plethora of details on sites not to be missed. Of the many mysteries is its authorship, though it seems to have monastic roots when tourism of the age was attracting a new breed of travelers, euphoric Christians on pilgrimage from various territories across Europe.

The library at Einsiedeln preserves the manuscript, written by a prolific individual all in the same hand. It is not considered so much a masterpiece of literature as an historic, detailed roadmap to the scores of Rome's monuments, buildings, walls and triumphal arches awaiting the spiritually determined. It suggests and tempts where one should start. While the full intent or aim of the work is uncertain, it hints the final resting places of the Christian martyrs, the tombs, catacombs and basilicas beyond the city walls, are the expected finish lines.

In centuries since and from the imposing north, trekking across the Alps was good spiritual training, a test of will and stamina for determined travelers. A stop for restful preparation, prayer and a blessing on the Swiss side could be warming and wise. The Benedictine Abbey in Einsiedeln is the most important baroque construction in Switzerland. A popular destination since the Middle Ages has been the Chapel of Our Lady with its famous and compelling Black Madonna, brought to its present shrine in 1466 replacing a Roman statue destroyed by fire the year before. Her dark complexion could be the authentic representation of the Middle Eastern DNA of Mother Mary or simply natural wood decay. Still, it may be a divine sign the Virgin's pigment, whether exposed to the sun in her trying travels or charcoaled by flames from a fallen candle, singed by the torch of an arsonist or a vandalizing invader, speaks to the resilience of all people and races making lifelong, curious and spiritual quests to be at her side. Solidarity with the pilgrim Black Madonna is renewing and rewarding, and they come by the thousands to make her blessed acquaintance.

A curator in the library provides wisdom without certainty. "Acceptance of limited knowledge, the unknown intent of the Creator, is not a bad start for any pilgrim. Answers may be found on the other side of the mountains, in Rome, or right back here on retreat. The most important thing for any pilgrim is to agree on a start."

In 1991 mountaineers trekking above 10,000-feet elevation on the Austria-Italy border came across a prehistoric corpse emerging from a melting glacier. He is named Otzi for the region he was found. Originally thought to be fallen on the Austrian side, 5,000-year-old Otzi is the oldest preserved human ever found, murdered just across the present-day Italian border. He is a scientific superstar, one of the most studied specimens in history, an arrowhead lodged in his torso with evidence of a bash to the head, and a substantial scatter of impressive belongings and tools at his side. Climbing out of the stone age, Otzi's DNA indicates he was Italian, a resourceful hunter and fighter who appears to have gotten entangled in a deadly skirmish over territory, and his ax head, trapezoidal and forged in central-Italian copper, suggests he was a man of high stature and means. The prized ax not stolen by his killers, robbery, it would be presumed, was not the motive. Otzi was an enemy trailed and executed, a trespassing pilgrim in retreat, a victim of vengeance or act of war, on the receiving end of some determined and due justice in his own fateful time. He left his mark in profound bodily fashion, literally, with over sixty tattoos on his incredibly preserved skin, parallel charcoaled markings, horizontal and vertical lines and two crosses, perhaps a branded record of the many ailments he bore. Down the center of his torso, la spina, run groups of lines that may have had their intent on easing his degenerating heart and chest pains. The ancient archer possessed deerskin quiver and arrows and the world's oldest-known snowshoes. The tomb of this well-known soldier is the South Tyrol Museum of Archaeology in Bolzano, Italy, in frigid conditions he would have found familiar in his alpine journeys fifty centuries ago. Multitudes of visitors pay belated respects through paneled glass contemplating his destiny and demise. Otzi the itinerant, assassinated and forgotten over the ages along a rocky Italian crest, now lies immortalized on frosty display wrapped in a murder mystery, the flocks of curious pilgrims wondering not so much who could be guilty of the dastardly deed, but what on Earth did our frozen ancestor do to deserve it?

ENGRAVED INTO the Marble Road in Ephesus is the Roman pictogram of *pes planus*, a common anatomical condition known as flat foot. Nearly one in five humans has some form of the condition, particularly prevalent among children when development is in full stride. The pictogram serves as a directional guide for first-century travelers entering the city's gates, providing a choice to pivot left or right, to the baths or the brothels.

The Roman linear measurements were astutely applied. The foot, *pes*, can be keenly observed at the foot of statues such as Cossutius and Statilius at a length just shy of the modern twelve inches.

The arch was a revolutionary construction method of the Roman empire, a centerpiece for development that would influence the very foundation and principles of architecture around the world. The innovation of the rounded arch provided for substantial stretches and heights, from towering buildings, aqueducts and bridges to the ever-imposing monuments to wars waged and heroics propagated across the millennia. This remarkable advancement in engineering provided for compressed pressure of the structures to be dispensed with marvel, thus remains of the Roman arches across the vast empire can be seen, or are in use, to the present day, their practical and aesthetically pleasing qualities replicated and employed as standards in modern-day design. The last stone to be placed in the Roman arch was the keystone, or capstone, the trapezoidal, irregularly shaped block forming the apex of the arch and providing stability for the entire structure.

The three keystone arches of the complex apparatus and anatomy of the foot, ankle and arch are the medial, lateral and transverse. Together, they are the shock absorbers for the entire human body, providing strength, stability and ability to move and, for the athlete and warrior, capacity to compete, leap and charge. Should one of these keystones be out of alignment the integrity of the entire arch collapses. For those destined to be excluded from, or with influential diagnosis avoid, military service and combat, a documented case of the ancient condition of *pes planus* does the trick.

In the human hand is a small, nondescript trapezoidal carpal bone in the distal row providing strength and structure to the incomprehensible integrity of the human hand. The irregular quadrilateral bone supports the complete movement of the intricate wrist and, most specifically, the integrity of the fascinating human palm. The Roman palm, *palmus*, is one-quarter of *pes*, or approximately three inches.

Roman palms of the enslaved and commissioned were skillfully employed in building the massive marble arch honoring Emperor Titus. The foundation was discovered by archaeologists at a far end of the Circus Maximus, a cluster of hundreds of marble fragments that once constituted and adorned the marvelous entrance to the world's largest track stadium of its time. Traces of the travertine pavement have been discovered along with plinths and four humongous columns serving as its base. In triumphant parades, emperors and generals would have proceeded under its capstone celebrating victories over Roman enemies.

Two arches were built to honor Titus. One still stands at the Forum's entrance, commemorating the emperor's victory over revolting Jews which ended in the epic act of mass suicide at Masada in Judea in the year AD 72.

Decorating this arch is a relief depicting Roman soldiers parading off with their stolen treasure, a golden menorah from Jerusalem, a boastful march absorbed by the arch, the spoils secured in the raised palm.

The last great arch was built by Constantine in AD 315 featuring old, recycled and plundered material. While the same architectural principles remained in play, the qualities and sensibilities were in full shift. Its panels depict the noble and wise Marcus Aurelius' head curiously reworked and reconfigured, etched to resemble an imposter, Constantine himself.

BUILT IN 1929, Royce Hall and Powell Library at the University of California at Los Angeles were the first two buildings constructed on the campus. Royce Hall is a striking example of Lombardian-style Romanesque architecture, the pride of the property and most recognizable symbol of the institution's prowess. On a high bluff anchoring the main mall, basking in the Mediterranean climate and sun-kissed skies, the locale echoed of Italy to the architects. The hall stands on the precipice of Janss Steps which lead to the athletic fields and Drake Stadium, the foundation of many national championships won by the outstanding UCLA track and field teams throughout its rich and prestigious twentieth-century dominance. During orientation tours the freshmen, budding wildflowers blossoming into maturity, are paraded to the steps and, ascending to Royce Hall, introduced to the majestic vista to hear of glorious triumphs, academically, athletically and historically, beneath the building's towering and intoxicating aura. Turning full attention to the crimson-brick hall and its dual towers, they are posed with a simple question of observation: "Can you identify anything unique, different or odd about the hall?" More times than not genuine appreciation of the art, engineering and beauty of the building, coupled by the breathtaking view, lead to a collective quiet. At this moment in the tour most students are stumped and, preoccupied by the obscure, they miss the obvious. The host will point out there are two open Roman arches in one tower, but puzzlingly three in the other. Traditional in the minds of the most astute and humble architects, however genius, is the purposeful incorporation of a defect, a contrived imperfection. "Man is not capable of creating perfection in the naturally perfect universe. It is in his interests, within his greatest achievements or pursuits, to discipline himself in humility, mindful of his mortal shortcomings," the wide-eyed young scholars are reminded, a primary lesson in their higher education.

Directly across the magnificent UCLA mall facing the Royce towers is the Romanesque Lawrence Clark Powell Library. Graced by its arches and columns, its porch featuring two supporting Atlantes, it strains in silence under colossal weight. Above the entrance is the Owl of Wisdom, with the God of Light and God of Learning bookending the welcome. Inside one can appreciate the mosaic on the wall below the main staircase's first landing where two men hold a book bearing the legend from Cicero's *Pro Archia, Haec studia adulescentiam alunt, senectutem oblectant* – "These studies stimulate the young, divert the old." Three arches draw visitors to the Main Reading Room. Surrounding the rotunda are others supported by tiled columns, their fine Romanesque bas-reliefs revealing the natural and wild world scrolled and on display in pigs, goats, peacocks, rabbits, squirrels and doves. The signature feature is the room's dome with dedicated inscriptions of luminaries and icons such as printing pioneer Johann Fust who, along with Johann Gutenberg, is credited with ushering in the age of publishing by underwriting Gutenberg's printshop and equipment. Fust usurped the operation in a suit, yet historically both are challenged as the true innovators, perhaps pioneering imposters swirling in a much larger circle of brilliant minds and businessmen caught up in fifteenth-century secret schemes and scams. What is known is they played central roles in the overall operations of making multiple copies of famous works, the Bible and Cicero's *De officiis*, the classical Roman masterpiece on ethics, morality and how to best behave civilly to advance the human condition universally. The library is named after noted librarian Lawrence Clark

Powell. "We are the children of a technological age ... Printing is no longer the only way of reproducing books. Reading them, however, has not changed," Powell imparted. His interests in the provocative and evocative was evident in his companionship and correspondence with the controversial, blackballed author Henry Miller, who took regular long walks as a penniless genius from his tiny abode in Beverly Glen into Westwood cultivating a profound connection to Powell. A catalog of the master writer's work has made its way into the UCLA collection. Likewise, it is fitting Ray Bradbury penned his dystopian novel *Fahrenheit 451* in these halls, educating the masses on the temperature it takes to incinerate books rendered profane, dangerous or simply unacceptable by censors and arsonists. Miller would be intimately familiar with such systemic dismissal and rejection of controversial publications, Powell one of his staunch allies. Powell also wrote and successfully defended a dissertation on the enigmatic and divisive poet Robinson Jeffers whose anti-war views nearly destroyed his public standing. Darkened or defined by his witness to twentieth-century atrocity, Jeffers reached deep to comprehend the presence of evil regularly intercepting the higher essence of beauty in our existence. He wrote of the grotesque and graceful, the fall of man and the call of nature, the decay of cliffs and endurance of stone. In a release which is not a surrender, but possibly the way out for man, he shares in *The Bloody Sire*, "Violence has been the sire of all the world's values. Who would remember Helen's face, lacking the terrible halo of spears? Who formed Christ but Herod and Caesar? Violence, the bloody sire of all the world's values. Never weep, let them play, old violence is not too old to beget new values."

In his final work, *The Beginning and the End*, Jeffers "can feel the beautiful secret, in places and stars and stones ... I wish that all human creatures might feel it. That would make joy in the world, and make men perhaps a little nobler – as a handful of wildflowers."

"I THINK '84 is probably the Olympics that I should have won, or that I could have won, I guess, had I not fallen down," the world-class long-distance runner Mary Decker reflected.

In 1984 the city of Los Angeles, selected to host the Olympic Games, returned to the classic, renovated Romanesque Memorial Coliseum where the 1932 games staged the main events, including opulent opening and closing ceremonies celebrating the world's most-talented athletes in the healthiest exchange of patriotism, pride and competition among nations. In the decades between the games the stadium still boasted its powerful presence in Tinseltown, a city otherwise recognized for its propagation of film and fantasy, its capacity to create the unreal among the real. On the east end are its colonnades bracing the symbolically imposing Olympic flame and the Robert Graham-commissioned statues, a headless male and female standing in confident pose as if anticipating the gold. The Roman elements hark back to a time and vision, regal if not royal, as the benevolent center of international competition where amateurism and fair play reigned as virtues, not impediments, in pursuit of the prize.

But George Orwell's dystopian novel hit its mark in 1984 in a resurgence of Cold War tactics, systemic surveillance and subversive activities, well in motion as the world's superpowers faced off for the first time in eight years, the United States having boycotted the Russia-hosted 1980 games in a decision both political and principled.

Ethics were on trial early, and if Big Brother in 1984 was watching he arbitrarily turned a blind eye, too. World-class cyclists by the score were swept in a scandal of widespread performance-enhancing drugs, a sports cartel of illegal doping well financed and fueled to provide significant and secretive advantages, in the most extreme cases by means of blood transfusions immediately before a race.

Then two unassuming sisters from Puerto Rico hit the track. Madeline de Jesus, injured in the long jump competition, feared her performance in the 4 x 400 relays would severely hamper or shamefully compromise the team's chances, so in her stead came an unlikely imposter, her identical twin Margaret who helped advance the squad by running the second leg in the qualifying heat. The Puerto Rico coach eventually got wise to the ruse and pulled his team from competition.

The ultimate drama came by way of competition between the world's two most-famous female runners, Mary Decker of the United States and Zola Budd of South Africa, who would be representing Great Britain with her native country banned from competing due its stubborn and shameful apartheid positions, the systemic separation of the races. Midway through the competitive 3,000-meter contest heading into the crucial curve of the track, the well-trained legs of each racer mysteriously, conspicuously or accidentally entangled, Decker falling into the track's center grass, Budd carrying on among a chorus and cacophony of boos from 100,000 onlookers and millions more watching by television around the world. Her heart and spirit torn in each turn of the track, her main competitor in visible despair and out of the race, Budd's pace slowed in each heavy stride. "I only knew someone had fallen. When I passed by the spot again, on the next lap, it was then I realized it was Mary," Budd confessed. "And the crowd started booing. That's when I gave up. Everything leading up to it, all the politics, all the hype, and then for Mary to fall … I slowed down deliberately. I didn't want to be on the medal podium. In a way, I stopped."

To the deserving land of the Roma went the spoils. The superstars fallen, the little-known and underrated Maricica Puica ran away with the gold, taking it proudly home to the unheralded, unexpected and little respected Romania.

Defeat did not embitter or hamper Decker's perspective. Life took its turns far from the Coliseum's colonnades and its headless statues, their backs to a famous if fading tripping incident on the perilous turn of the track below.

"I look at it as history, Olympic history," Decker reflected with calm surrender, "and it truly feels like it was another lifetime ago."

Completed in 1923, the Los Angeles Memorial Coliseum was dedicated to the veterans of World War I. When global conflict returned a few short decades later, attempts were made to combine the dedication to both World War I and II veterans, but strong, opposing and competing factions won the day. World War II recognition was put in its compromised if not relegated place amidst the rose bushes of Exposition Park.

Little remains of the complete inscriptions from the original, mammoth Colosseum of Rome, but an abbreviation from the fifth-to-sixth-century reveals *Imp. Caes. Vespasianus. Aug. Amphitheatrum Novum. Ex Manubis Fieri Iussit*, translating to "Emperor Caesar Vespasian Augustus ordered a new amphitheater to be made from spoils."

AT THE end of the Via San Gregorio is the Circus Maximus, 2,200 feet in length, 705 feet wide, once flanked by terraces of wooden seats on three sides providing occupancy for a quarter-million Roman fanatics, a quarter of the city's population. Rebuilt by Caesar, it was the largest, single structure for public entertainment in the world. As it gained in status it attracted more elites, the influential and the wealthy, the powerful and the royal. Trajan glorified and expanded its presentation and rebuilt seats for the privileged in marble. Spectators flocking to its entrance would pass the Roman shops and brothels, entering in a swarm of unbridled enthusiasm. Vendors sold cushions for the cheaper wooden seats. Senators and dignitaries settled into posh quarters ornamented in bronze, the imperial box boasting luxurious rooms and private suites. There they indulged in lavish days of recreation and reclining, eating, drinking and bathing. Gambling was feverish, exultation constant, and the roars and applause made for steady commotion. During the period of persecution the majority of Christian martyrs were offered here. Other entertaining episodes were the *venationes*, the staging of hungry and wild beasts brought from distant and exotic territories who would fight each other or feed upon condemned criminals, heretics and the falsely accused, including early Christians by the score. The circus would also host, in peaceful periods, a lively carnival-like marketplace, a myriad of booths and stalls featuring traders, fortune-tellers and buskers.

A precursor for courses to come, the Circus Maximus got its start around 326 BC, an enormous oval at the epicenter of the Roman

Empire, positioned nearly perfect in the valley between the Palatine and Aventine hills. Its full capacity of onlookers, emperors, senators and intelligentsia, laborers, commoners and the *liberti*, the freed slaves, were entertained and provoked, mesmerized and mortified over the course of nine centuries in witness and worship as the deity, royals, charioteers and competitors put on the show of shows. The *spectacula*, or *Fori*, were rising tiers three stories high, seating which separated senators from equites, the second-class citizenry, with the general public designated to the cheapest seats. Private, luxury boxes were reserved for the politicians and military.

The most famous races in their time took place here, some consuming fifteen days straight, the competitors and their horses dramatically entering through the *ostia*, or grand openings, on each end before approaching the *alba linea*, a white line of lime and chalk serving as both a starting and finishing line. Twelve *carceres*, or chariot stalls, flung open at the start of the races. Laps were recorded in dramatic display in the shifting of giant wooden eggs along the central *spina*, the ornate dividing barrier. The spina ran down the middle of the oval track, a feature twelve-feet wide and four-feet high, noted by the columns at its ends in which the horses and chariots made their turns. A great obelisk, 132-feet in height, stood towering and intimidating, a reminder of Rome's dominance and spoils. Egyptian, it was dedicated to the Pharaoh Ramses the Great but usurped and placed purposefully, pointedly and playfully in the circus after a heist across the Mediterranean. At opposite ends of the spina stood magnificent cones, the *metae*, twenty-feet in height adorned in bas-reliefs to look like cypress trees. They served as bumpers should the racers get too close and collide, risking damage to the treasured spina. Each charioteer strove to attain the best inner position on the left, racing counterclockwise. Exercising sound judgment in the motion was crucial, for if a wheel so much as brushed the spina's stone curb it could result in catastrophe, not only for the faulty and guilty but those crashing in the wake.

The opening processions were grand, a royal and nationalistic parade of Roman pride and propaganda. Images of the gods, hoisted and held in the palms of attendants, were displayed on carriages with performers on horseback and others on foot, followed by the combatants, dancers and musicians. Champions were treated in Greek tradition in the presentation of palms. The most popular, supreme charioteers were imperial superstars, known as *milliari* for having competed in over 1,000 races, many gaining bountiful fortune and fame. Scorpus completed a record 2,048 races before being killed. *Oh! sad misfortune! That you, Scorpus, should be cut off in the flower of your youth, and be called so prematurely to harness the dusky steeds of Pluto. The chariot-race was always shortened by your rapid driving, but O why should your own race have been so speedily run?* the Roman poet Martial laments in Book X of his Epigrams. *O Rome, I am Scorpus, the glory of your noisy circus, the object of your applause, your short-lived favorite.*

The party and drama would spill to neighboring streets, porticos and back alleys. Victors and the vanquished commiserated and consoled, celebrated and ceded in true Roman fashion in nearby taverns surrounding the circus in the hours and days post competition.

The great fire in AD 64 which tore through vast sectors of the city destroying many of the neighborhoods of the equites was started in the Circus Maximus. Rumors circulated the unstable and eccentric Emperor Nero was the culprit, a grand arsonist behind a larger scheme to rebuild Rome in his image. But the conveniently accused was the new and curious sect of Christians circulating tales of a Messiah and a message of universal peace, love and forgiveness, a pathway to the Kingdom available to all, including equites. These bothersome heretics told of the imperial power playing an unlawful role in the Messiah's crucifixion. Surely avenging Christians were motivated to inflict a blow on the capital's empire had they not fully and spiritually absorbed the Messiah's new commandment of loving they neighbor as thyself. Of ashes and to ashes all return, but out of the circus' inferno Nero took opportunity of a useful rumor, and brutal persecution of early Christians went hand in hand with the massive, ego-driven rebuilding and redecorating of Rome by his design, widening the streets and expanding the emperor's villas and palaces. Those following the Messiah were trafficked into the Colosseum, condemned without trial and, stripped and unarmed, faced wild and unfed beasts such as tigers and lions. It was a bloodier affair than their Master endured at the hand of Rome's Pilate and centurions.

Nero's appetite to compete took him into the rings of the Olympic Games in AD 67. Staged in a theatrical and comical display of faux athleticism, the imposter stole the show. While most chariot races featured four-horse teams, up to ten horses were drawn for the emperor to grab the reigns in a most disgraceful and fixed spectacle. Nero steered with overcharged horsepower collecting every prize and medal imaginable in his self-rigged Olympics.

As refined and sophisticated Roman senses dulled, carnal appetites increased and the Circus Maximus reflected the same. The barbaric mentality intensified in a downward spiral. The once glamorous, spectacular stadium reaching toward the heavens to please the gods had turned downward to bestial, bloody Hades, the only barrier between wild beasts being slaughtered by the thousands and the multitudes of enraptured, salivating fanatics was a cleverly engineered mote ten-feet wide and ten-feet deep, a churning purgatory of pretense and false security.

All that can be seen today of the grand Circus Maximus beyond its green-grass valley and cypress is the slowly decaying imperial box once occupied by benevolent and malevolent emperors and their loyal or disloyal courts, protruding its ancient nose out of the overgrown foliage into the Roman breeze, as if in haunting search or sniff of wild lavender wafting across its exhilarating but exhausted city, the ancient cheers faint, muffled by the constant blow of blaring horns and spinning Vespas.

CIVIS ROMANUS *sum* – "I am a Roman citizen" – was the self-assured proclamation resounding loudly in the Ancient World, a mutually benefiting declaration between the governing and the governed, the guarantee of civil liberties, protection and safety to be bellowed whenever a citizen was met with a bold challenge to inherent rights. The proud phrase would lose its volume, value and vitality in the Roman port of Ostia in the year 68 BC when an early act of orchestrated terrorism rocked the government's foundation with seismic vibration. Hardly executed by a foreign power in a feat of defiance, which itself would have been foolish for any competing state in that age, the damage was done by a misfit band of marginalized, despondent and desperate characters bent on abject destruction. What they could not have foreseen was the consequential Roman overreaction, the political, cultural and psychological turn that would set in motion systematic injustice and impropriety resulting in, ultimately, the epic downfall of the greatest government on Earth.

The German historian Theodor Mommsen called the anarchistic scoundrels "the ruined men of all nations," whose larger victory was an ongoing, self-perpetuated Roman state of heightened fear and anxiety where "the traveler on the Appian highway, the genteel bathing visitor at the terrestrial paradise of Baiae were no longer secure of their property or their life for a single moment."

In the wake of the fire and fury that torched Ostia and her harbored Roman war fleet, a few senators were kidnapped in good measure, and the bells of panic and alarm rang all the way into the inner chambers of the political elite. The result was a haphazard, shaky and tyrannical trip down the steep and swift slope of abandoned democracy as terror ushered in the destruction of the Roman Constitution, replaced with the hasty and unlawfully crafted and passed *Lex Gabinia*, an unprecedented slate of supreme authority, power and resources. In short order the entire treasury of the empire was bestowed unto the cunning, exploiting and opportunistic military hero and blood-thirsty warmonger Pompey the Great.

A life centered and preoccupied in battle, violence and conflict, there was still a fleeting hope among the rational that Pompey's periodic grandeurs and boasts of benevolence, such as cleansing the Mediterranean of its Rome-loathing pirates, would properly steer his thinking and lead to reasonable, positive outcomes. But his reputation preceded him, and etched into history is his eternal nickname, *adulescentulus carnifex*, the "teenage butcher," earned by his incessant, malicious impulses and ready dismissal of the people's wishes. Ultimately the sea he purported to have cleansed would swallow his headless and naked corpse, tossed overboard not by misfits but by powerful Roman insiders with sharp instincts and daggers of their own, steely, sharpened, bloody butchers themselves who had seen enough of their rapacious Pompey and his wanton assault on their civil liberties.

LOCKED IN the California Institute for Women are over 1,500 prisoners, hundreds above the designed capacity, a substantial percentage convicted of non-violent drug offenses. Ushered in by the War on Drugs, the age of mass incarceration made America the largest imprisoned population on the planet. The notorious do their time side by side with the anonymous. A course from nearby Cal Poly Pomona, *Contemporary Treatment of the Law Violator*, brings a class behind the massive, electronically charged barbed wire-laced fences and concrete walls under the watchful surveillance of modern-day centurions.

A silent procession of students halts fifty meters beyond an inmate alone in her concentration, undisturbed by the parade and reading intently during the day's open-yard hour. She is an aging woman in customary prisoner attire. The guide asks in low volume, "Does anyone recognize the lady we just passed, there on the same bench where we see her most every day?" The two dozen college coeds nod negative in unison.

"That is Leslie Van Houten, a member of the Manson family. She was sentenced to death but is serving a life sentence, behind bars since she was 19. She is over 70 today."

The students turn their heads back toward the bench to capture a glimpse of the famous convict.

"Many prisoners find redemption, spirituality and deeper purpose here. Some people question the sincerity of their faith, this newfound transformation and turnaround – wondering if the fresh outlooks and attitudes are but clever ploys to be played out in front of gullible parole boards, the patient manipulation of masterminds and imposters."

After a contemplative, long pause, the guide says as if to herself, "I must say in Leslie's case we have never seen or heard anything to suggest she is anything other than what she has shown over the decades, a very kind and peaceful person. She has taught and mentored scores of troubled ladies here. The devil once lured and possessed her young mind. I tend to believe the Lord now occupies her heart."

Van Houten barely survived a traumatic childhood, runaway years laced in drugs and the suppression of a late-term aborted baby she buried in the backyard at the behest of her mother. Coerced and manipulated into the Manson family, she took on several aliases leading up to a bloody, horrid deed.

Fifty years later, asked by students if there is any hope for freedom for a Manson-family member, regardless of the details of long-ago heinous acts, the tour guide is guarded. "This isn't Rome, it's California. We have judges, juries and parole boards, not emperors bending to the will of the gods. We're in the justice business, not the mercy business."

St. Paul authored in his letter to the Hebrews: *Therefore, since we are surrounded by so great a cloud of witnesses, let us rid ourselves of every burden and sin that clings to us, and persevere in running the race that lies before us.*

The Roman tax collector, murderous and brutal in his own right, turned his heart on the well-engineered Roman road to Damascus, illumined by a new spiritual law and light proclaiming a Kingdom offered to all if only hearts of stone transformed in a merciful commandment, requiring the deepest love possible of thy neighbor. Saint Paul made a turn and spent the rest of his years on a different track, one that eventually led to a Roman jail in Philippi. There he polished his ministry as well as appeals, changing the course of history and the arc of humanity.

LAVENDER, THE herb which incites emotion as no other, is a native plant from the mountainous region of the Mediterranean. *Lavare*, Latin for wash, and *livindula*, Latin for livid or bluish, provide the roots of its name, but it was Adam, Eve and Cleopatra who brought it fame. It has been cultivated, traded and spread around the world, yet its luring prowess and aromatic mystery resonates most commercially in the South of France, proudly displayed to legions of flocking pilgrims in the perfume capital of the world, the village of Grasse in Provence.

The Egyptians used lavender in cosmetics and as an embalming and mummification ingredient. To release its fragrant, calming qualities, mothers in labor were provided bundles of dried lavender to squeeze during contractions. Cleopatra, having learned of Antony's demise, resigned herself to death by the asp. Those coming upon her corpse found her chosen culprit and accomplice, the cooperating snake, lying in wait in lush lavender.

The poet Horace provided the masses a famous, celebratory song to accompany generous consumptions of wine, *nunc est bibendum*, "now is the time for drinking," composed on news of Cleopatra's demise leading to the subsequent Roman reward, the taking of her Egypt.

Dioscordes, a Greek physician practicing under the rule of Nero, was an avid study of the herb for its medicinal applications, relieving the many maladies plaguing the neurotic, ill emperor and his afflicted countrymen, the headaches, irritability, insomnia, wounds and burns, circumstantial or self-inflicted.

Exiled from the Garden of Eden, Adam and Eve stole off with the herb to protect them from evil, but it wasn't until Mother Mary laid Jesus' clothes on the lavender bush to dry that it emitted its perpetual scent. Spikenard, as it is known in the Bible, is its Greek name, where John recounts, "Then took Mary a pound of ointment of spikenard, very costly, and anointed the feet of Jesus, and wiped his feet with her hair, and the house was filled with the odor of the ointment."

The Romans made use of lavender in their cooking and bathing rituals and applied it in oil as a soap. But its real utility came by way of military applications during wretched wars and mass annihilations. The imperial campaigns required ample supplies to fragrant the air and mask the stench of rotting flesh.

Along the bloody Western Front, WWI doughboys were provided lavender by the bushel to dress horrid wounds and manipulate the putrid air wafting over the gaseous fields and rancid trenches, the destined-to-be graves of thousands of sacrificed souls. Military perfumery was contrived in a grand design to disguise and distort.

Wild lavender grows abundantly in the Somme Valley. In the cemetery at Courcelette just above the mass burials at Sunken Road a circle of lavender had blossomed to puzzlingly large size, perhaps as a result of abundant fertilizer, drawing the attention of gawkers and groundskeepers alike in a delightful combination of stirred and dulled senses, aroma and amnesia.

HE WAS an accomplished architect, well sought in the latter part of the nineteenth and early twentieth centuries. Thomas Hastings designed urban office buildings of grandeur with Roman touches, employing such skills in the Tomb of the Unknowns at Arlington Cemetery and the Pulitzer Fountain of Abundance in Grand Army Plaza in front of the Plaza Hotel in New York City. He detested modern skyscrapers as commercial, ego-driven monuments to profiteers with no redeeming value to the public or posterity. Hastings considered the American towers of steel and glass "bad in style and bad for the health of the citizenry."

His Pulitzer Fountain presents the Roman goddess Pomona, elegant and dominant in her gentle grace, facing directly across from the gilded military man on horseback, General William Tecumseh Sherman, who shares the same pavement.

The actress and model Doris Doscher posed as Pomona for the statue. In demand herself, she had played Eve in *The Birth of a Race*, an early, conciliatory film countering the controversial and disturbing version of America depicted in *The Birth of a Nation* where a terrorist organization, the Ku Klux Klan, was sympathetically if not heroically splashed on the silver screen. Doscher was also billed as "the girl on the quarter," posing for the coinage of the Standing Liberty twenty-five-cent piece. Controversy surfaced a few years after Doscher's death when it was socially if not sinisterly circulated she was an imposter. Another woman was rumored to have actually posed as the beautiful Liberty, the Broadway actress Irene MacDowell whose identity was concealed for decades due to a scandalous romance among the designers. Irene, whose name means peace, may have quietly chosen to keep the peace.

Whoever posed as Liberty, Pomona stands resilient and true, commanding the plaza with poise in a stare down with the general.

Pomona, or *pomus* in Latin, means "of the fruit," possibly coming from a term that more specifically means "to be taken, picked." In the Ovid myth *Metamorphoses*, Pomona is singly dedicated to her orchards and spurns all suitors. Courted by many fertility gods, she refused them all. Her beauty entranced and consumed the god Vertumnus who, desperate to penetrate her garden, became an imposter and tricked Pomona in his disguise as an old woman. As he gained Pomona's confidence and camaraderie he eventually won her love, all in dramatic acts of deceit.

She is a rather obscure goddess whose essence is a mystery, but her devotion remains undaunted. It is claimed a very good way to connect with Pomona is in periods of transition, the pivotal turns in life when substantial changes can be appreciated, as like seeds in her orchards when they turn to fruit. A tangible way to demonstrate the transformation, theatrically, is to take an apple or pear, find a tranquil location and relax, then call on Pomona to be present in the fruit. Slicing the pome one can visualize its pieces as both past and present, seeing the right paths and decisions as well as errors and mistakes, before separating the seeds and consuming the fruit. In planting the seeds one is returning them to Pomona with the energy of the goddess nourishing the new steps, seasons and stages of life, bearing necessary fruit for the ongoing journey.

Near the ancient, ransacked Roman port of Ostia, where coins and other loot were once taken by ambitious pirates, is a grove sacred to Pomona.

In the Roman occupied Judea wise men attempted to trip up Jesus in a quiz over taxes, authority and the law, a trick and test centered on the complex compliance with the occupiers. Jesus took a Roman coin bearing the image on one side of Caesar Augustus Tiberius, and on the other the emperor's mother Livia, widow of Augustus. "Render unto Caesar the things that are Caesar's, and unto God the things that are God's," Jesus instructed for the ages.

It was rumored after Augustus' death Livia was the suspected culprit, posing as a devoted wife while smearing poison on his favorite fruit.

In Newtown, Connecticut, located on a grassy triangular patch on the grounds of a former schoolhouse close to the center of town stands what is commonly known as the Sailors and Soldiers monument due to the six large, bronze plaques mounted on cement blocks circling its base, honoring veterans of the many wars of the twentieth century. But its original intent in the years following WWI was to glorify peace. The 36-foot-tall Lady Liberty stares out to the southwest brandishing a speared flag, an olive branch and chain. She was meant to steer her people away from war-time conflict and violence. According to a 1931 Newtown Bee article, "Any suggestion of arms or strife, so common in many memorials of this type, has been carefully avoided because it was not the actual conflict that it desires to commemorate, but rather the spirit and idealism that prompted the sacrifice of thousands of youthful lives, honor and principle."

Nearly a century later the village would be at the epicenter of a new menace to peace. One of its young citizens would commandeer a military-style AR-15 Bushmaster assault rifle, execute his mother and slaughter 20 first-graders and six educators in a matter of minutes. Survivors filed suit against the manufacturer, Remington Arms. The company filed for bankruptcy protection while under ownership of the private-equity firm Cerberus. Cerberus, in Greco-Roman mythology, is the three-headed hellhound guarding the gates of Hades so none of the dead can escape.

Newtown's Lady Liberty needed Rome's protecting she-wolf. Instead, her peace monument was usurped and into the quiet village's lanes ran the rabid and wild Cerberus. The town could benefit by providing Liberty a *mappas* as well, the white handkerchief of surrender and new starts, but it may be too late or do little good. It seems she cannot stop crying.

The dreamcatcher is a Native American protective charm resembling a web, a hoop and strings made of willow and decorated in feathers and beads. It captures evil spirits and frightening nightmares, allowing the good dreams and benevolent spirits to enter and flow. A special dreamcatcher has traveled from one school shooting site to another across America. Members of the Red Lake Nation, who had sadly suffered such a nightmare, drove nonstop through the night to deliver the dreamcatcher to Newtown. Inscribed on its frame is a message from the students of Columbine, young veterans of similar violence. "In the Circle of Life, we will all be together again."

WHITE PEACE doves are domesticated wild rock pigeons symbolized in iconography as the Holy Spirit. Early Christians often held pictures of doves gripping olive branches during funeral processions featuring the word *pax*, which has root meanings to both *peace* and *pace*.

The bird is associated with the Holy Spirit descending from heaven at the baptism of Jesus. The Romans were well-versed in divine signs which legitimized authority of the empire from father unto a son, the "adoptionist" view, and they sought natural omens which foretold military outcomes. The larger, aggressive bird of prey was the prevailing symbol of imperial power, the eagle. Suetonius, the Roman historian, depicted bird omens primarily from two perspectives, the rise and fall of imperial power. Thus, when Claudius entered the Forum and an eagle swooped down to rest on his shoulder, or as the army camped at Bononia and an eagle perched on Augustus' tent, history was interpreted and recorded. Tiberius' power was solidified when, according to Suetonius, "an eagle, a bird never before seen in Rhodes, perched upon the roof of his house."

An eagle flying with a scepter in its talons shares a Roman coin with the divine image of Hadrian taking the throne.

The symbolism of the dove, prevalent in Roman-occupied Syria and Palestine, was often associated as a foil or threat to the eagle. Coins minted in Ashkelon often depicted doves. But to the Romans there is no contest, as one is the mighty predator, the other a timid, non-violent and all-too-often victim. Ovid proclaims not all predators have bad intentions when, in pursuit of the nymph in Metamorphosis, he professes "I am not an enemy of thee ... In this way, thus the dove flies from the eagle with trembling wing; love is the cause of my following thee." In Horace's Odes the Roman dynasty is secured because "the fatherly Augustus is … imagined as an eagle that produced a succession of warlike eagles … ferocious golden eagles don't produce shy doves." The evolved Marcus Aurelius is credited for bringing peace and harmony to the empire, successfully allowing the Roman land and sky to be shared by sheep, doves, wolves and eagles, alike.

In the opulence and grandeur in bidding final, earthly farewell to an emperor, his bier was carried by the highest-born knights and the younger senators through the Via Sacra to the old Forum where an adorned house of wood was erected, similar to lighthouses in the harbors. The bier was placed on the second story and a militaristic parade – representations of historic figures, celebrated generals and kings clad in costume – would dramatically encircle as the heir to the throne would torch the house, devouring the entire building. At this point an eagle would rise high into the air from the top story as if from a lofty battlement and carry, according to the Roman idea, the soul of the dead emperor to heaven where he eternally partakes in the glory and pleasure of the gods.

The symbol of the dove is resilient in Israel in the Book of Antiquities as the spirit of forgiveness and mercy. In the apocalypse of Ezra, God has likened his beloved Israel to a dove and a sheep while the most terrifying beast, symbolically Rome, is described as an eagle. The dove is righteousness among the birds of the air as opposed to the eagle which is considered an abomination. Israelites are called to "practice righteousness," like the dove, and not "achieve anything by brute force," like the eagle.

Rock pigeons found their fame over the centuries, trained for homing and racing. Extraordinary senses and instincts guide them in their reading of magnetic fields, enabling them to effortlessly locate "home." They have been bred for their ability to home over long distances, serving as messengers in peace time and war. In World War I approximately 100,000 of the birds were used extensively by both sides, carrying messages from the trenches to British, French, American and German military headquarters. The carriers were often significantly more accurate and reliable than human counterparts scurrying on motorcycle or horseback. It has been indicated they had a 95-percent success rate in delivery, flying higher and faster than their masters engulfed in the horrors and violence below.

One particular dove gained unequaled infamy and is mounted and enshrined in the Smithsonian Institute. Cher Ami served the U.S. Army Signal Corps during World War I, receiving the French Croix de Guerre with a palm Oak Leaf Cluster for her heroic aerial service in Verdun. In her last mission, despite being wounded, the dove delivered Major Charles Whittlesey's desperate message contributing to the rescue of the so-called "Lost Battalion," hundreds of infantrymen left behind enemy lines. Cher Ami became a hero of the U.S. 77th Infantry Division, and with a shot through the breast, blinded in one eye and a leg dangling by a tendon, she barely survived. Healed, she set sail for her voyage to America, personally given a send-off by General John J. Pershing. Cher Ami, given wartime powers, was immortalized for saving lives and serving as an instrument for peace.

In time her new home, America, would adopt the other bird, replacing Standing Liberty on the quarter with the noted flyer of prey. The eagle, presently, is prolific in official symbolism grasping the intimidating fasces or arrows as well as olive branches, a confusing juxtaposition of intentions and means, an equal and binary choice of war or peace. The eagle etched on coinage is stationed for flight, the dove with a wooden leg is stuffed and grounded, one in fixed, measured value and the other priceless.

In the Book of Mark a divine adoptionist story is told, making a powerful and purposeful turn away from the eagle. The baptized Jesus rises from the water, heavens parting, as the Spirit is presented unto Him as a dove. A voice of authority is heard, "You are my beloved Son."

Some who were listening reached for the olive branch. Others, in habit, grabbed the fasces. Two-thousand years later both dove and eagle still fly, one common, docile and in abundance, the other armed as an icon and nearly extinct.

M E T A E

CHAPTER VII

"**I**, Darius, observed with serious concern but eternal hope. For Rome may have been encircled in a social storm, on the brink of surrendering to a sad and sorry fate, but Lucius did not quit on Rome. He led several restoration projects, the first, here, in the Circus Maximus. He became an expert craftsman in *opus sectile*, utilizing the finest marble and Tibertine stone in the refining of his techniques. He applied such in beautifying the Ara Pacis, Augustus' Altar of Peace, the Columbarium of the Emancipated People and its dignified urns and niches, the honorable resting place of thousands of our departed brothers and sisters.

Lucius had seen enough of man's violent, warring tendencies and the vile bents on corruption, the terminal race to subvert and outdo the other, the games of deceit, the ceaseless contests pinning neighbor against neighbor in lethal pursuits. A new Circus Maximus, under Trajan's design and intent, could be the restored epicenter that brought about the better part of man's natural, positive and competitive spirit. Here, we could race with considerable honor, pride and dignity, in fair contest, a measured degree of Roman allegiance and patriotism, entertaining the masses thirsty for joy and healthy gallantry. In truth, the people could gather in this great circle with roars and cheers, in peace and pride, versus wails of tears and fear. We gather today in his restored Circus Maximus. I pledge we, united in grief and appreciation, indebted to the fallen man, not weep but cheer for Lucius in his just return to the heavens.

Lucius served as foreman in the building of many of the great structures we delight in today. But he received his greatest joy and satisfaction among you, dear Romans, organizing the grand housing projects of the displaced, the dire poor, there on the gentle hills behind the Palatine, *suburbium*. Despite his growing stature and popularity, his presence frequently requested or demanded across Rome and solicited by the privileged, his business and political dealings bringing him into the elite chambers of his admirers, as high as the throne of the emperor himself, Lucius was at home building your homes, dining at your tables, conversing with your friends, drinking your wine. He was everyman's Roman, and he belonged to you. He belonged to the world, and now he belongs to the gods.

The gods witnessed his risky dealings, no doubt impressed if not amused. Greater sums and larger budgets were allocated to Lucius' blossoming projects, this commitment to you. His conspicuous and creative accounting is something in which I was well aware. In time we learned of inflated numbers, his pilfering of accounts that financed many unauthorized projects, also for you – never for personal gain – always, always, for you. These funds opened your new marketplaces, financed more labor for the upkeep and repairs of your streets, your bridges. He invested in your farms, your livestock, and provided compensation for your physicians and teachers as well.

In time we may have approved all such efforts, but Lucius was in a race against time and at your urgency, a speed he had chosen on a course that ferociously steered him. This was his pace, not mine. He was on the track that led to you, always to you. I was to learn we, the senators and my colleagues, were too slow, too tardy, for the momentum that drove Lucius. Indeed, we were too late.

We learned of your growing desires, the organized plans to see that your Lucius be a senator one day, and someday soon. While he had all the character, boldness, values and qualifications, the primary requisites to lead in this office, I believe now he was not meant nor intended to serve as such. The gods themselves delighted in his humble state and positioning, a role my fellow senators will never know. His immortal mark lives in the hearts and souls of you and all of Rome, and for all time. He may well race into eternity far ahead of me, and dare I say, the emperor himself. Such blasphemy I have the audacity to proclaim for I know intimately and deeply the divine powers possessed by the man. They charged in the grip of his hand, shot from his passionate eyes and sped the beat of our hearts. He was the best Rome had to produce, the noblest Rome had to offer, and his mark indeed shall never be forgotten as long as our united vision for a civilized, just and happy existence remains faithful and true, as long as we hear and behold his message, as long as his story is written and shared, for we are better in the eyes of the gods that Lucius lived, and in living, he now shall never die in the hearts of the Roman, everywhere. Yes, my dear Lucius, your mark is our mark, for all time.

Here, dear people, see my hand as I place it on Lucius' cornerstone. Note my fingers, my palm, at one with the impression of his eternal palm, casted in this cement. He was here. He was always here. He is here now, for you. Always, for you.

It was here Lucius and his beloved Flavia rendezvoused often to share their desires and dreams, vowing eternal loyalty and love, a love they shared for each other and for Rome, and in universal love for fellow man.

They would touch this stone, *palmus* to *palmus*, smile at the thought of such a simple act of defiance, Lucius in his craftiness to have imprinted an image of his own hand into the wet cement and casting himself upon the emperor's divine design. They were amused at this mild act of vandalism and mischief, this trite infraction to memorialize their place among the grand monuments, pillars and mausoleums of the noble, immortal Romans. Is it not, dear people, a most beautiful monument of all, this hand to help you, remind you, a hand outstretched to serve you, a hand to comfort you, a hand we must rightfully recognize that saved you?

I, Darius, was fully aware of the danger looming and mounting, as Lucius' outreach to you spread throughout the city and into the countryside. His popularity, a tide of hope and devotion to you, was interpreted by many of my peers as unlawful, poisonous, lecherous, a dangerous flow of undue influence and self-serving goodwill, capable of undermining the very foundation of imperial governess and power. For brethren in the Senate they felt cornered in a mortal test, and it was Lucius testing in a challenge to Roman power and process, considered by many a devious violation of Roman decree.

I, Darius, was privy to the discussions, debates and conspiracies, troubled and aware Lucius faced an impending wrath. I begged him to retreat, to cease the visible, lofty efforts rattling the highest command. I encouraged him to return to the villa in Todi, a country estate I secured for him after the Dacian campaigns. He refused. He had granted the property behind my back a year earlier to four families left homeless and destitute after the risings. Lucius, against my better judgment and advice, but with the loyal and loving support of Flavia, stayed here in the heart and at the hub of Rome's turbulent wheel, with you and for you. Always, for you.

His twin sons, loving, adoring and obedient, were given different skills and talents by the gods. Hal was a boy of letters, an intellectual, ambitious to study medicine, philosophy and the law. Hal stayed near his mother, Flavia, during those troubled days, comforting her worrying heart, reading to her, walking with her, dreaming of more peaceful days to come when his father's work would be complete.

Tobin is the other half of the circle, a boy of action, carefree and adventurous, at one with the natural world, the hills and riversides, on horseback or at his father's side, taking in his every movement or intently absorbing his few but well-chosen words, the wisdom of a loving father to an admiring son.

The boys were a bona fide reflection of the love between Lucius and Flavia, innocent and driven, sensitive and bold, worldly but dreamers, young yet wise. A rather perfect family circle.

My fears, your fears, came true on the fateful night when a team of marauders, armed and afire, violated the peace in a display of destruction far beneath Rome's dignity. It was there, while Lucius was near the Forum along with his son Tobin at a meeting of laborers, the demonic legions with rising authority and raging tempers, torches in the grip, set fire to the homes and marketplaces in the district of Lucius' Roman home. A hellish glow of red, orange and black rose into the skies just west of where we stand, there across the Tiber. The intended terror was successful, screams and cries awakening all of Rome. With the higher powers motionless and silent, the district burned mercilessly.

By the time Lucius and his son arrived in a frantic race to quench the flames, all was lost. There, they discovered the broken and burned bodies in the piazza's fountain and pool, Flavia and Hal, face down in the water, as if to not witness the final horror. They were afloat in the very pool Lucius and his artisans had constructed for you. Always, for you.

In the dark of night Lucius had his wife and son brought to this spot and buried them, here, where the love by his hand is sealed in this stone.

Lucius was a man of few words and spoke even less after the terror, allowing his mind to rest and heart to heal in his own time. He and Tobin retreated to the country village of Lucius' youth near the farm where he was raised.

In time Lucius adopted the ways of the farmers and settled for a while among them, embracing their skills and chores, following and listening to their tales. It was an honest but hard life. Taxes and rents were harshly imposed. Families who had worked the land for generations fell into entrenched suffering and painful poverty, greater percentages of their earnings redirected in taxes to support the inflating pleasures and unquenchable desires of Roman elites.

Blistered hands reached for help and hungry bellies ached for aid. These calls were heard and answered by the strong, quiet and kind man with the formidable presence, the good neighbor and guardian in their midst, Lucius.

Among the farmers were aging soldiers, veterans who served Rome in various military campaigns, battles and wars. Lucius was particularly moved by the ones whose stamina and spirits were damaged, the molested souls who had experienced and witnessed such brutality and unspeakable violence that their minds and faculties had left them. Some were reduced to terminal slumber, middle-aged men with sound bodies but little movement, requiring the care we provide to infants and the very aged. Others were unnaturally active, maniacal, repetitive talkers, screamers, agitated over everything and tolerant of nothing. They could be elevated to disturbing degrees of hostility with the simplest of prompting. Unpredictable, unnerving, and hardly *homo frugi* in their temperance, they sought sedation in excessive quantities of potent wine which *merum bibere* provides.

Lucius sought remedy and recompense for these countrymen whose numbers were many, their paltry military pensions inadequate to meet their mounting needs. Lucius' plan provided the dignity of steady work, jobs suitable to their unique conditions. They were given shelter in comfortably constructed barracks, fed and clothed with compassion, visited by physicians, teachers and holy men. While little could be done to repair the broken minds of the severely afflicted, an organization was formed to guarantee their basic needs were met so they could live out their years in respectable and dignified fashion.

I, Darius, stand before you as mourner and confessor, for it was I who determined the season was right to further the promise and pursuits of Lucius. His noble reputation blossoming once more, his legendary commitments more popular than ever, his loyalty fully proven, his availability to you clear and sincere, I concluded his time had rightfully come to lead Rome in a loftier position. In honor of his wife and son, in reward for his lifetime and dedication, I invited him back to Rome with the blessings and approval of a growing number of supporting constituents and colleagues. We had plans for our Lucius, ambitious goals to bring him into the inner circle of the leadership of the empire.

The betrayal was fixed and well executed. Understanding the divine power of our Lucius, a deep fear rattled my soul. Orchestrated by corrupt courtiers inside our Senate, I am suspicious of the plot and shall seek evidence justifying such suspicion. May righteous, just and swift be the punishment for this heinous act.

The assassins ambushed Lucius today in the center of the great circus, there at the spina as he stood with his brother and friend, Marcus, an act of grave shame and betrayal, an insurrection of dishonor to the highest degree in all of Rome. Our Marcus, here beside me now, stood bravely in front of Lucius at the moment of assassination to protect him. Lucius returned the loyalty and love, leaping in front of Marcus and deflecting the flailing daggers, usurping one of the shields in a valiant battle of one against many. It was in this instant, as many have witnessed and sworn to the gods by account, a great electric bolt from a single cloud in the heavens struck the shield. In a flash of radiant light went the life of Lucius. All stood still over the lifeless and faithful soldier, guardian, foreman, servant, laborer, farmer, the Roman in us all, embodied in our sleeping Lucius.

Apart from a disintegrated, vanished hand, cleanly removed at the wrist and taken into the clouds, leaving him free of weapon or armored shield, he lay in peaceful, immortal sleep, not a noticeable wound upon him.

The assassins scattered in haste, their treasonous, bloody deed fulfilled. It is with promise we shall find them. Honorable men delivered the body of Lucius here for us to bid farewell. It is little for us to bestow Rome's honor upon him now, an honor he had already, nobly and justly fulfilled by his life, a life committed to you, fellow Roman brothers and sisters. Always, to you.

It is rightful we inter him here, to rest with his departed Flavia and adored son Hal, beneath the stone with the imprint of his hand in the mortar, a memorial of his love reaching to them, and to you. Always, to you.

This is but one of the countless stones laid over his years of labor, in the lofty and loving vision to build a better and everlasting Rome. By our inferior hands we grant Lucius this honor in the Circus Maximus, in a sacred pledge our efforts be forever dedicated toward building a world the just and forgiving gods would approve, for the larger circle of all mankind, and for all time.

Should that foundation survive, may it be said its cornerstone was committed to peace, and placed on such promise, here.

Bene tibi, vivas, dear faithful and noble friend."

CHAPTER VIII

TUTELA'S PICTURE of Lucius proved vivid and fixed as we left
Switzerland, slipping into a deep and dark tunnel at nightfall
the lone passengers in the rear sleeper car. We drifted into a
welcomed doze, the hum of the train sedating our trek higher into the
Italian Alps en route, alas, to Rome. As the train picked up its pace,
racing along the slopes at intense speed, images of Lucius vanished with
a horrifying wail and screech, steel on steel, deafening and disturbing.
In one frightening moment the train streaked into a perilous tilt in an
ear-piercing whine nearly spilling us off the compartment bed. In fear
of derailment, I jumped then sprinted from the sleeping car and, with a
quick glance and palm raised toward Tutela, signaled for her to stay still.
Rushing forward in a panic, car to car, I bashed my bare foot against a
closing interior train door breaking the little toe of my left foot, all in a
farcical false alarm. Indeed, we were still on track.

Tutela, sitting upright on her knees in convulsing giggles watched in
unbridled amusement as I hobbled back to her side. I feigned a lightness
but dropped in heavy anxiety for several unsettling minutes, rocking
myself next to her as the train whistled into the mountains. I stared
straight ahead into nothingness, a rapid dialogue pulsing my throbbing
head.

I am fine. What was that?
I am fine. Is it safe?

I am fine. Get out, now!

I am fine. Cloe! ... Tutela! Follow me!

An injured foot, trapped, spinning in circles ...

... have you seen the others?

There, in The Bunker, the collapsing Rotonde ...

... huddled together, tossed and broken, torn and lifeless.

Metal, metal ... crash!

The train chugged in soft locomotion back to a steady and comfortable hum, leveling out of the tunnel and pressing forward at a sane pace. A conductor came by to reassure the passengers it was nothing of concern. I heard what he said but, hardly attentive, never met his contrite eyes.

Darkness, blind. Going too fast.

Tutela, where are you?

Here! Toby, come back, Toby ... here.

Can you taste the Swiss chocolate? Rest your head on my chest, as you did between the lakes. Come back.

Here ... here I come.

Quiet, quiet. It is getting so ...

... quiet.

The steady train rolled on peacefully as the heartrate slowed, the tender finger of Tutela tracing gentle circles counterclockwise along the heated circumference of my temple.

"Tell me, Toby, please, of your mother," she softly requested and, after a lost thirty minutes, I did.

She is 77 years young, the sacraments and Gospels her itinerary. Humor balances her days and accents the years, a life of past trials qualifying her imparted wisdom. A curious mind travels the world vicariously from her coffee table to the nightstand, an explorer inside four walls. An old soul guides the romantic and scholastic journeys, maps and beads tucked deep in the recesses of a well-worn purse. She glides in imagination from her front porch, a cup of coffee and a lit cigarette fortifying her outlook, reflection and vista. A heart of innocence bleeds unconditional love as she greets the long days with kindness, grace and humility.

Nearly all her possessions she has either stored or given away, family furniture, jewelry, the library of books devoured and digested. She is an organizer of life, seasonal and holiday decorations expertly sorted, packed and labeled, periods in her life chronicled, filed and stowed. She has collated the chapters of her life, and with a deep sentiment and attachment to her past allows each chapter to seamlessly stream into the present. She budgets her focus and interest in others by generous degree, curious and concerned, involved and invested.

A life spent giving leaves little to be expected. A pot of coffee to propel each day, cigarettes to stir contemplation, a pad of paper, a supply of pens and the daily lists of to-dos and to-considers, and she is economically equipped to launch another day. The lists, always the lists, gifts and knick-knacks to be provided, acknowledgements, announcements and greetings, personal and sincere, she shares with those in her world, including an expanding roster of loved ones gone, keeping a private correspondence in heart and prayer with the ghosts at her side. She has her calendar and address book. Not a birthday or graduation, anniversary or baptism, baby shower or first communion, confirmation or wedding, ever passes without heartfelt blessings and fond wishes.

She lives in a small adobe studio on the property of one of my sisters, nestled in the village of Arroyo Seco, New Mexico, the rising mesa above Santa Fe and Taos where the prehistoric and modern worlds collide. Peace and spirit fill the enchanting air, and she contributes to the mystic greetings of radiant-pink sunrises and soft-magenta sunsets in gentle smiles and fixed stares at her near and distant horizons.

Steady, rolling routines govern her movements, consistent as much as dependable, much like the landscape she gazes upon in reflection. Attending daily catholic Mass with her pleasant, prompt and loyal confidant Maria, more coffee and cigarettes are shared between them after the services as they perch on two simple stools on the front porch, a vista of pine peppering the hillsides as far as their wise and worn eyes can absorb, catching glimpses of the years behind and pondering uncertain days to come.

She enjoys the intimate musings between elders in the small village where secrets are impossible to keep, mischievously leaked. It is a crossroads of Native Americans, artisans and craftsmen, writers, retirees and ranchers. Woven within are occasional drifters, society's misfits wandering through Arroyo Seco in search of salvation or solitude. It is a place of unspoken and unwritten rules, where cooperation, cohabitation and co-existence are implied. References to harmony and peace are abundant. It has a market and one lone saloon, Abe's, and the modest, charming church surrounded by large patches of coagulating clay and brittle brush.

She makes her regular runs to each spot, the brief visits to Abe's for cigarettes or a new lighter. Her old brown sedan brandishes an age and resilience symbiotic to her own, called infrequently to serve but loyal and reliable as ever, a blessing with eyesight slipping and driving skills subsiding.

Life is slowing to a pace she once would resist but now graciously accepts. Her mental wheels roll as swift as ever, referencing her treasured books on history, spirituality and philosophy. At San Francisco de Asis Mission she volunteers as a teacher of religious education, and she pays attentive, caring visits to Casa de la Misericordia orphanage. Staying current on the turbulent but compelling state of the world, she maintains it still must be met and experienced with optimism and wonder, and keeps a personal plan to travel to Greece via Rome wielding a tour book on the region, earmarked with scrupulous notes as utility at her bedside. There the Lord Byron quote from 1818 is ornately framed above her nightstand, *While stands the Coliseum, Rome shall stand; When falls the Coliseum, Rome shall fall, and when Rome falls, the World.* No doubt in Roman times she would have kept proper company and commiserated with the elders and priests, the *presbyteri.* Today she awakens every morning with a greeting to Jesus, serves at His pleasure throughout her day and gives Him thanks and praise, bidding Him goodnight as she retires. Her day has a cadence and cycle all its own. One is invited to ride it with her for there is welcomed space and it is perpetually open, as is her abode and likewise Arroyo Seco. She bridges this locale spiritually and symbolically to Rome, Assisi, Athens and Ephesus, every place she plans to go in a delivery of herself, be it in books, goals or lofty, fading dreams.

Her grandfather is a constant companion, philosophically and in the journeys of the heart, for just as he and ancient merchants of Judea modeled, she lives by modest means, pursuing nor expecting treasure in the transactions of life. Her heroes and mentors are commoners, the workers whose hands may be dirty but souls remain clean, exploitation and greed foreign in the commerce. Are we not reminded Eastern Judea in Roman times had fewer slaves than any territory in the Mediterranean? She keeps a quote of Josephus tucked in her pocketbook next to a prayer card from her grandfather's funeral, *We are not a commercial people. We live in a country without a seaboard, and have no inclination to trade.*

Her bed is always made before her first cup of coffee is poured, a Native American dreamcatcher, aqua and pink, draped over the headboard. She carves fresh apples from the small orchard on her daughter's grounds and with precision and patience places them in her corn flakes. Her day can be marked by unchecked time spent with hard working, low-income folks in the neighborhood, some living in trailers, others in campers. She wakes to watch children playing in the fields with battered, soiled stuffed animals, or pulling rusted red wagons chased by country dogs, a raucous and circular caravan of laughter echoing in the Arroyo Seco canyon.

She browses the artisan shops and galleries, admiring local, hand-crafted jewelry, rugs, pottery and watercolors. Occasionally she buys a piece and tucks it away, remembered and tagged for a loved one on a list.

Her nature is such she attracts the fragile, broken and aimless, the lost lives planted or traversing the mysterious mesa. Some are veterans, members of the legions whose tarnished lives interrupted by war have left them on the margins, hapless and homeless. It is a steady pilgrimage of the orphaned, forgotten or unloved, others who ran and simply stopped, disarmed by the warm and hospitable woman welcoming them to her porch. The coffee pot may run low but there are always more grounds and plentiful sugar and cream in the cupboard of the tidy kitchenette. She listens to them often for hours and across turning calendars, and it is the passing of seasons that stirs her spirit as do the mountains, a link of the ranges of New Mexico to the crests of her far-away Catskills. Reflections inspired a recently completed memoir she

entitled *Now and Then*, a manuscript she has only shared with immediate family, a brave revelation of her pangs, longings and suppressed
sufferings concluding in bountiful offerings of hope and redemption.

One can now add author to her credits next to student, nurse,
teacher, philosopher, artist, traveler, patriot, citizen, counselor, philanthropist, daughter, sister, mother, grandmother, great grandmother,
giver, inspirer and survivor.

From the backyard she can look to the mountains, the ski slopes
of Taos to the quaint, dusty paths of Arroyo Seco, an impressive view
circling her corralled space. The vista permits her to travel sentimen-
tally where she can daydream into a distance toward the home that
never escaped her longing or belonging. Each day in Arroyo Seco she
transports to Haines Falls in the Catskills, conversing with her mother,
siblings and lost friends, and prayerfully cares for the one who cared
so deeply and delicately for the family throughout those difficult but
love-drenched years of her youth, the humble, gentle and generous Irish
merchant, her grandfather.

She was born and raised in a small mountain cottage adjacent to
the general store her grandfather ran six days a week, fifty-two weeks a
year. The youngest of three, her mother kept house as her grandfather
served as protector and guardian during the slow rolling years of the
Great Depression. He was from a small farm in County Meath in the
heart of central Ireland, having learned well the grocery trade on the
docks of Hell's Kitchen in the new country, operating a popular business
throughout the challenging decades post WWI. He had twelve children,
seeing two sons off to war, including James, resting in a grave shared by
tens of thousands of other young infantrymen in the Somme of France.

She never met her father, being just an infant when James died in
France during the "Great War." There were photos, medals, mementos
and the uniform cap as well as the occasional tale of his youth, but this
was the extent of her knowledge of him. Her mother became quite reli-
ant on the love, care and comfort of her father-in-law, prevalent in the
seldom-expressed but shared grief in the loss of their James.

Her mother kept an organized, tidy and warm house nestled between
the general store and Immaculate Conception Roman Catholic Church.

These premises would be etched in the corners and crevices of her memory. In the front yard of the cottage was a circular drive, at its center a grassy garden with roses and lavender manicured by her mother, fondly referred to as the "heart."

As a child Mom would embrace her springs and summers, play in the meadows, take long swims at North Lake, hike the trails to the grand old Mountain House, explore the coves and secrets of Twilight Park and tempt the cascades of Kaaterskill Falls.

In the brilliant colors of fall she would ride circles around the mountaintop on the school bus well past her intended destination, an amused and cooperating driver chauffeuring her into exuberance. Extending an elongated hold on the environment from her window seat, these images and scents would be sealed in her soul and treasured for a lifetime.

At Halloween she would trick-or-treat where the poor families lived in the flats by the creek known as the Cabbage Patch. When snow fell she would ride sleds and toboggans with her brother, sister and pals, one time sustaining a broken eardrum in a head-first mishap with a pine tree at the base of North Lake Road. Christmas was a magical time of ornamental splendor, the houses, shops and churches all across the mountaintop transformed in radiant red, green, silver and gold, lights and bells, carols and carriages illuminating her imagination, making a permanent impression of holiday joy and anticipation.

Her mother and grandfather sheltered her from the heavy and serious matters of the larger world, the unyielding Depression and another, pending World War. Albany, New York City, Europe and beyond remained, for the duration of her youth, a universe away. The philosophical maxims her grandfather imparted became capstones in her constructive thoughts, pillars of wisdoms she would carry for a lifetime, among the most tightly held, "Right is right even when no one is right, and wrong is wrong even when everyone is wrong."

She graduated with seventeen classmates, friends and characters known throughout her formative years, joining her older sister at nursing school in Albany, eventually landing an assignment at a Brooklyn hospital, both moves unleashing immeasurable homesickness. Weekly she would find her way to a payphone and, sobbing uncontrollably to her mother, plea for amnesty and a return home to Haines Falls. Her mother for reasons understood held back the compulsion to retreat. They faced an uncertain future with few viable options for a young, unmarried woman on the mountaintop, and one trusted path forward was the nursing profession.

After another World War, Roman numeral II, she met my father, a young veteran serving in the New York Fire Department. Her beloved grandfather had recently died. Among records left behind in the general store were receipts, a stack of IOUs from the Depression and war years. He had been supplying and feeding his neighbors across the dales, slopes and hamlets of the Catskills for years, the collecting of debts hardly a priority.

Two weeks after marrying my father she learned of the shocking death of her own mother, a trauma which instilled a deep drive to build a bountiful loving circle, dedicating decades to raising a legion of her own, twelve children, by the model and love she had witnessed and absorbed in the inimitable example of two towering figures now gone, her grandfather and mother.

She relied heavily on her faith and the saints, particularly St. Gerard Majella, the patron of expectant mothers. The mystical Gerard was prone to levitations, could read souls and was known to curiously bi-locate, miraculously appearing in two distant places at the same time. Gerard's mission was immortalized in an encounter with a young girl shortly before his death. The girl noticed he had dropped his white handkerchief and, adamant in returning it to Gerard, was rebuffed and instructed to hold onto it herself, for she "may need it someday." Indeed she would, for entering womanhood the young lady was on the verge of losing her baby when she applied Gerard's cloth to her womb. The pain immediately subsided and a healthy child came into the world. Additionally, Gerard came in handy for my mother when mountaintop gossip could turn to dangerous slander, ridicule and social alienation, being patron for falsely accused people and good confessions.

I was number ten of twelve, the seventh of eight sons and four daughters and a beneficiary of Mom's faith and resilience with St. Gerard on guard, making my entrance into the world through a long and difficult labor.

We did not have nor need much materially but we had something priceless, Mom would remind, and that was each other. Love permeated our childhood. She introduced us to faith with consistent application in a manner most subtle and hardly austere. Sacraments were completed for all twelve, their preparations managed by her consistent hand. The day we were confirmed the religious path forward was one of liberation, and each child was free to choose the direction. She fed, clothed and bathed us, got us to school and the medical appointments. Every birthday was celebrated and each holiday masterfully and mysteriously produced. Mom was Easter Bunny and Santa Claus extraordinaire.

It was crowded but there was room for others, such as Uncle Henry whom, in his intoxicated despair, she and Dad rescued from the battered backstreets of Brooklyn. We moved up to a larger house in California with a big front porch. The love and hospitality attracted multitudes of friends and visitors by the sheer magnetic flow, bountiful centripetal force and raucous joy emanating from a family home she and Dad created and generously shared.

In time she returned to her reading and scholarly interests. Enrolling in college at age 60, she earned a college degree and a California teaching credential. She taught in one of the most impoverished and challenged communities in America, South Central Los Angeles, where she loved and embraced class after class of elementary schoolchildren over the course of a decade.

In this period she cared for an expanding circle of family members as well as a terminally ill husband. When my father passed away Mom had his ashes interred beside Uncle Henry in a quaint hillside plot above town. Three simple words mark their final resting place under a Celtic cross. "He's my brother" is all it reads and all required.

A circus of collectors and a shoebox stacked with my father's medical bills, she reluctantly succumbed in a tragic turn of unethical real estate dealings resulting in the loss of her cherished home, a heart-ripping displacement that would upset the unity and knock the convening hub off her family's axis forever. Her world halted and reversed in many respects, but she found the deep resolve for occasional, enjoyable journeys with a mind and spirit feverishly curious and thirsty. We camped in the majestic highlands of Yosemite National Park and traveled to Ireland, tracing the roots of her grandfather and exploring the wonders of Connemara. We walked in the footsteps of Moses, Jesus and Muhammad in the Holy Land, drinking coffee in Jericho, dipping toes into the Dead Sea and climbing the ancient, snaking paths over the Roman ramps to the crest of Masada where two-thousand years ago the siege ended in historic horror, Roman legions discovering the encircled and trapped Jewish people having not surrendered to their oppressors at all, but lay dead in an epic act of mass suicide.

Now in Arroyo Seco she strives to keep up with a reeling, spinning world and her family rolling on its perimeter, clockwise and counter-clockwise, colliding in the confusing circulation. She peers into sunsetting skies afire in auburn and gold against the painted desert to a shared moon and ancient stars, the same ones that guided the Magi at the first Christmas, and on bright, clear New Mexico nights she reflects on the journey of the Holy Infant Jesus and the trajectory of His experience, the circle and turns her own life has taken, a correlation of service, sacrifice and suffering.

She enjoys more time now in solitude on her small, north-facing back porch to look out at the silhouette of the mountains at dusk or the soft, silent stillness in a Southwest sunrise. She cares not to look south so much, she confesses. To her, the south echoes of Los Alamos where they planned and executed a world-altering project named after New York of all places. The Manhattan Project split the atom against the backdrop of the beautiful Southwest desert, forever upsetting the natural balance in God's grand design, Mom reminds. They disturbed and ruptured the periodic elements of creation in a swap for the most destructive force imaginable.

Recently, authorities considered development in the region for a new nuclear waste disposal site. We are escalating at unchecked speed in a race to arm and occupy the universe, or perhaps poison it for a half-million years or more. An organized opposition is focused on the troubling challenge of where to store the lethal waste, though the lonely deserts are prone for prime selection. She is keeping a keen eye on this activism, sharing the anxiety, concern and, in fair share, collective shame. She budgets for regular but modest contributions to the cause out of her limited means.

She worries the common interest of good people may not win this round. She prays to the Lord each morn and evening He will carry this tremendous burden, the yoke we have placed on His shoulders, an immeasurable weight in kilotons terminally gaining reckless speed in our race to split and divide the majestic design of the Loving Creator. From her porch anxious thoughts mount, stir and spin.

Here, we have builders. Here, we have dividers.

Who wins this century? Fusion or fission?

Who loses this round in the race, starting point here for the next 500,000 years?

Remember Los Alamos. Victory propelling toward defeat, two faces on the same melting coin at a Fahrenheit somewhere between 50 and 150 million degrees.

Do we feel lucky?

Toss it, spin it, see where it lands. Monte Cassino to the Grand Casino and on to Los Alamos. Choose battles carefully.

Focus and remain focused.

Love and remain in love, with every element known or blown, in all creation.

As for Mom, she chose love in the moment it was introduced and offered and has fused its elements ever since, from the harmonic coves of the Catskill Mountains to the vistas of Arroyo Seco, alpha to omega, in revolutions of love for others. Always, for others.

Her God permits and provides. This God sits with her on the humble back porch, facing north to the mountains and the beautiful unknown beyond, and as a lone planet trembles and shakes in fear she prays for the lonely sphere and its inhabitants.

It calls and echoes across Arroyo Seco.

Take me home. I want to go home.

Then a frenetic bird appears, a hummingbird. Mother grips the butt of her dying cigarette and tips her coffee cup. A few of the last, cold sugary ounces spill onto a bed of chalky pebbles. The hummingbird dives to taste it and, just as quickly as it arrived, hovers momentarily for her delight and then disappears. Soon it is followed by a lone white butterfly dancing delightfully in the wind, a solo hora in her garden floating in counterclockwise circles, silent as a feather, lonely and free, until it, too, bids farewell.

Mom gently smiles in gratitude to the Resurrected Jesus and surrenders another day to her Lord.

Her day is done and its sunset, just as its sunrise, was nearly perfect. She watches for several minutes as the sun dips west of Arroyo Seco, its golden disc yielding to a corona of purple, magenta and lavender on the far and ancient horizon. She thanks God for the visit of the hummingbird and butterfly and in a whisper to Him and herself bids the spinning world and all its stirred souls, those in play upon it now and those whose turns have faded and gone, her faithful wishes for very sweet dreams, and a most gentle goodnight.

CHAPTER IX

MORNING BROUGHT the Roman sun blazing through our window as the train neared the Roma Termini. Tutela's heart pounded in anticipation of return to her eternal city. She exited in haste, her heavy baggage hardly a burden, easily maneuvered in an impressive hoist initiated by incalculable glee. As she swung it around her shoulder in one swoop of expertise, her bronze hair danced in the gleam of the bright summer light. She was in full stride and several paces ahead, eager to direct me to all the majestic city had in store. We passed innumerable souls in transit and rhythm with the city's pulse, beckoning us into the crowd of pilgrims and peasants, merchants and mystics, lovers and chasers, their handbags, backpacks and purses strewn over shoulders or balanced on their backs, the whole known universe well represented, its passengers coming and going, ebbing and flowing in rehearsed Roman trance.

We exited the grand station into the ancient and modern intersection, the old and very new mixed in its concrete, a unified architecture of structure and space surrounding the enormous piazza and parking lot. A portion of the Servian Wall, a defensive barrier of volcanic stone constructed over two-thousand years ago, was a fortified greeting, more welcoming than foreboding. Depending on the view, disembarking and colliding, coming or going, it is both an entrance and exit of space and time, blending into a perpetual carousel of cars, buses, taxis, motorcycles, bicycles, vans, trucks, shuttles and skateboards, endless streams blaring, passing and halting, accelerating and stopping, signaling to the whole disturbed, anxious and manic planet the race has once again begun, with haunting ruins ominously in sight. Past is prologue on the streets of Rome.

The cacophony did not impose nor bother, a trite hindrance to the spirit stirred by an urban symphony blasting through the caverns of the city. This was readily absorbed, a gravitational force of energy, the music of the spheres touching ground to greet each soul contributing to the orchestra at the intersection of arriving and departing.

I did not get far. My pace, lagging several meters behind a streaking Tutela, left me orphaned among several gypsy children, a red traffic light and a caravan of every possible vehicle jammed in the immensely wide Viale Enrico de Nicola, creating a virtual Servian barrier between us. The children were plentiful and tiny, a dozen or more no higher than my waste, Eastern European, perhaps Romanian, soiled and shoeless. They waved dirty palms as high as they could manage toward my puzzled face, shouting unintelligible beggars' requests, poking my belt line with cardboard, an urban altar to present offerings. They were boney thin, their sweet, deep and desperate dark eyes piercing behind long manes of jet-black dusty hair, suggesting a worldliness and wariness beyond their short years. The resemblance among them suggested they could be family. Over the juvenile mania I managed over and over a declaration of apology, *Mi dispiace. Mi dispiace.* I indeed had no cash or coin. In an instant I made a pledge to myself to return to this spot, whenever that might be, mindful of this precious pack and prepared to present a worthy contribution.

The long light finally turned green and I traversed the massive intersection where Tutela had halted her escape, a suggestive grin and a nodding of her head awaiting me.

"Romani. Gypsy children, Toby. They liked you. Perhaps you can adopt one. Or did they already adopt you?"

I turned back to catch a glimpse but the pack was gone. On the far side of the intersection, erect and poised in his tiny frame stood just one lone tot looking exceptionally somber and sad toward me. He had a secret. The child knew something I did not.

I instinctively reached down to tap the compartment in my waste pack, a reflex I had mastered on this trek over several weeks. The familiar feel of my leather wallet holding all my essentials, passport, credit cards and Eurail train pass, was met by an immediate shock, a startled, sober realization of its absence. In a quick glance I noticed the outside zipper pulled back, the inner zipper as well, the second line of defense breached. The children were not only the right size, they were imposters, master thieves of the highest order possessing expertise in the art of distraction and deceit. Suddenly, I looked back across the vast boulevard for the silent, sorry boy. He had disappeared, a clever trick, the game of hide and seek and hide again had claimed one more, another victory over the naïve, inexperienced Roman pilgrim. All roads lead here, the straight and the crooked. Among the dozen hungry little pirates it would appear at least one gave pause to the ancient art of raiding and release, and surely to the victor go the spoils. Sinners and saints rise and fall from these streets, and sometimes they are one in the same depending on which side of the street one stands, the direction of the wind or the turn of the hour.

I was not despondent nor angry. I was hurt in empathetic, shared sorrow, a solidarity with one lost and loitering boy, a recruited innocent caught and coerced into the streets of dirty deeds. Survival turns youth into criminals, young men to warriors, the desperate and misguided to terrorists. In the moment when apology is called there is the pull to join wayward comrades. Group suffering and consequence come later whether they make the history books or not.

Wedged between the traffic where the boy had stood sullen, a gently smiling image of Cloe flashed, younger as a child.

Forgive them. It is petty, only your wallet.

Everything is replaceable.

Notice the Roman sun. Bask in it, Toby. Bask.

Light, Toby.

Light.

Then she was gone, as swift as fleeing gypsies.

In an impressive and speedy deduction Tutela summed what transpired and turned on her heels to proceed, but I was heading back into the intersection against the red light, horns deafening. She snatched me by the shoulder spinning me to face her most-serious expression.

"You won't find them, Toby. They are the wind. The adults, the real robbers, are already in possession of your wallet and the children won't be seen for another several days if at all, and never in the same location for long."

A supportive smile crossed her reassuring face, the comfort and confidence of legal counsel clutched at my chest.

"I'm sorry. I should have given you proper warning. So excited I had lapsed. It seems to have gotten worse since I was here last. Do not let this burden your thoughts, Toby. It is common and can be fixed. It will be remedied. Just a matter of taking the steps."

I stood defeated and embarrassed considering the bureaucratic prospects, but solace soon won out in Tutela's calmness and surrender. A white handkerchief was in order, the little marauders stealing the day.

"A pain, yes, but not a catastrophe," Tutela affirmed. "Call the credit card companies now and freeze activity, then we'll get your travel and ID replacements in motion. But I know what you need now before a report to the police. A visit with good friends, then wine!"

I followed her wise and calm counsel, then Tutela insisted on a mandatory stop in her neighborhood, Borgo, the old trapezoid-shaped neighborhood on the west side of the Tiber in Rome's 14th Historic District. It was approaching noon when we stepped inside the Taverna Angelica, indulging in espresso and biscotti and sweet grape jam on toasted Italian bread presented on a high counter beneath an olive-green awning, allowing half shade and half shine to balance the Roman light upon our brows. Laughter and warm greetings showered the arrival, her friend Tomas serving the coffee, Lisa clearing dishes and a dozen other happy acquaintances and never-forgotten faces circled in a unified *salvete*. I was evaluated properly and fairly, sized up in a Roman instant, and in the lifting of espresso cups christened with approval.

Tutela shared the gypsy ordeal, her friends shaking their heads in parts both sympathetic and amused, the dual emotions such as one would have known in the great Roman Colosseum of old, where the spectacle offered victim and entertainer as one, much to the delight of the spectator but at significant cost to the one in the ring. Ultimately, sincerity transpired in the form of a collective apology from Tutela's friends on behalf of all of Rome and, in gratitude fueled by caffeinated jolts, sincerely accepted. In good coffee and company poured reconciliation and redemption.

I am fine. I am fine.

I am a victim and the entertainer.

All is fine. Look the other way.

The art of deceit. Hide and seek and hide again.

I cannot pay for the coffee, Cloe, but I am fine, as you smiled and as you said.

We agreed the children were victims, too, steered and coerced in the artful ballet of the ancient heist. The true pirates await in the alleyways and cellars, under the bridges and up in trees, counting and divvying up the loot, assessing the spoils and delighting in the bounty. Are we not all born gypsies tempted to roam and drawn to Rome, beggars, wanderers, famished and desperate, with satchels full and pockets empty, delinquents in search of treasure, returning as victors, victims or hungry paupers?

I told my new friends I had instantly forgiven the puny perpetrators which, according to this troupe of Italian electorate, qualified me to stand in noble stature with Cicero himself.

"*Optimus princeps*! To Senator Tobias!"

"No! No!" I insisted. "Senators attract assassins!"

So little changes dear, aging Rome, the pillaging and conspiring. It can be found in every nook and crevice, from the catacombs to the tavernas the evidence everywhere and nowhere like gypsy children in the Tyrrhenian wind. Rome, you have pickpocketed and robbed from here onto the outer spokes of your empire, across the coastal spans of the Mediterranean and back again. You have dispatched your children and they have returned to you obedient under the watchful gaze of Romulus and Dea Roma, bellies empty and pockets full, miscreants scattered like lost and leaderless sheep from your occupied Isles of Briton to Assyria. As I confessed so must you. All is forgiven when not all is lost. Your coffee is delicious and company good. The ancient sun and scorching bricks warm your heart and raise your spirits, the Italian hearths and ovens awaiting the yeast. We take the bread and drink the wine. Love one another as I have loved you – this the holy communion offered at your altar. My heart blazed in praise in the warmth of the camaraderie and friendliness of the first taverna. All was forgiven. If Cloe could hear me now would she agree it is almost perfect?

From coffee we turned to wine, a sacramental transfusion.

I raised a glass for Cloe, a private toast between the lost and found. Behind me a stranger tapped my shoulder and raised his glass to the larger forming circle in a collective, unified cheer.

Bene tibi, vivas. To absent friends.

A response across the taverna radiated in uniformed glee.

Bibamus moriendum est. Let us drink, for death is inevitable.

Spirits elevated, we found our way into the meandering paths beneath a radiant sun. Tutela bought four bananas, two pears and fresh flowers from a street cart, then we rounded several bends in the narrow maze and lazy labyrinth of the old city to a flat-faced, two-story apartment house with a low threshold, a thick wooden door presenting a tiny square window and an iron-framed peephole. She fumbled for keys but the task was unnecessary. A hatched window above opened with a startling shriek. A woman, not Italian, rounded in her fair-skinned face with long shocks of white-blonde hair in a distinct German accent bellowed out a welcome and raced downstairs for the enthusiastic greeting.

Tutela grabbed Melanie tightly, kissed each cheek and handed her half of the flowers, white roses and sprigs of lavender, and we were escorted up the narrow flight of creaking stairs. Married to Noah, who was not present, Melanie guided us to a small landing with pottery and several small plants marking a pleasant boundary between Tutela's domicile and their own.

The ladies joyfully initiated, a tad earlier than customary, their daily *riposo*, uncorking red wine as we sat on plush cushions on an aqua-blue tiled floor.

"Bien vida, Rome!" the German voice amplified.

"I am indebted," I said. "Indebted, with no money!"

I have been here sixty minutes.

I have been here for twenty centuries.

I have arrived.

I have never left.

I am sober. I am drunk and lucid.

I am burning and baptized.

The bananas are sweet as white chocolate, the white chocolate of Cannes.

Cannes?

I am indebted, Tutela.

I owe you. I am penniless.

I have a fortune.

I have been robbed and I am a thief.

All is forgiven, Toby.

Toby, you may settle. Nap with me for a little while.

Later we shall rise, Tobias.

Rise up. It is a new day.

The river.

We will walk to the river and cross the Ponte Sant' Angelo.

How long have I been sleeping?

Tutela, Cloe, Mom, Dad, Uncle Henry ... Grandpa?

While Tutela was well at ease, content and steady, I was atilt, restless and wobbly. Still, both of us shared a weariness from the travel and arrival. Was this my dream, the one I never had and always wanted? My exhaustion grew profound. Nightmares still haunted, reminded and randomly returned, sporadic and arbitrary interruptions. We retired to the quarters upon Tutela's plush bed falling into an afternoon bliss.

Bells from a nearby church awakened and called us to greet the Roman dusk. Hours passed, permitting a rebound and a bounce back into my step. I hardly recognized my gait. I leapt for Tutela in my heart, a pulse pounding *palmus* to *pes* as we galloped toward the River Tiber. It called for her. Assured in its current, to it we sprung.

We ought to marry, Tutela.

Must the holy sacrament be delayed?

The river ran swift and wide. I could not be lonely next to either, Tiber or Tutela, both flowing constant in my veins, supernatural if not impossible. Yet I could not remain another moment unpledged, bounded but separate, victimized yet free. There we danced in a delightful traipse across Ponte Sant'Angelo where the rites commenced, re-birth and reunification, death and life anew, bridged in the crossing, baptism, marriage and last rites blended and begotten in the Vatican's vortex.

Dunk me into the Tiber, Tutela.

Haste!

The river flows without promises in her race to the Mediterranean, on her time and awaiting nobody. Jump, and let go, palm to palm. In the risk comes Roman reward, hardly ill-gotten, looted or usurped. Have we the courage to let go or, judging by the current, have we not already?

Four days and a lifetime passed. Getting acclimated on the amusing axis and willingly lost in Borgo, I was consumed in the whirl. Meanwhile Tutela's occupation called for her time. I had not but a glimpse into her practical, legal and working life. I was anticipating the pleasure of walking with her daily to the office. Alas, she too owned a Vespa, and in reluctant indoctrination I climbed on and held tight to her waste, trusting and terrified. Free of helmets, the Italian air whipped our hair as we crossed countless Roman piazzas, ascending into steep, sharp and narrow passageways. We parked the apple-red motorbike next to two dozen or more, removed the lock on one another and entered the ground floor of her offices which housed an internet café. There were gracious greetings, embraces and more introductions, handshakes and double kisses offered on warm, friendly cheeks. The languages shifted, haphazardly and expertly, Italian to English and back again with the occasional layer and lilt of sweet-sounding French.

The upstairs was a tapestry of colors, scents and sounds. Bright hues popped from elaborate posters, artisanal rugs, masks and oil paintings adorning the halls. A universe of creativity decorated the impressively high ceilings, a museum of mosaics in a gallery of global delight. Etched in the north-facing wall in large bronze letters scrolled *SPQR*. Tutela explained in professorial tone how the death of Caesar in 44 BC and the accession of Augusta in 29 BC ushered in a period that witnessed the perishing of the republic, the end of the free constitution and the beginning of the decline of the great Roman Forum. Power of emperors replaced the senate of the people, and the benevolent letters *SPQR* (*Senatus Populusque Romanus* – Senate and Roman People) lost their larger meaning, a resounding result being the vibrant voice of the citizens silenced for centuries. *SPQR* was by noble intention the essential acronym providing the civil foundation of Roman ideals, values and principles of the citizenry, a sacred code between the governed and governing, the ultimate bedrock of the republic. It was inscribed on documents, monuments and coinage, and a citizen being detained or wrongly treated could always summon support or defuse maltreatment by publicly proclaiming, "*SPQR!*" But Augustus had manipulated the messaging and twisted the powerful letters by divine authoritarianism, and the echo of the emperor has influenced imperial fascists to this day. Mussolini modeled his intentions two-thousand years after Augustus. The dictator used *SPQR* widely in his propaganda, bellowing famously his incessant motto, "I'll make Rome great again."

"We are reclaiming *SPQR* after two-thousand years," Tutela declared. "If we don't, the tyrants will continue to corrupt it."

Indeed, alt-right white-supremacists and racially dividing terrorist movements from Western Europe to the United States had usurped the iconographic messaging and utilized the Roman eagle as a threat of corporeal domination. Toting the *fasces*, the ancient image of a bundle of sticks and rods with an ax ominously placed in its middle, it is aimed at intimidating declared or contrived nemeses. Should the sticks and rods fail they shall opt for the ax. The olive branch is nowhere in sight. In this new order *SPQR* and the fasces symbolically and euphorically are aligned with Aryan fascism and its threatening call to apply punishment, public flogging or, when decreed, execution.

Tutela reminded of Saint Paul being on the receiving end of the Roman fasces, documented in second Corinthians: *Three times I was beaten with rods*. The Christian convert expressed in self-deprecation to his loyal followers the need for solidarity, perseverance and unity – and while surrounded by tormentors, persecutors and executioners, implored, *Put up with a little folly from me* – and for two-thousand years, they have.

Folly, good humor and genius live side by side and in the environs of Tutela's intentions and schemes one could sense each in play as candles and oils emitted soothing aroma and effervescence amongst the banter and laughter.

"Lavender," Tutela readily informed. "It burns away bad energy."

The workplace opened and breathed in fresh appeal. Around a large oval of high desktops and stools convened people next to one another or facing each other, a terrace of activity looking down on espresso drinkers, internet browsers, impromptu tourists, local shopkeepers, cyber-surfing students and lively academicians in the public internet café.

"Is there bad energy here?" I provoked Tutela.

"It lives next to goodwill, always Tobias. Rome has been battling this duality forever. It is one we battle today as you do in America. We survived it after Caesar. We must survive it now," she responded with earnest.

"This is our intention with the building of my father's *Somnium*. But we must be aware of the reality and constant folly of human nature, the weaknesses of our vulnerable, undeveloped spirits and behavior. I cling to the promise. We Romans produced a practical alphabet, perfected a language, a code of laws, a network of roads, the great arches and domes and intricate city plans that launched a civilization, and yet it fell, Toby. Leaders listening only to themselves, deaf to the people, is deadly over time. Yes, Toby, I am a dreamer, but I am not naïve," she confessed with a tinge of sadness.

Indeed as she educated, it was in the Forum at the apex of this power that idle gossip began to lethally stir. Riches extorted from conquered provinces caused significant psychological changes in the Romans, followed by a palpable decay of morals and the loss of stoic virtues, discipline, industry and frugality. The army, formed mainly from barbarian mercenaries and commanders, churned up trouble and generated greed among the soldiers. Inflated salaries and obscene bonuses stimulated graft, and by priming the coffers of the military an emperor could buy his way onto the throne. A common form of corruption was the selling of imperial power to the top bidder.

"We know what can happen today," Tutela warned. "We saw it last century and we saw it twenty centuries ago. The *Somnium* will be built because the *Somnium* must be built."

There was no formality or dress code in Tutela's offices. It was fresh and free by design, today's Roman lawyers and architects expressing themselves confidently, liberally and boldly. Thirty people, some young, others aged, joined those on payroll aligned with pro bono professionals, volunteers and interns. They gathered around Tutela and inquired about the recent conference in Bonn, a collective appetite for reports and eager for updates on the project.

Soon, we convened in a tight, smaller conference room Tutela christened the Chamber of Ideas. Here, *contra virum*, the walls were blank, no computers, phones or windows, free of tables, chairs and artificial light. Several cushions buffered its perimeter.

"Where is the law library, your reference books? This cannot be a law office," I picked Tutela.

"*Corruptissima republicae, plurimae leges*," she replied in mischievous grin. "From Tacitus. It means the worse the state, the more laws it has. This is open space by design. The whole foundation of Western law comes from right here, Toby. Justinian and his Digests, the Twelve Tables, the legal codes of a thousand years past. The entire struggle between governing elites and we, the ordinary ones, the plebeians, comes from right here in Rome where you stand. Toby, we were the first ones to put law to paper. But more than all the libraries in the world, the true wisdom and spirit of the law is here," she made her case, pressing a forefinger to the temple.

I sat silent and attentive in a neutral corner as Tutela relayed to the team the momentum at hand, qualified in the successful conference at Bonn and responses coming in from influential attendees worldwide. Supporters and partners were growing in interest and commitment, and she was invited to several follow-up conferences across the continent, from Geneva and Stockholm to Brussels and Barcelona.

The vision of Mateo Sasso and his inspired daughter Tutela was now taking practical and progressive shape in both funding and state-sponsored promotion. In the days and weeks that were to follow I was intoxicated in the idealistic and surprisingly practical, well-oiled plan of the mission. An inner circle of geniuses and planners Tutela appointed as members of the *Prehenderat Somnia*, her dreamcatchers. By osmosis, emulsified in the oil and scent of lavender, they had encircled and captured me. The message was direct and clear if not complex. The effort was artistic and revolutionary if not basic. The plan was timeless and the attitudes upbeat. The energy was crafty and courageously optimistic.

Briefly, Tutela reinvigorated her evolving concept to the team, the circle of ambitious lawyers, designers and artists, programmers, contractors and developers, committed to a new run of the human race launched in the construction of the *Somnium*, its exhibits and convenings beacons of light for peace, freedom and civility to pulsate from a hub in Rome along all spokes out of Rome. I became an immediate and honorary member having never asked to join.

"All human beings are dreamcatchers by birthright," Tutela decreed. "Essentially, you can only relinquish membership by denying your place in the race, forfeiting your spirit! Invitation is unalienable. Participation is optional. Resignation is discretionary."

Tutela and her team prepared elementary codes of conduct exemplified in the crafted and economical use of few words. Each meeting was started and concluded saying in unison, "Peace be with you." All correspondence was expressed, somewhere in its contribution, with at least one expression of the word "love." Any point of error or contrition required the appreciation and articulation of "forgive me."

A motto in two-foot-high letters encircled the entrance hall, *Nil magnum, nisi bonum* – No greatness without goodness. A logo was designed as a spiral of colors radiating from exterior to interior, or interior to exterior, its beginning indecipherable from its end.

The campaign rose from the ashes of Tutela's father, the legendary Mateo Sasso, the immensely popular and prolific Roman architect of distinction who died at his drafting table in his office on the ancient banks of the Tiber two years prior. He was designing an enormous rotunda to serve as an art gallery, a modern gift to ancient Rome, that would feature selected works of art from every nation and faith on Earth. Submission of the pieces would require a single caveat. The primary crafted works had to be created by recognized leaders of each country and every religion. He called his masterpiece *Prehenderat Somnia*, the Dreamcatcher, and Tutula's web of determined dreamcatchers were now closing in on realizing that dream in the construction of its centerpiece, the hall of noble imagination and intention, his *Somnium*.

Tutela's eyes were welling as she recounted the vision. An only child never knowing her mother who died from complications at her birth, she successfully coalesced an endearing and dedicated nucleus of friends, colleagues and volunteers.

"These are my brothers, sisters," she whispered in unequivocal declaration, then turning her mouth to my ears vowed words of eternal love that sealed our place and direction. The world stood still for a moment on its wobbly axis. Twelve days later on a warm Saturday afternoon saturated in the Roman summer, comforted by a gentle, cool breeze from the north, I married Tutela Sasso in Bernini's Cornaro Chapel at the Church of Santa Maria della Vittoria in the company of her affectionate and close circle of adopted siblings.

It had been three months since an explosion had blown me off course. My toes now touched the rich Roman soil grounded by Tutela's gravity, anchored in Italian marble and willfully bound in the beautiful trappings every dreamcatcher can recognize.

"Forgive me, Cloe," I said aloud but low to myself. "I almost stopped loving."

Forgive me, Tutela. I almost lost faith.

Forgive me, Rome. I nearly went home.

Forgive me, father. I almost stopped serving.

Forgive me, mother. I nearly stopped believing.

Peace be with you. Four words. Four words for everyone and all time.

Four words at daybreak. Four words at nightfall.

Love is real, Cloe. You believed it for me.

I love you, Tutela.

Peace be with you, Cloe.

Forgive me. I knew not what I was doing.

May He commit you unto His spirit.

It is finished.

Are we not all wed in a universal dream?

I cannot escape you, Cloe.

I can never leave you, Tutela.

I will not run from you, Rome ... I cannot drift from you, mother, father, Lucius, Charles, Vinny, my brothers, sisters, and shall Jesus, supporting the capstone of His Mother Church, bestow His mercy, provide me sustenance, to never leave any of you.

Rome, Rome, Rome, take your hold and mercifully let go.

The Creator confirms when this is finished.

Until then, peace be with you and in turn, return to me.

Amen.

Tutela tapped my drifting head on the night of our nuptials with a small, faded brown book in her right hand, her thumb splitting its spine for words to be shared.

"Indeed, we have a few books, love," she motioned with a smile.

There she presented a passage from Ferdinand Gregorovius, the nineteenth-century German who had moved to Rome on the cusp of Italian reunification.

A violent transformation ... The convents are being turned into offices; the barred windows are opened, or new doors broken in the walls. After long centuries, sun and air again penetrate into these cells of monks and nuns ... Ancient Rome is fading. In the course of twenty years the world here will be a new one.

CHAPTER X

LOVE BECAME my contagion, the spirit pandemic. I wanted this dream to spread and may it be caught by all mankind, a forgiveness for collective past sins, a remedy for terminal ills, a repair for all we have broken. To put the atom back together again, fusion in the confusion, a surrender to the Creator, a just return for what had been split and forsaken, was this too much to ask for as a catcher of dreams?

If all roads lead to Rome may all man's blood, the life-giving rivers in his veins, carry all his matter, his secrets, genetic codes, the history, recorded and hidden, remembered and lost, his present and his future to the River Tiber. May every capillary and artery pump life into his broken heart, reviving and resurrecting him here in Rome where in the mystery of the spin it revolves and recycles with every element known, nourished, fed and cleansed, a transfusion from the Mediterranean to the veins and back again, to be purified if not perfected.

We were all in, vowed and deep in the dreamcatchers' designs. It was a calculated campaign of beauty and peace, the late Mateo Sasso and his daughter its qualified authors, loving revolutionaries returning us back to the hearth, the cave, the common dens, cribs and tender incubators of our infancy. Where better to be born anew than in the loving wonder and wisdom of the womb? She provides the cradle to rebuild civilization. Thus, dreamcatchers seek universal civility, shepherding lost sheep, netting the drifters, orphans and desperate gypsies to rediscover and redefine Rome and home again.

In short order over the subsequent months Tutela's passion drew desired results. Several world leaders submitted original pieces of art created by their own hands, watercolors from Sweden and France, a sketch from Switzerland and a ceramic ornament from Italy. As she exhibited and spoke at peace conferences a growing slate of supporters signed a Declaration for the Common Dream, a crafty fifty-word commitment to unify the human spirit. The document was translated into thirty-two languages as a start, beginning and ending with the phrase *Prehenderat Somni* – Catch the Dream.

While not the main focus nor the priority, buttons, magnets and pins were produced featuring the spiral logo and the concise phrase to employ, *Nil magnum, nisi bonum* – No greatness without goodness.

Four total words encompassed the entire mission, a mandate with no end, a call for what can and must be. It recognized no viable substitution was to be had for direct and creative human interaction, the intimate and personal, for face-to-face human connection was rapidly dissipating in a digitally driven, socially isolating environment of the modern age. Accepted was the reality and potential of the internet in all its benevolent promise, but acknowledgment of its demonstrated folly, the misuse, abuse and escalating isolation, corruption and pollution of the mind and spirit had to be recognized and addressed for its clear limitations. Additionally, the project was to be liberated from the chase of advertising revenue as a core tenet of its values.

The premise was adopted for its welcomed simplicity. Upon submitted works of art, offered to the donors would be the encouragement and channel to sign the declaration. Accepted were financial contributions from sincere sources, small to the substantial for the engineering, design and construction of the heart of the project, the gallery and convening chambers of the great hall, the *Somnium*.

Expanding on her father's vision Tutela decided the *Somnium* would feature a ring, half subterranean, embedding it literally and symbolically into the Earth. It would feature a glass ceiling for a view to the heavens. In its center would be the *viridarium*, an open garden, a parkland featuring flora and foliage, a representation of samplings from every nation on the planet. It would be encircled in a *peristylium*, its north side featuring a steep, rising portico. A series of spiral staircases would lead to a large auditorium surrounded by various art studios. Here, an open invitation would exist for world leaders to greet and commiserate with one another civilly, creatively and freely, liberated from agenda, pretense and the press. Instruments, equipment and tools would be bent on the artistic, canvas and easels, paints, oils and watercolors, ink, pottery wheels and clay, glazes and kilns, chalks and pencils, yarns and brass, beads and shells.

Initially, the idea of conventional writing with pens and tablets was rejected but with Tutela's blessing included would be a poetry studio.

A location had not been selected. Various prospective sites were shortlisted and proposed. Several prominent families offered acres on estates, a generous slate of benefactors around the world lining up for the honor. These were summarily and respectfully declined. It would remain here, Rome its rightful home.

"Is it true, Tutela? Dear love, tell me it's true!" I sought confirmation one late Friday afternoon.

"Yes! Yes!"

In wake of commitments secured at summits and conferences an explosive response from nations and globally recognized interfaith organizations had positively responded to the appeal, adopted the language and absorbed the project's idealism and methodology.

At last count fifty-six nations and twelve of the world's top religious leaders had signed on, committing to the two primary aspects to be embedded in their official communications:

a) To begin and conclude formal communications in the wishing of peace on one other, coupled with an expression of love

b) To incorporate a spiral circle as a symbol unifying the human race in a common dream of world peace and harmony.

Additionally, each was committing their leadership to participate on site in the *Somnium* for creative and dedicated time with one another on dates to be arranged upon completion.

This was a fire lit for the distressed and distracted soul of man, an economy of words, imagery and artistic actions to be repeated over and over again, igniting and warming deep into our collective heart and conscience, combatting the cascade of destructive language and attitudes that had polluted ourselves over the course of centuries, drowning us in violence, war, despair and sorrow. It would invite and ask one another to begin again, rejecting any focus on a terminal finish line. We can revisit the promises of Eden, our noble, natural callings, simply by a leap back into the spiral, rewinding and returning which, paradoxically, provides a direction forward to take notice of the compulsion of Jericho, Ur, El Dorado and Atlantis, every village, town, hamlet and cave, each towering metropolis we ever systematically raised or summarily collapsed. Repeating the spiral, clockwise and counterclockwise in a rediscovery of our higher selves, there shall be sputters, stumbles and falls, but through centrifugal force is the universal law allowing a way out on the other side.

Tutela knew intuitively the power in the economy of words. Where have all the thick tomes, resolutions and treaties, declarations and constitutions, revolutions and recycled world wars gotten us? Indeed, her very profession, a maze of texts and volumes of case studies nuanced in wordplay, saturating the brain and suppressing the soul, blending and stirring, mixing and mashing, had contributed immeasurably to convoluted conflict and mass confusion.

Words can be harmonic, a lilt in lyric and poetry. This mission would not serve as an institutional substitute for such art but, ultimately, it would beg the slates be wiped clean.

"It forgives as it invites," Tutela opined. "Thank you for sharing in the dream, Toby. We adopted a poetry room through your passion, and I can hardly wait for a new Ovid to appear."

I wished to join Tutela at the approaching conferences. To obtain a replacement passport, I was wisely reminded, required a police report of the expert gypsy heist at the Roma Termini months ago. This I had been procrastinating, swept in the passing weeks and winds at Tutela's side and immersed in her project, a man in a dream and of no country. Welcoming my new place and identity, the husband of lovely Tutela, my imposed delays freed me of origin, nationality and passport. Beyond forgiveness I was symbolically and spiritually liberated, deeply grateful to gypsy children and their inadvertent act of amnesty.

The days were a swirl. I was transfixed in the circulating air and stir of Rome. Whenever Tutela was extraordinarily occupied, it fell to Melanie and Noah to graciously and generously host me around the city. The taverna was a regular rendezvous. I was willingly lost in the tumble of time, stopping now and then to remind myself where I was on the calendar, the day, the month, the season. I passed the tempting headlines on front pages of the international newspapers stacked on sidewalk kiosks, a reluctant pause just long enough from my excitable pace to catch a glimpse of an outside world astir all its own. Television was ignored entirely, though the rare respite into a cinema house I permitted, usually catching a classic European noir. I wrote poetry and read fiction, walked aimlessly for hours observing and daydreaming well into the nights as young, fallen lovers and elderly, adoring couples took their aim and turns toward the tempting moon. I ate copious amounts of pears, grapes and bananas along the narrow pathways and backroads and on Sundays made a soft morning routine strolling the ancient passages on the way to Mass with Tutela, never in succession to the same house of worship, alternating contemplative hours in a chosen chapel, church or cathedral.

The headlines, despite all attempts to ignore, would interrupt or steal my attention. Warriors were circling like buzzards, thirsty for blood in new calls for revenge. Cannes and the devastation of the Rotonde served as the adequate if not exploited fuse. It was lit and hot, its sparks and embers flying from France to Britain, NATO to the UN. America fanned the growing flames, a seemingly unquenchable inferno, and in due time the well-armed and angry would target the Middle East. Some called for another Roman numeral, III, to be attached to a necessary and overdue world war.

Having seen enough I retired one Sunday afternoon with Tutela to the warm, green hills of the Borghese. We settled upon a favored knoll under a heavily shaded grove of Italian stone pine. She provided the blanket as I shared red grapes and bites of gimblettes, the round cakes sold by local bakers on the quaint backstreets of the Borgo. Resting her head on my chest a gentle breeze danced in soft rhythm with Tutela's slow breathing. We indulged in our chosen pastime in the park, the sweetness of idleness, the joy of doing nothing – *dolce far niente*.

"Tell me, Tobias," she requested softly. "Your loves, the ones won and lost. How did your heart open to mine? Was there a special one, a love of Toby in his former life?"

Before I could collect my reply she had a revelation for me. Our bond omnipresent and sealed, we had not paused to open such doors, confessions to past romances. Now on this carpet of late-summer splendor the testimonials flowed.

She suffered from lupus, a latent form of the silent, insidious disease. Occasional fatigue and a weakened immune system once stifled her plans and altered her direction. She had discovered in time the proper lifestyle, habits and diet to help counter its effects. The regimen required rest and, above all, a spirit of acceptance to chart a reasonable and proper course, given the serious and unpredictable recurrence of symptoms. Lupus, Tutela said convincingly, is a hidden tag latched secretly to millions of her body's cells, but she refused to be defined by its shadowy nature, publicly or privately.

"Other than you Toby, today, there are four people on this planet, physicians, that know this about me."

A soft tear fell, trickling down her cheek where I caught it on my thumb. I kept it there for proper absorption into me, rubbing it into my forefinger until it evaporated over the Borghese.

She was engaged once at twenty to a man sixteen years her senior, a career military officer from Sardinia. He made many promises that her young and innocent heart believed, and she was hopelessly betrothed. He was in the Italian navy, his tour of duty shipping him on long stretches to the Gulf of Oman. He wrote once to her in their first weeks apart while daily she sent emails, letters, postcards, trinkets and thoughtful gifts in efforts to harbor a distant, fleeting love. She never heard from him again. It would be eight years before her heart re-opened. Even at that the romances were brief, empty and shallow dalliances. She ended all of them, admittedly, breaking a few innocent hearts herself along the way, not so much in retribution as much as migrated habit, well trained by love adrift. The naval wayfarer had taught her a lasting lesson about love – ships passing in the night can leave long wakes.

Landing a husband was proving to be fleeting, and with a heart guarded and a father ailing, she dedicated time to his care and the increasing demands of her law-school studies. The onset of lupus steered away thoughts of having children and further postponed notions of finding true love.

"I disciplined myself well," she admitted. "But the mother in me still asks questions and I fib back to her. Yet, my new family does grow. Fate from that park bench at the Singing Fountain in Marianske brought me to you, Toby. Was I not courageous to sit down, yes?"

"Oh yes. I thank the gods and you, Tutela, for a fallen handkerchief. A brave moment for both of us, right? I was an aimless coward in so many ways. I had loved before. You know much of Cloe whose love was on a different, cosmic plain. But I had a distant love, too. She trained my heart how to release and let go. Carla," I started.

She had made her way into my thoughts through windows Tutela opened. Carla was my college love in California. We once dreamed of being wed followed by a honeymoon in Italy. She kept a painting of the kissing bridge that spans the Venice canal, two lovers in passage, their bodies wrapped as one as the gondolier rows beneath a crescent moon. It hung above her bed. We would turn our bodies to stare at it and utter aloud, "Someday … someday." She was sunny, light and beautiful, an open-hearted free spirit, a lover of life who expected little and demanded less. Her Latin fever and my Irish fire made for passionate years but stubbornness defeated us. We pushed and pulled then tore at each other over a decade until, in the end, the heart strings stretched and snapped and Cupid took his proper flight in an opposite direction.

I had misread, not taking full note of a love so clearly present. In the blindness of career climbing, whipped in the media circus of Hollywood, selfishness surrounded my moves and I lost her in the spin.

Fate was merciful as she eventually married and had a beautiful, healthy little girl. The gods bestowed generous and forgiving fate in a second chance at love, for her and now me, when they arbitrarily or justly could have been cruel and punitive.

As our revelations came to a close the Roman sun was sinking. We finished pouring our souls on the Borghese knoll kissing ancient wounds. We fell asleep as children played on the sloping lawns below in a race to steal each moment of illuminated joy before night ushered in its dominance. We departed locked in arms strolling slowly in the wake of parading children and their spent energy.

In the hypnotic flow of another golden Roman experience I passed on a Sunday afternoon plan to visit the police, which would be a slow day at the station, to finally file the report to replace my passport. Another appointment utterly more stimulating and spiritual was pulling. Tutela and I made such passionate love that night I was sure the Roman moon, Caligula and Nero himself were blushing. The jealous poet Ovid smirked and took detailed notes. Venus paused then gawked. Tutela and I witnessed the Archer brace, and dutifully on target strike his pose and plant his mark with piercing pride and cosmic approval.

Falling into deep slumber in Tutela's arms I dreamed of my childhood home in California. I shared the largest bedroom with my brothers, the sisters in another and our parents in the third. In the dream the house was extraordinarily large but completely empty, the Roman columns at its entrance bracing a tremendous balcony perilously rocking and swaying. Tiles on the porch were eroding and breaking, insects the size of my palm climbing from the cracks and running under a widening gap of the tremendous front door. On each of the house's wings, flanked by floor-to-ceiling French doors, the shutters swung violently open by powerful winds blowing not from the outside in, but from the inside out, a tempest of maddening cyclones tearing through the hallways in counterclockwise commotion.

I stood paralyzed and lost in my strangely threatened home, alone, with invasive and insidious bugs coming from one direction, the wind gusting from another. The earth began to quake, the walls to rock, side by side at first in slow then elevating force until they yielded to the floors pounding in jolts, horizontally then vertically. I was at the top of the grand staircase holding on desperately to its rail but my grip failed, the girth much too thick for my palm, so puzzlingly small. I was a child. Bricks started falling about me from atop the chimney to the kitchen chute. I tried to call out but I could not utter a sound. Great waves of water could be seen outside the shattering windows. From the second story they had reached the sills twenty feet high, a cascade coming from a pool across the street and a hundred meters distant. I saw a familiar little girl from the neighborhood, alone on her toy raft crying in the rapids. Insects in the water, grotesque and larger, surfaced then dove. They encircled the terrified child and spilled into our house, crawling their way up the stairwell to the base of my bare and water-logged feet then latched onto my ankles.

My father appeared at the landing. He looked to me but he, too, could not speak. He motioned to the corner room where the waves could be seen as if to warn me of a catastrophe to come. Dozens of wild dogs appeared there in the room as he kept his steady and serious focus, lobos, wolves and coyotes circling in search of prey or marking and claiming a turf once ours.

Dad turned to descend the stairs but hesitated in the retreat, a painful grimace on his face, biting his lower lip until blood spilled from his mouth down the mid-rift of his blinding white t-shirt. He started to fall as the dogs rushed. They snarled and snipped at my father's legs and he began to teeter in the imbalance. He shouted he was fine and that I must leave.

He is fine!

He is fine!

His house fell around him in a crash of concrete and frigid water. Suddenly, I was standing in the muddy rubble. Only the Roman columns remained, their concrete foundation and reinforced rods firmly in place by caementicum restorative work he had masterfully completed years ago, perhaps in expectation of the fall.

Standing in the ruins I muttered unconvincingly to myself.

I am fine.

I am fine.

Awoken by the nurturing nudges of Tutela I grabbed for her in a desperate embrace.

"Are you okay, love? My God, you were shaking."

"Yes, yes. I am fine," I assured in my fog.

"You were calling out, 'Lucius. Lucius. Lucius.'"

Puzzled and panting, I could hardly breathe.

Holding me tight in the shudder, Tutela said she had a dream of her own, powerful and specific, vivid and instructive.

"Do you have a birthmark, a wound, a scar, somewhere near your foot or ankle, Toby?"

"Yes, why? My right inner ankle, since I was five."

Staring intensely into my eyes she said she was told in the dream to look for it. She knew its color, shape and location, describing it in perfect detail. I was sure she had never noticed it before. We had certainly never discussed it. It is a faded, nearly round impression just above the inner-ankle bone and practically invisible to the naked eye, camouflaged beneath my body hair.

The Roman morn just beginning to offer its illuminating sunlight through the open window, I bent my right leg toward her gaze, rolling the pajama pant leg to reveal the mark. Holding my foot with both hands, Tutela guided it within inches of her eyes, closely examining the ancient scar.

I was five years old on the back of a bicycle with my sister steering. We were going down a steep driveway racing our friends when I violated the cardinal rule. My legs tiring in their spread away from the swiftly rolling wheels, I brought them to rest on the frame near the back wheel. In an instant my right foot was sucked into the spinning vortex of the spokes essentially causing the bike to suddenly brake. My sister soared over the handlebars as I tumbled to the left, spilling into the street's curbside before coming to a stop on the neighbor's lawn. She landed safely and miraculously in the road as I remained in the wreckage of the bike, my right foot above the ankle jammed in the hub and spokes. The other kids and my lucky, injury-free sister scattered in a rush of screams seeking adult help. It was a workday afternoon and there wasn't a father to be found. The children and their mothers gathered around me, a horrible sight of a bloody, ripped-open ankle unmovable within the twisted bike's frame. My mother calmly called for someone in the crowd to get a screwdriver. Several unforgettable minutes later she lifted the frame and freed her little, wounded rider. A nurse in her earlier life, she washed and dressed the flesh proficiently then calmly put me to bed. All healing happened there, back at home with siblings at play, the simple and happy normalcy that always returned after calamity. Mom was here and Dad would be home soon, all the mending and security ever required in the world. The only leftover from this crisis was an awkward round impression above the inner-ankle bone that no one would ever notice.

There, faintly behind my lower-leg hair, my worthy scar was presented for confirmation by Tutela's careful inspection, set free by the healer, branded over thirty years ago and divinely revealed for the Roman dreamer in my midst.

"Remarkable. Amazing, really. The dream is true," she softly attested.

Without hesitation in a bow to her charioteer's reveal, she put her lips to the ankle, puckered and placed a gentle kiss on the blemish. The sun danced on her hair through the open window as I brushed it away from her brow, exposing her rich, ebony lashes and golden-caramel eyes. We locked in a kiss without utterance.

I rose to wash my face and together we made coffee, opening the shutters as a burst of Roman sun filled the apartment and blessed the plants on the sills. As she bathed I dressed then set off for the police station to file the ever-lapsing report and, consequently if not tardy, obtain the necessary documents for a new passport. Replacement was no longer optional, however postponed by my own delay. I would need to travel soon enough to accompany the project's campaign, the presentation at conferences, summits and exhibits across several borders alongside Tutela and her team.

Arriving at the aged, dank and musty station I was surprised to see the reception room nearly full to capacity, fifty or more restless souls, many appearing to be tourists and travelers who had met one type of mishap, crime or another. Those speaking English were on cellphones as "pickpocketed," "train station" and "gypsies" could be overheard in multiple degrees of description and anguish. Amused if not tickled, I smiled to myself and took my place in the queue, offering not my account nor seeking details from others as an uneventful three hours passed.

"Tobias Tyrone."

"Here," I signaled.

"Sir, remain. Stay here, please," the young Italian clerk ordered in clear English.

She returned shortly with a portly man with little hair, thick glasses, a poorly fitting tie and a very visible sidearm pistol. He was short in stature and hardly imposing, save the revolver. I was brought through a side door to a desk behind a high counter. Together the two of them squinted into a computer, my eyes affixed to the back of its monitor, curious and slightly unnerved. Asked to confirm my full name, mother's maiden name, date and place of birth and U.S. Social Security number, I cooperated with proper, heightened concern.

"What does this have to do with gypsies pickpocketing me several months ago?" I asked, breaking my patience.

The officer walked around the counter and held my elbow. With kindness but authority he directed me down a long hall cluttered on each side by cardboard boxes and stacks of files, its walls littered in bulletin board postings, the stench of long-ago smoked Italian cigarettes still wafting into the humid canals of the station's maze. In a momentary lapse of hope, I was beginning to believe they were in possession of all my lifted belongings and bringing me deep into the vaults to retrieve.

Instead I was placed in a closet-sized office, empty but for a table and four wooden stools barely fitting the confines. The door locked behind me. A window was open but barred. I heard the sounds of the Roman morning outside turning into the noon hour. Church bells began to chime ushering in the *postmeridianus*. Two doves came to perch at the window's ledge. Soon two men, well dressed and younger with steely looks in their eyes, entered as the portly officer directed a sympathetic if not worried glance my way before closing the door behind him. One of the stoic men stood with his back to the shut door. The other walked around the cramped perimeter of the table and latched the shutters of the sole window, bringing an ominous darkness to the intimidating quarters as I heard the flaps of two departing doves..

"Welcome to glorious Rome, Mr. Tobias Nathan Tyrone," he sarcastically stated, keeping his back to me. "You're under arrest."

CHAPTER XI

NOON THAT day began a nine-month detention. I could not seek nor was provided conventional, legal counsel. I could not receive visitations from Tutela or anyone else for that matter. I sent and received messages only through intense screening, review and censor, Tutela my steady and reassuring correspondent.

Transferred to an unknown facility, I was placed somewhere in the inner bowels of a baffling, inquisitive Rome. It was all a monumental mistake of pathological proportion, a sign of the new and readily ushered-in imperial times, where cross-referenced data, faulty and unchecked analytics, common suspicion trumping common-sense rule, government to government, agency to agency, officer to officer, now reigned. Refuge came by the occasional reading material but never a newspaper. I shared my experience and kept close company in Roman books of poetry, Ovid my ally. The most famous poet in his time in the first century AD, he had been banished by Augustus from Rome to the remote town of Tomis on the far edge of the empire in present-day Romania for reasons still unknown. It has been suggested he simply saw something he should not have, a witness to an emperor's indiscretion. Tomis was a prison all its own as Ovid could hardly commiserate or converse, none of its citizens versed in Latin. Loneliness and longing were the true punishments. He wrote substantially about this punitive form of emotional torture, the heavy toll on the soul and spirit, a penalty more harsh than common criminals and convicted murderers endured as inmates back in Rome. Ovid declared his wrongdoing was hardly a violation of the law but rather simply *carmen et error*, a poem and a mistake. He suspected his authoring of *The Art of Love* may have been at the root of the contrived crime, similar to the commercial banishment the heroic Henry Miller would suffer two millennia later for amplifying raw romances and brazen carnal desires in his self-imposed French exile. Unlike Miller, exile destroyed the misunderstood genius Ovid, the authentic romantic paying a spiritually lethal price for possessing a burning heart. A reclamation of his rightful place, the just return of his soul to his city, was eventually delivered for the poet. The Rome city council revoked Ovid's exile in AD 2017.

At the onset I had regular investigators approaching me in my lone cell, perhaps six, eight or ten in a day. In a few weeks it was reduced to only one, maybe two. The questions were ceaselessly repetitive, ad nauseam, a recycle of inquisition spun in a vortex of redundancy.

"What do you know of the bombing of the Rotonde?"

"We know you have information. It is in your interest to share it now. Is there anything you wish to offer regarding your actions leading up to and on that day?"

"Why have you waited all these months to report your alleged pick-pocket story? Why the long delay in renewing your passport?"

"Will you share your exact itinerary over the past six months?"

"Tell us what you know of this woman, Tutela. How did you meet her? Where?"

Randomly but rarely I got a minor peek into their humanitarian side.

"Would you like another blanket, sir? Are you comfortable enough? Can we get you something specific to eat?"

They awoke me in the middle of the night two months into my detention. I was impressed and proud of my resolve under these circumstances. Perhaps the Rotonde trauma, the many months on the road bed to bed, meal to meal, a rucksack over my shoulder and Tutela by my side, prepared me for the endurance of this trial.

"Tell us, sir, how a man dedicated to peace can explain such disturbing literature in his possession?" they persisted, providing insight with a new line of questioning.

"I don't know what you're talking about."

A red, black and white flyer was flashed abruptly into my face. Folded, creased and worn, its ugliness was apparent even in the flash. It was the leaflet I had picked up outside the church, Eglise Notre-Dame de Bon Voyage in Cannes, in the confusing moments just after the blast.

Had I had it all this while? Did they manufacture a copy? What was happening here?

Stop.

They are trapping.

Stop. The blast!

Explain yourself, myself. Who am I?

Who was I?

The temperature rose in the seething heat of the moment, the interrogation room a sauna, a Roman bath. Blood in my veins began to boil. I felt faint and exhausted, beaten and done. I reached for surrender, *mappa* and St. Gerard.

Exhale. Heavy. Exhale.

Give it up. Forgive. Give all.

Peace be with you. Peace be with me.

I love you. Forgive me. Peace be with you.

Cloe! Cover! Take cover ... Cloe!

The girl in the church she cried alone, in the minutes before the whole world cried in return as it made its way toward waging a bloody response. For the most part the mongers are blowhards, braggarts and imposters, war hawks and pundits exaggerating their impulses. The catastrophic events in Cannes would not deliver the disproportionate violence many promulgated and pursued.

What to make of me who claimed to catch dreams, to have all the answers yet huddles so disturbed and shakes at each accusation, the innocent appearing so surely guilty? I wanted to shout and scream in a plea to Tutela guarded by the ghost of Lucius, to brace me and take me to the sweet green knolls and grasses of Villa Borghese. I wanted the fire within to melt the iron on my wrists and the bars on the sills and through the inferno and smoke declare me libertus, my elusive manumission shouted for every freed slave to hear from the peaks of the Palatine to the far corners of the fallen empire.

Death feels near.

Mom? Mom? I want to go home.

I live to love. I know I am loved.

Caged, in love. Ovid? Carmen et error ...

It was leaked with patient but cruel intent their trail of supposition, that the awful events in Cannes had driven me circuitously and suspiciously to Rome. In short, I was a person of critical interest, huddled just like scores of others in various interrogation rooms across the continent as the plethora of data demanded. The weeks were fading away along with body weight, energy and hope. Some say time drifts slowly imprisoned. I found the opposite. It was if all the world outside was revolving in fast motion making purposeful passage of their lives as I rapidly wasted away idle, isolated and aged. Time here should be tortuously slow, painstakingly dripping minutes from one's time, sucking the lifeblood out of the spirit in sadistic sequence, hourly yearning to be free, loved and remembered. In the tepid pacing wall to wall, waiting, waiting, waiting for the blessed, nebulous and due pardon, I prepared for a merciful and relieving exit from this colossal mistake.

Though it was not summarily granted, a peace, undiscernible and welcomed, grew like a lone lavender bush in the barren soil of my soul. Brief but regular messages from my love weathered the tempest. Tutela reminded me of the good, historic company I shared, the epic confinements of brethren Martin Luther King Jr., Socrates, Jesus, Paul and Thoreau. Tutela helped me stay steady in the counting of hours and measuring of days, anticipating shared wine, pears, olives and cheeses at exile's end. She told me in her calm and faithful correspondence a greater love awaited us, providing a picture of the silver statuette of the Gallo-Roman goddess Tutela, a replica her father, Mateo, had kept since her childhood, the original a second-century piece in collection at the British Museum. The protectress of the city dons a mural crown and cornucopia, erect and steady on a twelve-sided ribbed base. In her right palm is a *patera*, a balanced libation dish, her long wings helping to support a stand in which rest seven busts depicting the gods of the days of the week. The goddess Tutela was my calendar and calling card for a freedom and fairness to come.

For all the data and information compiled and crossed, the expensive, sophisticated lines of intelligence, the records, phone monitoring, wireless and analog, internet surveillance and satellite imagery, no official could determine or conclude much less reveal what it was I had actually done and who it is that I am. I felt self-empowered in my few garments, limited meals and sixteen-square meters of space. Armed with my thoughts and pen I expressed my love in poem, the ongoing vision of Tutela, her father and dreamcatchers, doodling and scribbling day after painstaking day. All these men credentialed with their shields, holstered in pistols, stoic and adrenaline-infused, at guard behind two-way glass, equipped with modern toys, earpieces, cellular devices and flat screens, seemed no happier or freer than me, imprisoned in their professions, caged in indoctrinated suspicion, hardly breathing the open Roman air and rarely tasting in its daily delights. Deaf to its children's laughter echoing from the city's streets and off its imprisoned walls, they are no more in tune with Roman harmonics than those confined whom they incessantly berate. They have descended deeper into these colorless corridors than I, even the few whose human instincts were still relatively unmarred and occasionally signaled an awareness of my innocence. They are members of a system run amok, a tiger in the dirty ring chasing its own tail, a colossal waste of human drama lacking the amusement of the performer and void of an appreciating audience. Humility is the primary victim, the simple acknowledgement that one could, despite mounting data, be very, very wrong. It is an entire globe locked in a secret foil, a recycled, polluting game of hide and seek, seek and hide, over and over again. Whatever they saw in me, as clever pirate or naughty gypsy, meant surely there was a treasure trove somewhere to be brought to the surface. The new economy of global intelligence and surveillance required suspicion to permeate and feed the beast. Basic faith and belief in fellow man were casualties in the crime, unabashed, collateral damage in this modern marketplace of data gathering run roughshod. Propertius prophesied such. *But now the shrines are neglected in empty groves: Religion is vanquished, all men worship gold, For gold faith's broken and justice up for sale: Law follows gold: law gone, soon shame goes too.*

I continued to greet the accusers politely. I forgave them daily and loved them spiritually. Where they go after these hours, to what houses and families await them in the labyrinth beyond, breaching the River Tiber or the Appian Way I could only suppose, thinking them lonely, cold and fear-fueled environments of their own making, goblins in the ruins, apparitions appearing in rear-view mirrors. I was free to sleep with me, the company in my heart being Tutela and everyone I once loved, do love and wish to love. While the pounds shed and energy waned, I stretched each morning and exercised every eve in a regimen of sit-ups and push-ups, feet pressed to the walls and floors, rising into speedy paces, a race against me in comical, tiny, concentrated laps in the cell, my arches and palms serving as propellers until all to be heard were the slaps of soles on cement and pants from the lungs. I counted the laps, three hundred counterclockwise per session, until my increased stamina raised the bar to a thousand. The echo and cadence of Tutela in my head pushed the elevated pace. I placed her in the center of my confines at the spina of this track. Resolved more than ever I was a solo charioteer in the circus, within reach but untouchable as the raucous audiences beyond in collapsing tiers crashed down. Never escaping the wrath of Nero and his insecurities and fears, they stir eternally, anxious and broken wondering where else to turn or how to begin again. If I could have invited all of Rome and the entire circus of the human race I would, to join me in one moment of self-imposed peace and solitary confinement where in collective witness we'd hear each other's hearts beat – a drown of the world's crying cadence, the march to the wayward warrior's drum – and I'd recite my cellmate Propertius, *I will speak out – and may I prove my country's truthful prophet! Proud Rome is being crushed by her own prosperity. I speak the truth, but none believe.*

I bent to a thunderous sky as another Roman day elapsed and longed for homing pigeons to bring word of overdue surrender. In each electric strike and shattering clap from the gods a stark truth illumined my inner citadel.

I am free, my dear captors.

I am fine, Marcus and Lucius.

I am ready for doors and hearts to open.

Dreams to be caught.

Civis Romanus sum ... I am a Roman citizen.

Free, calls this world.

The strongest and most resolute message from Tutela kept despair in check and spirit intact. As I inquired about the outside world and ongoing investigation of the Rotonde bombing, the climate astir among the people and press, she delivered fearless insight and perspective. The great Roman fire ignited on July 18 in the year AD 64 started in the Circus Maximus and spread rapidly. It burned for nine days and nights in a raze of two-thirds of the city. The emperor Nero was accused of adding fuel to the fire, scattering incendiaries to inflame it, watching the inferno blaze away from the comforts of his tower of Maecenas, dressed in stage costume while singing gleefully, anticipating a grand rebuild of Rome to his own specifications and renaming the city after himself. In Tacitus' account Nero, amidst an infuriated populace, directed blame on *a race of men detested for their evil practices, and commonly called Chrestiani.* Derived from the One who *suffered under Pontius Pilate ... a dangerous superstition spread ... the common sin into which everything infamous and abominable flows like a torrent from all quarters of the world.* Nero found *wretches who were induced to confess themselves guilty; and on the evidence of such men a number of Christians were convicted, not indeed on clear evidence of having set the city on fire, but rather on account of their sullen hatred of the whole human race.* Tortured, mocked and publicly burned to death, their charred corpses were often left dangling along Roman streets or as amusing displays at Nero's festive parties. But Nero's arson and false persecutions backfired. *At length the brutality of these measures filled every breast with pity. Humanity relented in favor of the Christians,* Tacitus reported.

Tutela made a case that poetic justice, rhyme and reason today would prevail, and soon enough justice would bend, in due, rapid and reasonable speed in the proper direction on its long, forgiving arc. Further, she professed, all the pain, suffering and loss at the Rotonde paled in comparison to past Roman tragedy. After Nero's ignition the Circus Maximus would endure catastrophe in Diocletian's reign a few centuries later when the top tier of its seating collapsed, killing 13,000 spectators. "There is collective guilt in the Roman conscience," she concluded. "We condemned Saint Paul and crucified Saint Peter upside down, beheading the rock of our faith in the Circus Maximus. Conscience will bring reason and truth to these matters, with ready resolution, Toby, and absolution in your innocence."

She was right in the prediction, her intuition keen and sharp. I needed this stimulating fodder to counter cruel anticipation and diminished hope. Tutela forwarded more writings, including those of Marcus Aurelius which were consumed in earnest as well. I was particularly attached to his *Golden Thoughts*, the *Ta eis heauton*, the "to-himself" chronicles written in the intervals of his travels, battles, revolts and tribulations. He would claim the understanding of the universe lives within the same order and power possessed by man. *All things are implicated with one another, and the bond is holy ... There is a common reason in all intelligent beings; one god pervades all things, one substance, one law, one truth ... Can a clear order subsist in thee, and disorder in the All?*

I clung to Aurelius as I stared at the cell walls, remembering God has given every man a guiding *daimon*, or inner spirit, by which we must tap and in discipline ask for reliance, be it in the bask of sunshine or shadow of despair. Spiritual laziness is fateful suicide.

Nearly seven months in this criminal circus and alas came a tear in the tent. The light came through by way of the dirty and demonic leaflet. The soiled piece of ominous, disturbing literature lifted from the steps of Eglise Notre-Dame in Cannes just as the mysteriously troubled girl was discovered in her despondence unleashed a torrent of suspicion. Was she Russian, this frazzled, traumatized young lady, staring at me and flailing in hysteria?

I had never fully absorbed or comprehended the context of the content. I dismissed the flyer as amateurish and sloppy, one of many nasty messages in circulation, the reactive sloganeering that surfaces in the election cycles of Europe. In the confusion and haste of the bombing and its aftermath it was one of thousands of foggy memories that had clouded my mind. Clearly, though, it was a hate-filled propaganda piece, plastered in imagery of sadistic anarchism. Had I stuffed it into my possession, my shirt or pants at that moment? In the roar, chaos and confusion had I not put such pieces together? Despite my few belongings and the limited garments I had worn since that day, had my traumatized superstition inclined me to avoid wearing those same clothes again, for indeed I had not, and could the shirt and slacks now in possession of the interrogators be unleashing runaway theories and investigations all their own? What was the possible link?

Tutela informed months ago in the immediate days after my arrest authorities had raided her residence and combed through the offices, files and computers, securing everything they wished.

The flyer! That ugly, provocative leaflet, its bizarre sketches, the circles of streets making a maze of the map of Cannes and its harbor, arrows pointing in all which ways with a bold, black x in its center, raised substantial suspicion but was not the only red flag.

Why did they not ask me about this months ago? Why the delay, this game of grab and go, catch and release, secure and reveal?

This truly could not be the single item justifying my detention. Why?

Three more weeks passed and the matter got clearer, the fog lifted, the puzzle pieces coagulated, but my sleep was interrupted and fragmented by episodic dreams.

The puzzle. The puzzle. Solve it for us, Dad.

The house, it falls, only your columns standing among the ruins.

She-wolf, come rescue me ... Cerberus stands guard.

Nipping and biting. Dad, he stands silent.

I can only nod to the door, there in the corner, where escape awaits.

A wound on my ankle. Dad, is he near? Mom, cut me free.

"Again, do you know this girl?" the official snapped, his palm slamming the table, a photocopy image of her face presented under my nose.

She is young but the trouble in her eyes has aged her, bags blue and black. She is fair and attractive, a lean face revealing high cheekbones, too lean to be healthy. She is a girl on the run, inside and out.

"I do not know her, but yes, I did see her. I saw her. I spoke to her. Yes. Yes," I affirmed. "She is the girl I told you about before, many times. She's the disturbed one I encountered that morning, on her hands and knees outside the church. She fled, jumped I think, from a vehicle. Or maybe she was pushed. A delivery truck I think. Yes, a delivery truck. The passenger door was swinging open. It was very dangerous. Scary. She stumbled from its floorboard, there to the curbside, and then I saw her at the church."

The interrogators held still in my latest account. The room's air lifted in each utterance. I was free in my recollection but unsure how it would be received. It mattered little at the time, the liberation and revelation having its own reward.

"She struck me as, perhaps, intoxicated, drunk, maybe on drugs. A few moments later she was there, in the back of the old church, alone, restless, weeping uncontrollably, inconsolable. I remember asking her if she was okay. I handed her my card and said if she needed help to contact someone, and that I would see what I could do, too. She rejected my help. Waved me off, shaking her head. She was very upset, muttering, shivering. The girl was in some kind of personal or deep psychological trouble. She was back outside there, on the steps when the bomb went off. It shook the steps, knocked me off my balance. When I turned, she was gone. I suppose you know the rest."

"And the flyer?" one of them asked. "Do you care to share anything more about the flyer?"

"Is it hers?" I asked.

Their faces were blank, glaring into mine like lasers, unblinking and fixed.

"Tell me, by God, is it hers? Is she involved?" I begged. "Is she involved, one of the bombers? Was that the reason for her being so upset? Tell me!"

There was no movement in the room, the very air still and lifeless.

"Do I not get answers, now, please, from you? I deserve answers! I'm the one deserving of answers!" I pled. "And, I am innocent," I offered in softer tone. "For an instant could any of you believe I would be behind the mass murder of my friends, my colleagues, people I adored? And I ask again, now, when do I get proper counsel. I am an American and this is Rome. I deserve a lawyer, yes?"

"We are the legal minds here, my friend, and we are the ones who get to ask questions. Or, as you say, deserve to get answers," the tallest one imposed. "Are you still insisting this was your only encounter with this girl, in the immediate moments just before the explosion?"

"Yes. Absolutely. Yes! I had never seen her before. That is why I was drawn to her. She struck me as being in very deep trouble. Am I accused of being compassionate to a criminal?"

My tall interrogator rose slowly and stoically to leave the cell. One of the others, a middle-aged woman, perhaps Danish, certainly not Italian, turned and said something direct and clear for me to absorb in the lifting fog.

"Many are wondering," she said suspiciously, "how is it you have been receiving phone messages and emails since the day of the bombing, hundreds of them actually, from this young, little friend of yours? How it is her social media searches for many weeks were for you? Why you, or is it some clever imposter, Toby, who traveled as you, with your passport to very interesting locations, attempting some exceptionally strange purchases from Eastern Europe, all as Tobias Nathan Tyrone? The same Tobias who quit his job so curiously and has been off the grid since Cannes, and allowed so many months to pass before reporting his missing passport? Many wonder how it is you conveniently left the Rotonde at such a perfect time, and is pictured with a known accomplice? It was to do what, Tobias Tyrone? Ah yes, you are such a noble boy. You were on your way to church after a trip to get goodies. Such a sweet do-gooder. Church and chocolate, was it not, Toby?"

She closed the steel door, the clamping of its lock splitting the fleeting notions of peace and hope, and I sunk lower in the immediate silence that followed. A dove landed on the sill, and while usually arriving with companions, this one stood alone. It limped, pacing back and forth as if its leg just above the foot had been bent or pierced. It tried to utter a coo but, like this room and me, was mute. The Roman afternoon sky turned a dark-charcoal gray. A hard rain pelted sideways against the thick walls, a repetitive, deafening patter creating the only sound breaking a silence between me and a broken dove.

Did my face register shock or, worse, exhibit a pretense of guilt? I begged Tutela and God to come and deliver me now. I was guilty of surviving and the mortal crime in believing. I would run from this past if I believed it could not catch me. Tutela outpaced me, just as she escaped the hungry reach of the gypsies.

For the first time in my detention I failed to sleep. The days that followed were more or less the same, a monotonous flow of repetitive questions all drawing to the same assumed conclusion, a guilt by an association I could not adequately explain. But if I was only guilty on some cataclysmic cosmic level, I was surely beginning to look the part. I lost additional weight, stopped my exercise regimen, tucked Ovid away and wept.

The justice, healing and understanding would come several weeks later though not soon enough, from actions and forgiveness of a very courageous and complicated young lady. It would diffuse the rabid media, the countries and allies, coalitions and their militaries that for months spouted and flexed, gyrated and geared to take on declared or contrived enemies and conspirators in the Middle East, reflexes to the bombing of the Rotonde which amplified the alarms on other supposed targets that never rang true, military barracks, consulates and embassies. It would quiet the tolling of calibrated bells in the towns, villages and cities across the airwaves and cellular towers of the Western world. I was adequately aware of the momentum building and rage that had been rising, but had consciously denied myself even in detention an ear to this ringing, a stinging surge, a drumbeat to the concussing jets fueled and pointed to bomb, bomb and bomb away and again.

For at the moment Cloe and hundreds more were taken, also vaporized was any inner call in me for revenge, and something instinctive, a quiet but crystal-clear voice said the world was at another critical intersection of choice, and carnal retribution, the mistaken one, could win the day. I chose to believe Cloe in alliance with her widowed Philippe whispered in that instant, "Do not kill for me as you killed me." Thus I laid claim to a newfound reagency, focusing on a journey that, while recognizing our violent past and tendencies, could steer us to a different, higher plain in the resolution of our conflicts, dealing with one another, loving each other. The first step on that journey would be a rejection of the road I had been on, a shallow, materialistic, nihilistic and ego-driven path surrounded by the energy of pomp, fame, comfort, faux popularity, wealth, objectification, testosterone and adrenaline and, fanning the blaze, amusement and technology in mass proliferation, my insatiable, unhealthy appetite: bread and circuses.

For some years, as Cloe was aware, I flirted with the notion of leaving the multimedia marketplace, saying due farewell to the film frenzy and its red-carpeted carnival of the Rotonde. In that great billow of black and orange smoke, when Cloe collapsed as the Big Top came down, my decision was clarified in catastrophe. The circus had left me and I had left it – all its petty, ugly, dishonest, cruel and trite habits, the methods and schemes, plots and plans, conspiracies of comradery wrapped in complacency, were exorcised from my soul in the rise of the holy smoke pouring from my soul, not black or orange, but in sweet, pillowed white and soft purple, the aromatic plume of wafting lavender. How was I to decipher a young, troubled lady in Cannes would steer me into the arms of a destined love, introduced in an overdue surrender in the dropping of a handkerchief in the small Czech village of Marianske Lazne?

Then, from a simple cell in Rome, complicated answers came to me from questions I never posed, the troubled girl's profile provided and appreciated, an avalanche of information descending upon my puzzled plight. The authorities let it spill, a flood of thawing intelligence, information and detail. Propertius was resilient and concurred with my resolve, *Do not petition me with humble letters: At the last my oath shall be as it was at first. This my perennial law: unique among lovers, I neither quickly give up, nor rashly begin.*

The young woman was a runaway from Ukraine, a broken, damaged spirit, aimless, bruised and abused. She was nineteen, parentless and orphaned, a trafficked, itinerant child. A distant uncle raised her until she turned fourteen when she was roped and tethered into an ugly torrent, a deathly spiral of drugs and prostitution. She was victimized in a vacuum of the human underground, a ruinous road that took her across the Urals and Eastern Europe, over the Alps and into the basins of the Mediterranean. The Russian underworld johns profited as she was sold into the marketplaces of the macabre, and from dingy railroad and bus stations to the mansions of millionaires she became acquainted with the world's hidden, horrific and unchecked appetites.

She had several operating names and aliases and no one had determined with certainty which was genuine. She had come forward with her brave revelation as the planet armed for Revelation. The Rotonde blew up at the hands of just seven misplaced and misguided servants of anarchy. Seven angry, hateful, broken souls, the eldest twenty-three, were swept into an ideology of chaos and cacophony, wholesale destruction, fueled by alienation, neglect and resentment, motivated by envy, avarice and jealousy, a want in the world to be noticed and counted, a deafening call for attention and to make a mark, be it a final but lasting mark, any mark on the elusive landscape of the revolving human race, their broken ankles hobbling across the troubled terrain of Earth in the belief their turn on its turf shall and must be known and impressed if only to themselves by shout or whisper, declaring "Take notice, I was here. I was once here."

It was a few years prior the young lady peered through the Ukraine darkness with eyes on Paris, the City of Light her sharper focus. But she ran into a bitter and hideous circle in Marseille then followed its dangerous arc into London. Most of the pirates in the gang were British, plus one Moroccan, Bulgarian and American. In the alleys, streets, flophouses and bars she was offered, swallowed and absorbed in a radical, contagious indoctrination. The world was a cruel and unfair marketplace, overfed, unbalanced and disproportional in its graces and gifts. Love was withheld and pain advanced, and the promoters, pilferers and profiteers must pay. A ferocious, fanatical and effective engineer of the mind as their lead, it was a charismatic anarchist who set to unleash and free a new generation, designed by destiny in grand acts of demolition with a bullseye on the Rotonde, the centerstage of the entertainment world.

They were prepared to die in the effort, martyrdom part of the methodology, striking a resolve to like-minded young revolutionaries the world over in a calculated online call of solidarity, to react, respond and repeat. Their literature and website would feed the fire and unleash an unholy smoke, a signal to their generation to embrace the menacing mission. The subtext to their cause was emboldened for all to see, "A race against time but one we must win ... nothing to live for, everything to die for!"

The inventory of the literature and the online presence made its way into fanatical circles. The organization was weakened in the surprising magnitude of the devastation, drawing a heightened interest and investigation across the global network of international intelligence. The truck bomb's construction was aided by an operational toolkit offered in subversive, dark-web back channels of the internet, in detail providing resources for materials, devices and detonation. The Russian girl had come forward and steered authorities right to the source, blocking its channels of communication and, in turn, possibly saving untold lives in copycat acts of similar violence.

She went public poised and well-groomed, composed and prepared. The regional tabloids and worldwide news media heard and shared her *mea culpa* and specific knowledge of the plot. Her uncle in the Ukraine denied her involvement, claiming the confession to be an attention-motivated stunt. She was with him in Kiev when the crime happened, he insisted. She was never sold into prostitution. He maintained the misled niece was simply a colossal liar. Now, illuminating light on the subject revealed the uncle to be a source of soul-shattering deceit, profiting himself by her trafficking.

Suspicion of me was fused by a most unlikely circumstance. A British couple, seeing her youthful, familiar face plastered on the news, retrieved a digital photograph from their trip to Cannes. Dated, timed and logged in sequence, just before their many captured images of the Rotonde's destruction, standing next to the girl in full clarity was me, locked in a concentrated and pivotal dialogue with the suspect on the steps of Eglise Notre-Dame.

The evidence and her indisputable, intense knowledge of other facts known only to the authorities, including the acquisition of explosive fertilizer from farmlands in central France and details of the stolen transport truck in Marseilles, solidified the girl's legitimacy and bona fide account of the terrorism. Only a last moment's rattling of the conscience spilled her out of the suicidal truck. With no time to alter the course of events she scampered into the church, confused and scared, hoping to make a desperate plea to anyone who would listen, including the elusive gods, and so it turns, me.

The business card contributed to the folly. While I was staying off the digital grid the shattered girl was not. She had been frantically emailing me, connecting to my social media accounts and leaving suspicious and problematic messages on my business voicemail, all outside my knowledge but compiled in a sea of surveillance. My abrupt resignation and subsequent disappearance only added to the mounting intrigue and swelling curiosity of the investigators. The bizarre trail of attempted online transactions using my name and accounts had been regularly intercepted across Western and Eastern Europe, a nest of activity from cash withdrawals to the purchasing of illegal weapons wrapped in a complex web of nefarious underworld figures. When the Roma children committed petty robbery outside the train station they could not foresee the wrath a Tobias Nathan Tyrone imposter would bring upon the real one.

One more month of detention followed as they sorted the evidence, details, facts and depositions. Through legal maneuverings arranged by Tutela and the mystery girl's legal counsel, eventually the truth, enough truth, surfaced with merciful but dangerously delayed justice.

The girl signed affidavits and testified I was a stranger to her with absolutely no knowledge or involvement in the circle of anarchists. In the course of three weeks she wrote me several detailed letters of her lost dreams, confessing she was sorry for what I had been through and all I had suffered or lost. She was exhibiting inescapable signs of self-harm, scraping in alternating tracks left to right, vertically and horizontally the flesh of her wrists with her fingernails and pulling out long locks of her fine blonde hair. The jailers had no choice but to cut her nails every few days and shave her head for her own protection. She had been asking me in relayed notes if I had room in my heart to forgive, though she feels God will ultimately judge her "severely and rightly." Kindness and compassion existed in the brief moments we connected in those fateful moments at the church, she shared. This was something she saw nothing of across the scattered, broken years of her childhood. She thanked me for these few but lasting moments, and I thought if I had to testify against her in a court of law someday I would hope she would not think differently of me for having done so.

She wrote she wished she could roll back the calendar of time and walk through this life differently, slowly and steady, instead of chaotically as a runaway. She loved animals, American musicals and theater, and while in custody had the opportunity, under supervision, to visit Tutela's new website and the progress of the *Somnium* project. She liked what she saw. She said the world could be a better place with more websites like it. Of course she is not a president or religious world leader at all, she admitted, but it would be quite special if one day she could go to its studios, draw or paint, and discover if she had any talent at all inside. In reality, she observed accurately, she would most likely never get to see or do any of this for the future would be one of imprisonment, isolation or worse. She included in one of her notes a glimpse into a story she was reading, Uberti's *Dittamondo*, the account of an imaginary voyage. In it the ancient geographer Solinus, accompanied by a poet, arrives to find a young lady weeping. The woman is Rome who shares a longing for the untouchable and unreachable years of youth, and in such reacquaintance with innocence hopes to recover her former beauty.

In her fantasy of rolled-back time she would have joined the circus. She dreamed of being in the happy and hypnotic troupe Cirque du Soleil or any circus that would accept her, where earth-shaking joy comes by way of herds of elephants, horses and lions, each gallant entrance of the carnival an opening to a new and imaginary world, traveling the globe as one in a new and adopted family where magic and music radiating in a kaleidoscope of colors would be in weightless flight as she soars. She would spin and dance with tigers, cats, parrots and cobras, and from the trapeze she would finish in a leap of courage to the secure and trusted net below, the audience erupting, the whole planet exploding in grateful, astonished joy and applause. The growing legions of amused guests would know her true name among the bands of musicians, mimes, dancers and jugglers. Admiration would come by way of jesters, rope-dancers, acrobats and flyers, happy men and women on high, wingless and aloft like the Roman ancients on their *petauron*, the flying machine engineered centuries ago, its miraculous mechanics still a mystery today. Where once the dwarves were taught to fight in amusement for the emperor here they would dance in glee and security, and she would join them in a new hora of the day, counterclockwise from the direction that spun her into darkness to the rim of the Rotonde and stark incarceration. She wrote of historic and famous circus performers, Isaac van Amburgh, the lion tamer, Jules Leotard, the flying trapeze artist, Zazec, the human projectile, and her favorite, Charles Blendin and his flamboyant high-wire act, dressed in Roman garb and pausing on the line above the perilous Niagara Falls, his onlookers awestruck as he leans back in a casual pause, confidently balanced above the roaring cascade for a simple sip of vintage wine.

But now it was the wheels in this circus and its revolving spins of justice capturing her space and time and ceasing forward motion. As she braced and awaited her fate, nine months and twelve days in the hub of my purgatory I was freed from its spokes.

It was on the morn of my liberation I received heart-ripping news in a note passed to me from one of the authorities as I drank coffee at the cold cell table. The nameless, mysterious, dreaming girl from Ukraine was dead. She had gotten hold of a dull metal instrument somehow, a final magic trick, cutting her wrist so deep and just below the palm it nearly severed her hand. She left a brief message for anyone left to listen.

"I am sorry to the world. I am sorry to God. Forgive me."

Please forgive us, broken and abused stranger.

I already had forgiven you.

I had! But for time. Time. Passing time!

You were too late, Toby.

She was too broken.

The young lady could have ignited persistent war but now may she rest in overdue peace. By her surrender, the white handkerchief in the left hand, may it be said at her finish line she poured cold water on a world's hot fuse.

Tutela greeted me in the reception hall of the jail. She placed a small beret on my head with a kiss. Members of her staff had knitted the cap for me, embroidered with the letters *SPQR*.

"My Toby, my love," she whispered, locking our arms at the elbow and clasping our hands in the tightest of grips, palm to palm. "You are libertus, a freed slave – *vindicavit in libertatem* – freedom by the rod."

Tutela informed in imperial Roman times the felt cap, *pileus*, was symbolic of liberty, worn on the clean-shaven head of the freed slave and signaling to the citizenry his redeemed position and class. It is seen on Roman coins of Antonius Pius, the figure of Liberty holding pileus in the right hand.

I stared back at the caged quarters that nearly stole my soul. Her grip still on me and mine on hers, Tutela turned me toward the exit and the bright Roman sunlight, an awaiting and newfound manumission my just-earned reward.

To fully understand the definition of liberty one needs to face it nearly stripped, having it dangled at the nose while hungry and alone, bare but within earshot of children mere meters away freely at play while the dove comes and goes at will to the sill, pitying your plight before taking wing over the ancient hill of Palatine – only to return, day after evaporating day – until they add up to centuries for anyone with the time to pass and hours to count as they vanish, as you realize you are left but two choices – to either free your soul in a plea and deal with your gods or slip into the abyss of forgotten, tortured spirits who hold onto a fleeting idea the Earth itself is idle in its orbit waiting for your return in order to make proper revolution. The last few times I asked this of the Earth I swore I heard a rumbling ruckus, a chorus of chuckled amusement, the kind heard in the circular rotunda of the circus in its full motion when the clown flirts with the tiger and the audience reacts instinctively if not superstitiously, knowing not if the joke is on the clown or the tiger, or most peculiarly, themselves. The spectator can be the last to know until that one, faint but crystalized moment of realization and illumination sparks the soul, the split second between rehearsed laughter and certain demise when the whole tent folds in on itself and collapses down in a dramatic puff of musky dust, where utter stillness and silence reign in a millisecond of time and all once known ceases, instantaneously, just as all left curious and yearned to understand is revealed by the reigning Ringmaster. Libertus was never fully to be had or realized in this dimension though its pileus be tauntingly extended, out of reach on the other side and fully out of sight in the distracting beauty of the circus.

It stands to reason in the grand scheme of things the performance should be nearly perfect.

Cloe should know, awaiting with open arms on a terrace in the comforting clouds on a backdrop of baby blue, to embrace one lonely, drifting trapeze artist on the wire, dangling dangerously and desperately in need of a hug or a catch – a young, fragile dreamcatcher from Ukraine who only asked for one wistful walk in the sky, but for a moment to know the glee and view from above, so high above she can watch white doves sail where angels dance – to join them hand in hand in dizzying joy in counterclockwise spins in the heavenly hora, where weeping yields to roars of joy, followed by deafening, delirious and approving applause, be it for a life well lived or one act well done.

CHAPTER XII

TUTELA AND I walked the streets of Rome for three hours sharing the multitude of details turning in our heads at this moment of rebirth and, alas, crossing the Tiber we turned the familiar corner into the trapezoid of the Borgo to the friendly and familiar front door where we belonged. There, on display, was a cradle in the entryway framed in marble-white with a baby-blue ornament, a dreamcatcher, adorned at its center. Noah and Melanie were standing in conspired silence with mischievous smiles, a tiny babe tenderly asleep wrapped in soft-pillowed cotton in Melanie's arms.

Rushing to offer my embrace of congratulations I was interrupted in the raise and halt of Noah's palm.

"He is yours, dear and free friend," announced Noah. "Toby, meet your son."

I did not move, stilled in my tracks. Melanie extended her arms to present the miracle, gift-wrapped in a soft blanket, molding him into my hold as Tutela stood at three-paces distant with arms folded in peace, tears streaming down her sun-kissed cheeks.

I heard his gentle exhalations. I felt the rhythm in his steady breathing, the rapid beat in his pulsing heart. I was locked on his perfect head, his peach-fuzzed scalp and olive-crested brow leading to peacefully shut eyes. All of creation was in my arms. My eyes welled as I strolled with him from the entry to sit on our bed as the universe collided in a

moment of atomic fusion, its suns, planets and stars, the divine constellations, lightyears away to the eight pounds in my arms, the infinite
atoms of the galaxies, the Big Bang to the supernovas, split and fused
into this tiny mass of elements wrapped in soft cotton, delivered to me in
this chamber and onto this bed, here in new-born Rome as Tutela stood
in triumph and solidarity with the goddess Pomona as Saint Gerard
whispered in each ear to welcome this babe, our babe, the world's babe
to take his rightful turn on the grand track.

Tutela needed not to explain. I knew the unspoken reasoning. She
knew my soul and shared the imprisonment with me over these months,
the babe our key to freedom and redemption. She had often hinted at
this in our correspondence, teasing of the "growing love awaiting us all."

How greater my prison, how larger the crime, to be aware of her
stress and condition, pregnancy and lupus, and free not to aid or care
for her? She knew as did I the necessary limits of information in such a
circumstance, and the greater recusal is often reflected in a higher love.
Her instincts and discretion paved the path to a finer surprise.

She carried the babe quietly for both of us. I wept at this thought,
Tutela joining me in the emotional release. Melanie and Noah shared in
the flow, a river of crying in unified joy, the heavens opening, too, with an
infant child so still in his peace, the most content creature on the planet
holding court in tranquility at the center and hub of the returning and
forgiving circus, poised and prepared for the uncertain turns to come.

The natural first steps were for Tutela, the babe and I to meet Rome
in a unified first stroll, and may it be Rome to serve as the audition
where all humanity and the gods delight in each step and every bounce
above her cobbled paths, the Appian Way, mindful Forum and haunting catacombs, calling us forth to roads at our feet and paths before us
mysterious and unknown, the babe an itinerant with a direction and
purpose uniquely his own.

Tutela briefed me on the state of our lives. Despite turbulent circumstances matters had turned to a relative calm.

"Your mother called and wrote constantly, dear Tobias. She had
all the confidence you were on the right track and would be okay. She
prayed for you daily and placed her faith deeper in God, if that is even

possible. This trial she put in His hands. She sent regular messages, some of which you received, and writing a book is stirring her heart. It is about the Greeks and she said her next trip must be soon to Athens. In her pilgrimage we are to expect a stop in Rome."

I listened pleasingly without removing the gaze on our child.

"Your former employer is suing you for breach of contract. They submitted absurd terms in a separation agreement which includes a return of two years' salary. We can settle, or we fight it all," she said with a sly grin.

I decided at that moment they could have it all, and soon, in the pulling of my pension funds, depleting it whole if necessary. Free of it I would be lighter and liberated. The Roman gypsies had nothing on the masterful thieves of Hollywood, but a much larger emancipation would be won on this end.

Tutela's team would pick up the mantle and lead the *Somnium* project in her well-deserved absence. Not a step would be missed with the foundation formed and momentum building.

We passed by the merchants, kiosks and playgrounds, the flower and fruit stands of Piazza Cavour, the offering of gimblettes and the warming of chestnuts in symphonic rhythm to the ringing of church bells in the breezy air. We turned toward the taverna, new friends and old gathered in greetings abundant, a sleeping babe lifting his tiny nostrils to inhale the persuading perfumes of flowing wine and fresh-sliced cheeses. We traversed the Galleria Alberto Salvi as pilgrims and itinerants in tow. Our babe, welcomed on the steps of Piazza di Spagna by legions of travelers and admirers, brought pause to a carnival of Romans and tourists, a caravan of doters offering every creative expression of approval, passion and love they could muster in stride. We made way to the Trevi Fountain where the pools glistened and whirled in blessed sunlight, the rays dancing off the monument and onto the bundle now cradled in the crescent of Tutela's arms. We entered the Giardini del Quirinale and rested on a shaded, cool and familiar bench. Laughter from scores of Roman children at play stirred our babe's sleep until a sweet smile of solidarity joined their joy.

After the passing of another hour we made way to the office of Tutela's dreamcatchers who were busy on its mezzanines and terraces, phones ringing in harmony with church chimes across the bustling lane. Tutela informed of the many blessings that had surfaced throughout this tumultuous trial. A generous philanthropist in France, learning of the plight and plan, adopted the mission and had embraced its purpose, pledging with his investors a considerable and bombastic sum, over three million Euros to help spark the organization's next phase of development. The funds were to be wired in the coming days to commence construction of the *Somnium* in a spirited and public demonstration of Roman-centric purpose, staged by common citizens on site driving their shovels into the ancient turf as the first act.

The generous donor had made a fortune over the past year in the explosive, worldwide dramatic production of the musical *Eden Revisited*, making serious and successful runs on Broadway and London's West End, with Paris and Tokyo to come and a multimillion-dollar film deal in the works as well. His name is Philippe Hilaire but he requested the gift be accepted anonymously, free of fanfare and publicity. The contribution is to honor the memory of a lost love, one whose sweet, radiant light shed joy, love and peace on his path and moved his world in a most spectacular direction.

The municipal leadership of Rome had made complete commitments, too. The inertia led to a speedy execution of architectural drawings, engineering plans and the ambitious timeline for an official groundbreaking of the structure. The operation moved swiftly through the channels of government in granting approval to the location of choice – upon the sacred grounds and at the true center of the great Circus Maximus.

"There we shall build it," Tutela had declared to her team in assured voice and tone. "There it was meant to be, and there it is destined to be."

Onward we went fulfilling the day's itinerary. Willfully I was lost in the circuitous route, and should I be forever spun in Tutela's orbit in eternal Rome, our child looking up to us as the sun started its descent into the Mediterranean, then all would be eternally right and corrected in the universe, the gods granting reprieve and kissing our foreheads in magnanimous manumission. I found myself tugged by Gregorious, walking his path past the churches, monuments, fountains and towers as he whispered into my ear, seduced by the statue of Venus, *which is so indescribably perfect that she almost seems to be alive.*

We paraded the perimeter of the Mausoleum of Augustus, sharing amusement at the sight of the litter, Coke cans and fast-food wrappers strewn in the dry grass and weeds dominating his once-ornate concentric circles securing his ashes, the emperor unworshipped as the traffic rushes and passes. Martial the poet properly reminded as we moved on, *The Mausoleum tells us to live, that one nearby, It teaches us that the gods themselves can die.*

In the historic, restored Enrico Fermi complex in via Panisperna we stood in silence where once stood the Royal Institute of Physics, a Roman laboratory where Fermi advanced the first experiments on the phenomenon of radioactivity induced by neutrons, setting the wheels in motion that ushered in the atomic age. The Italian physicist would be central in the Manhattan Project and the dropping of the world's first nuclear bombs. Here he initiated the work mostly alone, but on occasion could be found racing down the corridor in hyper-excitable demonstration and competition with fellow physicist Edoardo Amaldi.

To the Pantheon we strode, which brought a giggle at the thought of Pope Urban VIII using material from its roof for guns. The Holy Spirit and the soldier, the dove and the sword, the olive branch and the fasces, always within reach at any spontaneous moment, a simple choice to bend or turn, to the left or to the right, clockwise or counterclockwise.

On the banks of the Tiber we took respite on a patch of grass, curiously but predictably in the shape of a mammoth heart, for why not? Love was the compass and compulsion and we were riding free and in front on the Archer's chariot.

"You and your poets. You know of Propertius, yes Toby?" the new mother quizzed.

"He is familiar. Do share, love."

"He enjoyed drinking his wine right here on the riverside with his loves, where he could be *seated on a throne amid merry women.* He appeased his hawkish patrons with false bravado, plucking his lyre, praising the exploits of war, but to his love Cynthia he shared deeper desires and sung a different tune. All the military glory in the universe could not equal the delight he knew in a single night with his Cynthia."

"That makes you my Cynthia."

"Propertius told her, *Why should I raise sons for Parthian triumphs? No child of ours shall be a soldier.*"

Lest we forget our poet laureate Virgil, I reminded Tutela, who took no delight in war either and never lived to witness the enduring success of his masterpiece, *The Aenid*. Nor shall we dismiss the gift from Augustus who published the work after Virgil's death making it a source of Roman pride ever since. The poets were delivering a dove overhead, raising Tutela on a proper pedestal as Virgil's words danced off the stones in direction of the great circus. *These shall be your skills; to impose peace.*

To the Circus Maximus we made haste. On both old and modern pathways our gait intensified, driven and compelled, eager and enthused as the great track called in a race with the setting Roman sun. Our babe between us at the ancient festive gate, we paused. Here, two thousand years ago the circus would open with *pompa*, a procession of musicians and bands followed by the officiating magistrate in his chariot, clad in costume as triumphator, holding in one hand an ivory scepter adorned with an eagle. Attention would turn to the chariot cages, the *carceres*, as the imposing umpire on high would give a sign commencing the beginning of the race by throwing his white cloth, the *mappa*, into the arena. There would be up to twenty-four races, elapsing the nearly perfect amount of time in a day's provided light.

Along the turn of the great track Tutela and I found a thick patch of grassy turf, laid our backs against the ruinous walls with feet pointing north, and took a treasured rest with our sleeping babe.

Tutela shared the larger influence and source of her grand creation, the account of *Somnium Scipionis*, the dream-vision of the legendary Roman general who foresaw the destruction of Carthage in 146 BC. Scipio's future was foretold in a nocturnal visit in which his deceased grandfather informed that loyal duty would result in death, but it would be richly rewarded in *that circle that shines forth among the stars … the Milky Way*. Staring at the infinite wonder of the universe, Scipio began to hear a *loud and agreeable sound*, the *musica universalis*, the music of the spheres, a cosmic symphony produced in the revolutions of the planets. The Earth does not move, motionless at the center. Overcome by the vision, Scipio absorbed a larger understanding that Rome in all its glories and expansiveness, power and prowess is relatively insignificant in relation to the entire world, which itself is dwarfed by the vast, mysterious and eternal cosmos. Humility reigns where perspective is present, in a glimpse at the beyond to the eternal destiny of humanity on the other side, to the gods in motion on golden-gilded chariots of peace, joy and love as they race on the outer arcs of the Milky Way, making each and every being in creation a splendor and wonder, a gift to behold and an amusement to treasure in each spin on this one lonely and cherished orb.

The *Somnium* would be right here, Tutela decreed, pointing to the spina, the very center of the circus.

"And may it be that in the spina we delight in a living viridarium, an orchard of olives, pears, apples and cypress trees, enveloped in aromas of lasting lavender."

Our dream was unfolding. I turned to my two loves and opened my eyes. There, in the ancient stone and within reach, discernibly clear in the groove of mortar set centuries before, an embedded palm print was evident above our babe's head. I placed my palm into its caementicum then Tutela placed hers upon mine. I whispered our babe's name for the first time into his listening spirit.

"Lucius Mateo. Lucius Mateo. Love of love, Lucius Mateo."

The names of my past, all the names in my life lost and found, some here and others gone, all the faces, places of yesterdays and years, throughout the periods of lost and found time joined in the witness, palm onto palm into the ancient stone, and I kissed Tutela's palm and she did mine, our babe on my chest in the grandest Roman oval and its imperfect circle. I heard compassionate whispers of angels overhead and in the sweet puffs of breath from little Lucius the song of Ovid could be heard in agreement in the forgiving breeze as the fire in the restless Roman sky recessed into the cool-blue and surrendering sundown.

I heard Marcus Aurelius, the good and patient emperor, straddle the perimeter of the circus and bless the moment. *These are the principles of the rational soul. It traverses the whole universe, and surveys its form, and extends itself into the infinity of time, and embraces the cyclical renewal of all things, and comprehends that those who come after us will see nothing new, nor have those before us seen anything more; but in a manner he who is forty years old, if he has any understanding at all, he has seen, by virtue of this uniformity, all things that have been or will be.*

Maybe in Marcus' uniformity we would begin again – all the old, tired, attempted and failed, ventured and gained, won and lost competitions – ceding in proper surrender, a drop of the white handkerchief to hard lessons learned.

Maybe all of the speediness, the reckless inertia and rapid races, the rushes to battles and returns to wars, the tugs and pulls, the games and challenges, dares and duels, hiding and seeking, what is yours, what is mine, taking and fleeing in perilous turns, would give way to new rules of revolving on the tenuous track. Maybe the pirates and thieves, gypsies and knaves, charioteers and beggars, kings and paupers, Olympians and defeated, the vanquished and the victor would start here again, recognizing one another in the adorned, singular shade of perennial love on the points in our lives when spontaneously in time but eternally drawn, singularly and superbly, we meet a finish when it greets a start.

Maybe all the spirits in the whole furious and fanatical human race would triumph in the worth of lives well lived, creating and constructing a carnival of alternative desire.

Maybe in that race, each one, be they in sprint or stroll, on the high wire or in the marathon, thrusting the javelin or chasing the chariot, be noted they served their fellow man and the gods well, played fairly and lived righteously, generously gave and courageously loved, and when fortune feigned immortality came the merciful mindfulness all gains, however glorious, are fleeting.

Maybe the whole race would be measured from Rome to the farthest sun in the search and strive for renewal, each lap mapped, properly, fully and fairly drawn, each rider the right to a glorious run – once upon a Circus Maximus – and perhaps the stops and starts would only be recognized in the beauty of the indistinguishable, where present and past are propelled forward as much as they harken back, a circle so supremely impressed and nearly perfect it cannot be determined by the start nor the finish.

If so, the circus knows no end at all.

Contra virum, it breathes eternally in rhythmic revolutions, counter-clockwise to an end that is masterfully an amusing resemblance to the start. It is a recurring call to live again – *principium*, a new start – as fresh as a birth in the warm Roman sun.

It is that sweet familiar line traced in the race to the finish.

The beginning.